Pinch of Love

The Sunshine Breakfast Club
(Book 2)

KARICE BOLTON

PINCH OF LOVE

PINCH OF LOVE

Cover Design by Didi Wahyudi using © Patryk
Kosmider ©dfikar

Interior: Adobe Stock © Phoebe Yu

Interior Formatting: BB Formatting

Edited by Valorie Clifton

DEDICATION

To my readers! Thank you for making this series soar. And to
my family, I love you more than words could ever describe.

Chapter One

Maya

"You've got to be kidding me." I wiped the sweat puddling on my dark brows and blew out a sharp breath of frustration.

As I punched the code into the door lock again, the angry squeal of rejection came back at me. In frustration, I kicked the wheel of my suitcase with my sandal. My bags collapsed next to me, and I breathed a grunt of pain and annoyance. This moment in time framed why I was grateful I wasn't born grumpy. Things would always go wrong, and I'd get hurt.

"Just great." I sat on the suitcase closest to me while I dug in my purse for my cellphone to call the property manager. This magic code was supposed to let me into my vacation rental, yet here I stood.

I glanced at my phone, saw a million missed calls from Rob, and rolled my eyes.

Rob. Fiancé and business partner extraordinaire.

Crusher of dreams.

Demolisher of hearts.

Or maybe it was the other way around.

Either way, my heart, body, and soul had quit the opposite sex.

On cue, my phone rang again.

"Right, like I'm going to pick up your call." I shook my head and let out a heavy sigh as the front door magically opened.

I turned to see a tiny face poking out the door with scrunched brows. She had two lopsided blonde braids and what looked like spaghetti sauce smeared on top of her cute nose.

"You not Daddy."

I stood quickly and shook my head. "No, I'm not your daddy, but I am supposed to be staying here for the rest of the summer."

The little girl looked surprised and shook her head. "Nope."

She slammed the door in my face, and I sat down again in complete defeat.

Maybe they overbooked the house.

I shrugged and started to dial the property manager's number when the door swung open.

This time, a woman my age poked her head out.

"May I help you?" Her plump cheeks matched mine, and I instantly felt like I'd found my savior.

I nodded. "Yes, I mean, I hope so. I rented this house through October, or so I thought."

The woman stepped onto the porch as I stood with my suitcases again.

Her blonde hair had been slicked into a ponytail, and her white jumper was encrusted with a red handprint on it, probably from the blonde kiddo holding down the fort.

She folded her arms over her chest and playfully scowled. "Well, my husband has some explaining to do if he rented our house out from under us."

"Darn it," I muttered. "I've been scammed. The cab dropped me off, but my sister lives in town. I'm so sorry for imposing. I'll be out of your hair before you know it. I'll give her a quick call."

She shook her head and studied me for a split second. "What's the address you're looking for?"

I showed her my phone, and she smiled.

"The good news is that you haven't been scammed.

The bad news is the rental house is on the other side of the lake. Happens all the time, partly because we always let our tree limbs overgrow and block the sign. Our house has a one in front of it. See? The driver must not have paid attention. You're looking for 450, and we are 1450." She smiled and shrugged. "I know Cash, the owner. He'll come pick you up, no problem. He's a little jaded with a dollop of grumpy, but he's a sweet guy for the most part."

My brows arched. "For the most part?"

She laughed. "Don't worry. I didn't mean like he'd come stab you in the night or anything."

My eyes widened. "That thought hadn't even crossed my mind."

She touched her forehead and groaned. "Sorry. I've got this really crazy mind that goes places no mind should ever go. My husband thinks I'm obsessed with true crime." She scowled. "He could be right. Anyway, not to worry. Cash is not some type of slice and dice landlord. There are no women in his freezer. In fact, I don't even think he dates."

I hid a laugh and wondered whether I should have ever left North Carolina. Maybe this entire trip was over the top. I shouldn't be the one running away from my life. It should be Rob fleeing for his.

The woman reached into the pocket of her jumper and

scrolled through her phone. "Ah, here he is."

I shook my head. "Really, I'm okay. I'll have my sister come pick me up. I've caused enough of a disruption."

"You're not even a little bit of a disruption. Besides, out here, I can pretend that my toddler isn't painting the walls with spaghetti sauce." She dialed the number and winked at me. "We'll get it all straightened out. I'm Becky, by the way."

"Nice to meet you. I'm Maya Bailey."

Her eyes widened. "Millie's granddaughter?"

I nodded and smiled. "One of them."

Becky's toddler walked onto the porch with more sauce on her face, and I couldn't help but laugh.

"Millie is such a character." She grinned as someone on the other end of the line answered the phone. "And I love Grace. We're both in a book club together."

I couldn't hide my surprise. Grace never struck me as a book club kind of gal. Granted, I didn't know that much about my sister in recent years. Our family mainly consisted of three siblings, all girls, and we orbited around Grandma Millie since our parents hadn't really lived up to the guardian title. Once we hit our twenties, we scattered like fleas on a freshly bathed dog. Grace moved to Illinois, married, and had a daughter, but she recently moved to Buttercup Lake. Nina was my older sister, and she lived in New Mexico. When I

5

thought about where to hide out for the next couple of months, Wisconsin's cooler temps called to me.

"Hey, Cash. I've got a guest of yours here. I think it's time I tell my husband to clear the branches off our address sign again."

A low rumble of laughter vibrated through the phone, and I couldn't help but drop my gaze to the porch. Cash sounded a lot younger than I'd imagined him to be.

Not that I'd done much imagining, but if I were to, I thought he might be sixty, living in a cabin down by the lake with a mutt named Oscar.

I turned my attention to Becky as she guided her little one back onto the porch.

"Thanks, Cash. I'd drive her over, but my little one is covered in spaghetti sauce, and a bubble bath is next on the agenda."

Becky thanked him once more, and I brought my eyes to hers.

I winced in embarrassment. "Thanks again."

"He should be over in a couple of minutes. Come on inside. You can leave your bags on the porch. No one'll take 'em."

I'd forgotten how friendly the residents of Buttercup Lake were, and I suddenly wasn't sure if I was ready for it. I had a lot of pouting and plotting ahead of me.

"I'd offer you lunch, but I'm pretty sure no one should touch what my little Melanie manhandled." She patted her daughter's head, who pointed at my suitcases.

"Minnie Mouse," the little one squealed.

I glanced behind me, but I didn't see anyone looking like the mouse, so I shrugged. "Uh, yeah."

"Oh, speak of the devil. Here comes Cash." Becky gave a quick wave as I turned to see a white Jeep turning down the drive. The Jeep's top was off, and a guy with a baseball hat and sunglasses sat in the driver's seat. He had an ice cream cone in his left hand and turned off the ignition with his right.

For no apparent reason, my heart skipped a beat when he parked and gave us a wave as he hopped out of the Jeep. He was wearing a loose pair of khaki shorts hitting his knees and a grey tee that happened to cling to his thick biceps. I ripped my gaze away as if I weren't inhaling the man in front of me like he was inhaling his pink ice cream.

"Ah, that's why he got here so fast. He was getting ice cream," Becky informed me as if that explained the world's problems.

I smiled, remembering how much I loved grabbing a cone of butter pecan when I was a little girl visiting my grandma here at the lake. It was such a simpler time.

Spotting an older man slowly pushing a walker on the road in front of Becky's house reminded me of my Grandpa Renny, who'd recently passed. My chest tightened, and I looked away.

"You must be Maya," the man said, walking quickly to the porch.

I smiled and took a step forward. Forgetting that my suitcases were piled in front of me, I fell flat on my face with a thud and a porch full of gasps. The smallest bag tumbled down the steps and landed with a thud as Melanie giggled.

Within an instant, Cash's large hands looped under each armpit, lifted me up, and plopped me on the ground next to him like I was nothing more than a tulip he'd plucked from the garden.

"You, okay?" he asked, taking a step back to assess me while still firmly holding onto my arms.

My entire face was on fire with humiliation, and heat started thrumming through every fiber of my body.

"Looks like you got a keeper there, Cash," the elderly man hollered, stopping his walk and watching us as I smoothed down my floral mini skirt and brought my gaze to Cash.

He looked half horrified and half amused. "Never mind Carter. He's the town gossip."

"One of the many town gossips," Becky corrected.

The sexy landlord watched me and tried again. "You okay?"

"Yeah. I'm great. Totally fine. I used to be a gymnast when I was twelve so I'm good."

"I'm Cash, by the way."

I nodded, knowing his name from the reservations but mesmerized by the man standing in front of me nonetheless.

He was all man.

All male.

One hundred percent testosterone. The dark hair tucked under his hat looked slightly wavy.

He didn't have to smile to be sexy. He just was, which didn't matter because I'd been burned by the male species. Fool me once and all that.

"Nice to meet you. I'm Maya, and I'm so sorry for bothering you and Becky." I tore my gaze away from Cash's so I could take a breath without him reading my mind.

Which was currently filled with all kinds of things I shouldn't be thinking about with a mother and child toddling around us.

And then I gasped when I saw it. "The ice cream. What happened to your ice cream?"

Cash chuckled without smiling and glanced on the

sidewalk where his cone was turned upside down, and the pink ice cream pooled onto the concrete.

"No worries." He shrugged. "I shouldn't have stopped by there for the second time this week, anyway."

"I owe you one," I said, shaking my head as Melanie wandered over to the cone and attempted to pick it up.

Becky dashed over to her just in time before her daughter was about to take a bite of the dirty treat. Instantly, a sob of tears came flooding down the toddler's cheeks. Becky scooped her into her arms and smiled, glancing at us both.

"Way to go," the elderly gent hollered as he started his route up again. "Let her eat it."

"And that is my cue to exit. It was nice to meet you, Maya." Becky smiled kindly.

"You, too." I grimaced and nodded, feeling extremely guilty for not only disrupting these kind people's day but also for making a child cry and an old man angry.

I turned to stack my suitcases back up and let out a slow and steady breath. This wasn't the dream I'd had when I thought about coming back to Buttercup Lake for the summer.

I was a hot mess, and my toe throbbed for some reason.

Cash knelt next to me and reached for a bag when our knuckles brushed, and I felt my body heat up again.

I don't need a rebound guy.

I stood and pulled the biggest suitcase up and glanced at Cash, who'd somehow managed to stack two on each of the remaining ones and started toward the truck with them all.

"You did such a great job of telling me the door code and where I could find everything and sending the map to the town, and then I still show up at the wrong house." I followed Cash to his Jeep, but I sensed him smiling in front of me. The first one of the day, and I didn't get to see it. "I'm so sorry."

"It's not the first time, and I'm sure you won't be the last." He shoved two of the suitcases into the minuscule trunk and placed the others in the backseat before turning to mine and plopping it on top. "That should do it."

And I realized Becky was right. He might be a little bit on the salty side.

I tried once more. "Again, I'm so sorry. You didn't sign up to be my cab service and—"

Cash's head tilted sideways slightly, and he studied me for a split second. "You don't have anything to apologize for. My job is to take care of the guests who rent my properties, and I had nothing better to do."

The way his gaze lingered on mine made me wonder what was going through his head. I couldn't tell, and I was usually really good at reading people.

Well, maybe not that great since my fiancé-slash-business partner stood me up at the courthouse altar, but generally, I could tell what people were thinking.

And I knew what thoughts were pummeling through me.

He was a towering male with a muscular build, and I'd just been put through the wringer of emotions and humiliation. Cash seemed like the perfect distraction. Except that I'd never let myself have a distraction until Buttercup Lake. And the lake was supposed to be my distraction, not the property owner.

Cash opened the door, and I smiled as I climbed into the passenger seat of the Wrangler when he noticed my knee.

"Ouch. That's gotta hurt." His gaze rested on my knee, and I looked down to see my left knee all scratched up and bloody. "We should get something on that right away."

I shook my head. "I'm totally fine. I'll worry about it when I get to the house. I must have gotten tangled with the zipper or something. My sister can bring something over."

"Your sister?"

I nodded. "She and her daugher live here and rented a place temporarily."

His brows slightly rose as he circled the hood of the Jeep to get to the driver's side. "Is Grace your sister?"

"Yup."

Cash shook his head and climbed into the seat. "It's a small world. That's one of my properties."

I laughed and glanced in his direction. "What did you do? Buy up the town?"

His gaze caught mine, and he nodded. "As a matter of fact, I did."

Cash turned on the Jeep and put the SUV in reverse as he looked behind him. "So, you love Minnie Mouse, huh?"

My brows scrunched, and I shook my head. "I don't know why everyone keeps saying that."

He pulled onto the road and pointed his thumb to the backseat. "Probably because all your suitcases are red with white polka dots. It's a signature Minnie style."

I snorted and glanced out the window as the warm wind ruffled my hair. "Well, that explains it."

"Did you just snort?" He eyed me.

"Suppose I did." I turned to him. "Why are you such an expert on a mouse?"

He shrugged. "It's pretty much common knowledge."

My brows rose. "Oh, yeah?"

"Just sayin'." A smile almost touched his lips.

He pulled down a road that I didn't recognize, but it was close to the lake, and my jaw dropped. "What the heck happened to Buttercup Lake? What is this?"

Cash nodded. "We got a new downtown complete with restaurants and shops."

When I'd come here during the summers, there was a market attached to a gas station, an ice cream shop, a mechanic, a laundromat, a diner, and a small gift shop.

"It's like a little bit of civilization erupted out of nowhere." My cellphone rang again, and I ignored it, but I noticed Cash noticing that I didn't even bother to see who it was.

Cash just continued on. "It kind of did. There was nothing here before, and nowhere to really develop a main street near the gas station, so the mayor and a developer worked on this together."

"My sister said Buttercup Lake had really changed." I glanced at Cash as he slowed to let a family across the street with their ice cream. "How long did it take?"

"About five years."

I noticed faint lines around his beautiful green eyes and some crinkles along his forehead. I couldn't quite tell how old Cash was, but the way the lines rested told me he used to smile.

"This will be the perfect getaway for me," I said more to myself than anything.

"Yeah?" He glanced at me as he turned the corner near the lake. "What are you trying to get away from?"

I licked my lips and drew a breath, wondering if I really wanted to get into it.

A bit of the grump left his gaze, and I smiled.

"Just life." I shrugged.

Cash looked a little concerned, but I turned my gaze out my window to catch glimpses of Buttercup Lake through the thick woods.

"I get it." He tapped his steering wheel and let out a deep breath. "I really get it."

Chapter Two

Cash

"For the love of all that is holy," I muttered to myself as I reached into the trunk to grab her suitcases.

Why did my renter have to be so beautiful?

Just the thought soured my day, and the fact that I'd left my ice cream upside down at Becky's didn't help things either.

I glanced at Maya hopping out of the Jeep and shook my head. Whenever our eyes met, mischief dripped from her gaze, and her little sprite body sprang into action. She was like something I'd see in a damn fairytale rehashing, where she literally floated from one destination to another. Apart from tumbling head over heels atop her suitcases, she seemed like a vision.

A sigh escaped my lips as I snuck another look at her. All five feet of her were full of curves and softness. I only knew this because I was nearly six-five, and she was like a foot and a half shorter when I dug her out of her suitcases and set her in front of me.

My jaw clenched, and I shook my head.

Nope. Not gonna do it. Not gonna go there.

Maya pulled out the big suitcase from the backseat, and the Minnie Mouse bag nearly squashed her as the heaviness fell into her arms. She couldn't be an inch over five feet, which was the complete opposite of her sister. Beyond the dark hair, there wasn't much linking these two. Everything about Maya was soft. Grace was more defined. I liked soft.

As Maya steadied her bag, I held in a smile. At least she shouldn't wreak too much havoc on my place. She's a single, calm woman who wants to find herself or something.

Her cellphone rang, and she didn't answer it, didn't even bother to look at who was calling, just like before when it rang. I didn't know whether she was just being polite in front of me or truly avoiding someone's calls.

"You know, I have a smaller place that's a bit less money if this is too big for you," I told her. "It'll become available in a few weeks."

She turned and scowled at me. Her beautiful caramel eyes nearly knocked me off my feet. "I like space, and money isn't an issue."

"Duly noted." I nodded and wheeled her suitcases to the porch. "Well, you'll have plenty of it here. Five bedrooms, four bathrooms, a chef's kitchen, and several sitting rooms."

Maya snuck up behind me, and the sweet smell of flowers wafted over my shoulders. I closed my eyes at the door and told myself to get it together as I punched in the code.

The lock screamed at me.

Damn, wrong number. I punched it in again, and it was wrong.

Again.

What did this woman do to me? I had to pull myself together. I knew these codes like my social security number.

She chuckled. "Here, I have it on my phone."

"No. I got it. I just . . ." I finally punched in the correct numbers and pushed the door open with a grunt. "There."

I stepped inside with most of her luggage as Maya took in the front of the house before coming inside. "This house is so adorable. You'd never know it was so spacious just from the front."

I nodded in agreement as she took a step through the front door, pulling her suitcase behind her.

Maya gasped, and her eyes widened as she took in the home. "This is perfection. I love the wallpaper. Did it come with the house when you bought it?"

I shook my head, happy that she'd noticed the little details. With every house I picked up over the years, I'd always spent a tremendous amount of time and money rehabbing them. It was nice that it was noticed once in a while.

Maya's small fingers ran along the banister leading upstairs before she spun around. "This is a beautiful home. I promise to take care of it while I'm here."

I gave a quick nod. "Thanks. I appreciate it. The lake's out back. I'll let you be so you can wander the property alone."

She frowned and shrugged. "I don't mind company."

Shit.

"Okay." I nodded. "Let's start here to the left. We've got the dining room with a fireplace in the corner. You can step through the door here, which leads into the kitchen. I took down the wall between the kitchen and the family room there, so it's a more open concept."

I stopped walking, realizing Maya hadn't budged and was nowhere to be found. I retraced my steps and found her staring at a statue. It happened to be a bronze casting of my childhood dog sitting in the corner of the dining room.

She glanced at me. Her doe eyes flicked between the bronze statue and me. "That's beautiful."

"It's Buster."

She cocked her head slightly. "Buster?"

"My dead dog from when I was a kid." That did not come out how I intended.

Her eyes widened. "You mean, that's him? Like he's in there? His ashes or something, or bones?" Her voice dropped to a whisper. "Or is it like a sarcophagus?"

Before I had a chance to answer, her eyes darted to a row of vases on the mantel in the dining room. "Are those more relatives? Grandma or Grandpa? Or like the cats of the family in those urns?"

I chuckled and shook my head when she pointed her finger at me.

Her pretty eyes narrowed on me. "Wait a second. You *can* smile."

I shook my head. "Huh?"

"Becky mentioned that you were a little crusty," she explained. "And I noticed your mouth never once leaves that straight line, even when you laugh. Not even one lip curl in the northern direction."

"Crusty?" I repeated, shocked.

"She didn't use that exact word, but she assured me that you wouldn't be slicing me up and storing me in the basement, at least."

Well, there's that for a character assessment. Was that

really how my friends saw me?

I shoved my hands into my back pockets and stared at Maya, dazed. "How long were you at Becky's?

Maya shrugged. "Not more than ten minutes, I'd say."

"And you managed to cover whether or not I was a serial killer?"

"It wasn't me." She shook her head. "The thought never crossed my mind. At least not until Becky mentioned it, and then I have to confess that I wondered if coming to the middle of nowhere was a really a bright idea."

"And?"

"And then you showed up in your Jeep, and the rest is history." She clasped her hands together and studied me. "But I've never met a man who could giggle without a smile."

I straightened and frowned. "I didn't giggle. For the record, the vases are empty. My grandparents are very much alive. They summer in Arizona."

She folded her arms over her chest. "And your parents?"

"They are the ones who gifted me with the Buster monument, and they are doing quite well here in Buttercup Lake enjoying retirement. My siblings are currently spread throughout the state and abroad. Not dead."

Maya's smile widened, and I couldn't help but notice

how full and luscious her lips were. They were naturally pink with a lavender hue on the bottom lip. Nothing I should be observing when I'm handing over my rental for the remainder of the summer. This was a purely business transaction.

Her caramel eyes narrowed on me, and she kept smiling. "You're peculiar."

I laughed, and she pointed at me again.

"But I love your smile when it does surface," she added.

"I've been called a lot of things in my life, but peculiar was never one of them." I smoothed my hands over my shorts. And same went for *crusty.*

She twisted her lips into a contemplative pout as she eyed a painting above the mantel.

Oh, no.

Not Henry.

"I love that painting." She lit up and wandered over to the picture of my yellow parakeet from when I was seven. "The yellow is so vivid, even though it's watercolor."

Please, move on. Please, move on.

She squinted at the corner. "Knox. Isn't that your last name? Did you paint it?"

I shook my head and sighed. "No. My mom painted it."

Maya nodded and started to step away when a thought stopped her. "Wait a second. Why did your mom choose a parakeet to paint?"

My gaze dropped to the wood floors as I hid a laugh.

"This isn't a rental property. It's a shrine to all your pets." Maya snorted, and she slapped her forehead in disbelief.

"I'd never really thought of it that way before," I explained, trying to hold in my laughter at her snort. There was something so cute about the noise, and she didn't seem the least bit embarrassed.

Maya nodded and let out a whimsical hum. "Interesting. Really interesting."

I nodded in agreement. "I suppose that's one way of looking at it."

I just prayed she didn't notice the pawprint hanging in the family room of Benny, one of my other childhood pups, or the black and white photos of Cherry canvassing the hall upstairs. She'd been a beautiful cocker spaniel.

My mom was an artist, so everything had always been done beautifully and very artistically, but as Maya pointed out, they were all still reminders of the dead animals in my life.

What was wrong with me?

I bit my lip and sucked in a deep breath, watching her.

"If you want a different place, I'm more than happy—"

Maya shook her head frantically. "Nonsense. I find it fascinating. Now, show me the kitchen."

Fascinating? What was I dealing with?

I walked into the newly remodeled kitchen with white granite countertops, light grey kitchen cabinets, and a white subway tile backsplash. I'd done most of the work myself, and at times, thought about moving to this rental and renting out my current house in its place.

"The view of the lake is absolutely breathtaking," Maya said, sweeping her fingers along the silky countertop. "And this kitchen just sets it all off. Wow. The pictures were beautiful, but I wasn't prepared for this."

"Thanks. I did most of it myself."

She turned to look at me with curiosity dripping from her expression. "You did this?" She waved her hands around the room.

I nodded. "It's what I do. I pick up wandering guests who are lost and remodel my rentals in my spare time. I even got that thing working." I pointed at the door in the wall.

"What is it?" she asked.

"A dumbwaiter. It goes from the basement to the primary suite." I opened the door where a platform hovered, waiting for snacks to be served.

She giggled and leaned against the counter. "I've just never met a man who's so handy. Shoot. Rob had to call a handyman to change a lightbulb in the ceiling."

"Why didn't you just change it?" I asked, realizing that came out wrong too.

Around this woman, nothing came out of me smooth, polished, or even somewhat polite. It was like this female had some sort of mystical powers that turned me into a bumbling jerk. What was it she said? Not even a lip curl in the northern direction? Just the thought made me smile, but I didn't.

Maya straightened and let out a sigh. "Believe me, had I known he was calling someone to do it, I would have just grabbed a ladder and changed it myself. I only found out when I walked in on a stranger balancing on the top step to change out the lightbulb. Rob always acted as if money grew on trees."

I didn't realize I was studying her so hard until her cheeks pinked up all the way into her forehead.

"Who's Rob?" I asked without thinking and quickly added, "Not that it's my business."

"I'm an open book, Cash. Ask me anything you want. As for Rob? Good ol' Robo? He's the asshat who left me at the altar." She let out a grunt. "And, unfortunately, he's also my business partner. Grandma Millie told me not to do it. But did I listen? Nope. I was young and in love."

My jaw dropped open. I couldn't imagine any jerk leaving Maya anywhere, let alone something as sacred as a wedding. I recognized both the pain and embarrassment in her words and looked out toward the lake.

"It's his loss." I brought my gaze back to hers.

She flashed a smile in my direction. "You think so? I thought I'd probably ban myself from all meet-cute encounters."

I licked my lips and nodded, trying to regain some semblance of order with my thoughts. "I know so, and what the hell is a meet-cute? Sounds ridiculous and like you're not missing out. Is it some British lingo you're dropping on me?"

She laughed. "Just so happens that a meet-cute is generally the first romantic brush between two characters in a romantic film or book. I happen to read a lot, so . . ." She shrugged. "It just sounds sweet and innocent and so much better than purely hooking up."

"Whatever." I batted the air between us for absolutely no reason at all. How did this woman make me feel so vulnerable and like a babbling idiot? "Any man would be lucky to have a cute meet with you, or a hook-up, so don't say that."

"It's a meet-cute." Her gaze softened, and she nodded

her head. "But thanks. I think I needed to hear that from a male." She wandered toward the family room. "The mind can play terrible tricks on a person, but that's why I needed to come to Buttercup Lake. I just needed time away so I could get my head squarely planted on my shoulders again. Because I know there'll be a fight ahead, and I have to be ready for it."

I watched her wander into the family room, and I couldn't imagine anyone just dumping someone so rudely. But I'd seen a lot in my forty years, and I was learning not to let it all surprise me.

Maya's phone rang again, and I realized who was on the other end.

Rob.

And I knew there was a lot left to the story that Maya just didn't want to tell.

Chapter Three

Maya

"Oh, my gosh. It's so good to finally see you," Grace gushed.

She finally let go of me and took a couple of steps back. Izzy, my niece and Grace's daughter, came in for a hug too.

I'd barely settled into the house before I got the first call from my sister, and thankfully, Cash had already left before they arrived. To say I was in love with my place to stay for the next few months was an understatement. Between the amazing kitchen, gorgeous view, and cozy library I'd stumbled into on my own, I wasn't sure I'd ever want to leave.

"Do you mind that we brought our dog?" Grace asked, and I glanced at the poor thing.

"Is that what you call it?" I teased.

It had a flat face, floppy ears, hair that made the pup look more like a dirty mop than a canine, and a constant snort that accompanied its tiny self.

Izzy let go, and I noticed just how much different she looked from the photos I'd been sent over the last year or so. Izzy had looked so angry and aloof in so many of the pictures I'd seen, and this teenager looked like sunshine and rainbows. I saw a bit of her dad in her features, but I saw more Grace than anything.

"We call her Pancake for obvious reasons," Grace informed me, closing the door behind me. She had a plastic pitcher and spotted the luggage, and her brows furrowed. "I didn't know you were a fan of Minnie Mouse."

I rolled my eyes and laughed. "I just liked the polka dots. It only came to my attention recently that Minnie and I share an affinity for the pattern."

Izzy chuckled and nodded, picking up Pancake. "I think it's a cute set, Aunt Maya."

For some reason, I loved the way that sounded. It had been so long since I'd been around family that hearing those two little words from my fifteen-year-old niece made my travels worth it. I'd given up so much for Rob, and yet I never felt that he'd cared.

"So, I thought if you didn't mind, I could have

Jackson come over with dinner later?" Grace's eyes lit up when she mentioned her boyfriend. He was a professional golfer and often on tour.

"Absolutely. I'd love to see him. It's been so long. What about Grandma Millie?" I asked as we wandered into the family room.

Izzy giggled and glanced at her mom.

"Well, Grandma Millie is on a weekend trip with her boyfriend," Grace informed me.

"Aw, the one that got away so many years ago." I smiled, remembering when Grandma Millie told me about her first boyfriend. She didn't say much because Grandpa was still alive, and he was all that mattered in her world. I knew she loved our grandpa with all her heart, but I also found some love letters one time when I was visiting her that showed there was one before Grandpa Renny.

Grace nodded. "She said she'd tell us that story sometime when we're all together, but not before."

I snickered. "Grandma Millie is one of the most manipulative people I know."

"But with a heart of gold," Grace added.

"Which is exactly how she gets away with it," Izzy added, and I laughed. "When we pulled up, I saw a wing of some sort. What's in it? A bedroom?"

I grinned as they followed me into the kitchen. "That, my lovely niece, is a fully stocked library. I'm in book heaven."

Izzy's eyes widened. "Seriously? It looked huge from the outside."

I nodded. "And there's a screened porch to the side of it. I may never want to leave this place." I pointed through the family room where a closed, ornate door begged to be opened. "Through those doors, and you'll be in awe."

"And in the meantime," Grace added, "I want to catch up with my sister."

Izzy rolled her eyes and chuckled. "Not before I get some of Grandma Millie's lemonade."

I handed my niece a glass of ice as Grace poured the refreshing beverage for her daughter. I handed my sister two more glasses with ice.

The faint smell of lavender lemonade filled my nostrils, and I was instantly whisked back to my childhood.

"I don't know how she makes this, but it's amazing."

"Imagine how rich we'd be if Grandma bottled it," Grace teased as Izzy opened the door to the library.

"Wow. Just wow." Izzy spun around and looked at me. "You can't leave this house until we finish every book inside here."

I chuckled and nodded as she bounded into the library.

"Your daughter seems extremely happy being here in Buttercup Lake," I whispered.

"I think it's the combination of the lake and a boy named Caleb." Grace smiled and nodded. "But it's night and day being here. It's why we decided to stay."

I grinned. "Ooh, Caleb. He sounds cute."

"He is adorable." Grace smiled. "But he's also a teenage boy, so I know what's on his mind."

I cocked my head and playfully frowned. "And yet the thought would never occur to your angelic daughter."

Grace groaned and took a sip of lemonade. "That's precisely the problem. She's my daughter, and I know precisely what's going on in her head."

"Ah, to be a teenager again."

Grace looked horrified. "I'd never wish that on my worst enemy."

I shrugged. "I don't know. The thought sounds pretty ideal to me. No worries. No men to dump you or try to swindle your business away from you."

Grace's jaw dropped. "Maya, are you serious? He's going after your company?"

"Isn't it grand?" I rolled my eyes, trying to suppress

the anger roiling through my veins. "I should have seen this train wreck coming."

"But love." She nodded. "Love clouded your vision."

"Not just clouds. It was more like a hurricane or a tornado. I'm not sure which is worse."

Grace pressed her lips together and shook her head. "I'm so sorry, and I suppose now is not the time to mention that I never liked him either. Or are you going to get back with him, and then I'll awkwardly attend the wedding, pretending I never said those words?"

I chuckled and took another sip of the perfectly tart with a hint of sweet drink that my grandma had made.

"Not a chance." I winked at her. "It's crazy how something as simple as Grandma's lemonade can make me feel like all is right in the world again." I smiled and shook my head.

When the truth about my life was anything but that.

I had an ex who was threatening to take me to court for his share of the company, which he felt was more than fifty percent his. Meanwhile, I was trying to pretend that my heart hadn't been shattered to pieces, burned with a torch, and then buried six feet under with the rest of me.

"It's crazy that I run an online therapy app, and I'm such a mess personally." I shook my head and took another sip of lemonade.

Grace nodded sympathetically.

"The one thing I don't want to become is bitter, Grace." I let out a sigh. "But some days, it is extremely difficult to be Pollyanna."

"It's only been three weeks," she offered.

"True." I nodded and smiled. "But some days, it feels like just yesterday, and other days, it feels like an eternity has passed. So weird."

A funny look came across my sister, and my brows scrunched.

"Why are you looking like that?" I asked, getting nervous.

She leaned over the kitchen counter as I sat on a stool. "What did you think about Cash?"

I cocked my head slightly. "What do you mean, what did I think of him?"

She waggled her dark brows. "You know . . ."

Not taking the bait, I smiled. "Becky across the lake assured me that he's not a serial killer, so I take that as a great sign for a potential landlord for this short-term rental I'm in."

Grace groaned and looked at the ceiling. "You know what I mean. Give me a read of him."

I snorted. "Grace, I'm a therapist, not a psychic." I

brought my gaze to hers and grinned.

She stomped her foot and chuckled. "Come on . . . tell me."

"I know exactly what you mean, so I'll tell you all about me. I am a hot mess who has no business dragging some poor, innocent man through the fire with me."

Grace smirked. "I've heard he's not so innocent."

My stomach fluttered for absolutely no reason.

Actually, that wasn't quite true. I'd been thinking about Cash from the moment he drove his sparkling white Jeep in his shining armor to rescue me from Becky's. In between my throbbing big toe and my stubbornness to avoid Rob's incessant calls and texts, Cash was top of mind.

"Fine. What I think about Cash is that he's a sexy and smart guy." I took another sip of lemonade. "Who is a bit of a grump and has an affinity for his dead pets."

Grace scowled. "How is that a bad thing?"

I folded my arms over my chest and chuckled. "I didn't say it was a bad thing. It's just my observation."

"So, you're saying you're into him?" Grace prompted with a grin as she briefly glanced over my shoulder.

"I'm saying that I'm a mess, and Cash seems not interested. Very not interested." I folded my arms. "I've become a textbook case of jumping into someone's arms too quickly, and I just know that whatever he has to offer is next-level."

A man's gravelly voice nearly shot me off the stool. "What's next-level?"

I turned to see a man I recognized immediately.

Jackson Locke Jr.

My sister's first love.

And right behind him . . . Cash . . . and behind him, the elderly gentleman who had been using a walker earlier. Carter, maybe?

My cheeks instantly flamed red, and I prayed with all my heart and soul that the guys hadn't heard much, if any, of the conversation. The beats of my heart thrummed so loudly my ears rang, and I was one step away from the room spinning. I attempted to wiggle my bad toe to remind me that I was present.

I slid off the stool as Grace kept a smirk plastered to her face.

Jackson set several bags of food on the kitchen counter. "I thought since I was bringing dinner over, and this guy was groveling on a street corner, I'd let him come along. I hope that's okay."

Carter scowled. "I wasn't groveling. I have a damn walker I'm supposed to push all over the place, or Daisy threatened she'd come back to live with me. I can't handle her. She's way too perky."

Jackson laughed and pointed at Cash. "I wasn't talking about you, Uncle Carter. I was talking about this lost boy."

"I wasn't groveling. I was trying to get some ice cream since I managed to dump my last one all over the sidewalk."

"Who's Daisy?" I asked, glancing at Jackson.

"My younger cousin," Jackson informed me.

"And Cash used to date her," Uncle Carter chimed in.

Cash's brilliant green eyes met mine, and my breath became stuck in the back of my throat.

Like seriously stuck.

I started hacking, and Grace dashed past Jackson and started banging me on my back.

"I'm okay," I said between coughs. "Totally okay."

"Sounds like it," Cash said with a raised brow.

My gaze shot to his. "Are you always this full of sunshine?"

Cash's eyes locked on mine, and a scorched intensity shot through his gaze. It looked like he had so much to say but thought better of it before his full mouth turned into a thin line.

And then . . .

The grumpy man smiled.

Carter cleared his throat. "Usually, the man just grunts in caveman around town, so you're lucky you got words."

I snickered and looked up at Cash. His expression didn't change.

"It's nice to see you again," I said, clearing my throat and wiping the tears away from my coughing fit. "And I do have a question for you."

He stepped closer. "What's that?"

I pointed to the wall in the family room where a paw print hung among a painting of tulips. "Is that also a pet from years past?"

Cash closed his eyes, and the most beautiful smile threaded through his lips. "Yes. He was my dog named Frankie."

When he opened his eyes and his gaze found mine, a flutter of excitement rippled through me just as my sister cleared her throat.

"Jackson, Carter, and I'll go start the grill," she informed us.

I nodded my head, not tearing my gaze from Cash's. "Sounds good."

Cash studied me and took a deep breath. "Sexy and

super smart?"

Dang it.

He'd heard.

"And a bit of a grump," I added.

"I'm not grumpy. I'm just not a ray of sunshine every single second."

I chuckled. "Tomato. Tomahto. And if anyone should be sulking around this beautiful home, it should be me."

Cash nodded and sucked on his bottom lip briefly. "Fair enough."

"You know, you're even sexier when you smile."

Cash let out a low rumble of a laugh and shook his head while crossing his arms over his chest. His large biceps curled into a lean mass of flesh. "I'll keep that in mind, but I wasn't too concerned with being sexy."

I laughed and shook my head. "Don't even give me that. Any guy who has as many muscles as you do obviously cares about his physique. Your hair has the perfect flip at all times." I tapped my foot. "And you have more confidence than Wisconsin has mosquitos."

He smirked. "Well, I carry lumber around for my workout."

"And your hair?"

He grinned, and it about knocked me off my feet.

"You wouldn't believe me if I told you."

My brows rose. "Try me."

"I don't know . . . I might lose a bit of the cool factor."

"I never said you were cool." I chuckled. "Just sexy. Want some lemonade?"

He nodded, and a few seconds passed, so I tried again.

"Does your mom cut your hair?"

He rocked back on his heels and grinned. "Nope."

"Then what?"

"I use a Flowbee," he confessed.

My jaw dropped open. "You use a vacuum attachment to cut your hair?"

He scratched his chin. "Sure do. It chops it and sucks it right up."

I stood in complete awe. Cash truly was a fascinating human being.

Pouring some more lemonade, I stared at my glass. I didn't want him knowing just how impressed I'd become by my sexy landlord. "Wow. That's pretty awesome."

"Awesome?"

I nodded, handing him lemonade. "Completely awesome. I always get a little weirded out when guys spend like two hundred bucks on a haircut." I shrugged. "It's nice to see that a vacuum can do just as good a job." I smiled. "I cut my own hair too."

"No way."

"Yup." I grinned. "I just twist and chop. Twist and chop."

Somehow, through all our chatting, we were less than a foot apart.

Cash took a swig of lemonade like it was honey whiskey and smiled before setting his empty cup on the counter.

Definitely all man.

The scent of his soap wafted between us, a hint of pine, possibly. It was nearly intoxicating. I looked toward the open door to the library before bringing my gaze back to his.

There was something conflicted in his smoldering gaze. "I'm sorry about barging in on your family reunion tonight. Jackson was pretty relentless."

Shock registered through me. "Oh, my gosh. I'm happy to have you. You're a good distraction with everything going on. Plus with Carter around, I might need a decoy for him to target."

He nodded, but his brows furrowed. "Distraction?"

His voice was husky.

I leaned in and smiled. "You know, easy on the eyes . . . and it's fun to try to get you to crack a smile."

The right side of his mouth curled into a sexy smirk, and I let out a laugh. "See? I did it again. You smiled. If I shower you with compliments all the time, I just might get to see more of it."

He nodded as my sister and Jackson came back inside, but his smile instantly dropped.

Grace's hand came up to her mouth. "Oh, did we interrupt something?"

Cash jerked away and shook his head. "Not in the slightest." He sounded gruff, and I had to keep in a chuckle.

His green eyes flicked to mine, and it felt like I was flying down a zipline with no way of braking.

Chapter Four

Cash

Reason four hundred and thirty-six that living in a small town could be rough for a guy who wanted to remain single and in solitude for eternity was that four hundred and thirty-five other people wanted to set you up.

And they had set up poor Maya as their next victim. The moment I got the call from Becky about a lost tenant, I had a sneaking suspicion that the limb blocking the number on Becky's address sign was meticulously placed. After all, it wasn't my first run-in with the Sunshine Breakfast Club—our sneaky little book club that paraded around as a bunch of book lovers when, in reality, they are wicked and ruthless matchmaking fiends.

Their last attempt to force me into love resulted in an unsuspecting newcomer in town named Daisy being mysteriously placed wherever I happened to go. I couldn't believe they'd try to push me on a date with a girl who hadn't even reached thirty. Needless to say, she and I shared a good laugh about the situation because she had no interest in marrying a man who was one step away from drinking Geritol.

Okay, maybe I might be exaggerating a little bit at the age of forty, but that age difference can sneak up on a person. Some days, I felt a lot older than forty.

I shook my head and kicked my heels up onto the stool in front of me and watched a paddleboarder navigate the lake behind my house.

Maya.

Definitely a woman out of my league.

But there was something about her that kept creeping back into my thoughts. And the truth was that when Jackson persuaded me to join him at Maya's for dinner, it didn't take much in the way of arm twisting. I tried to play the invite off as if I didn't really want to go, but I couldn't wait to see her, and it had only been a few hours since I'd left the rental.

I let out a deep breath and leaned my head against the chair as I thought about how endearing her little snort was whenever she laughed too hard or discovered something. What worried me was that I wanted to know more about her.

I wanted to know every single detail that had led her to Buttercup Lake. Why she left her house. What she did for a living. Her favorite color.

Everything.

I also understood that if I asked about every detail of her life that I was dying to know about, she'd probably flee Buttercup Lake and never look back, and this trip was about her. I was merely the property owner who needed to make her stay as comfortable and uneventful as possible.

But for the first time in a minute, I didn't hate that the Sunshine Breakfast Club was up to their usual tricks.

Lifting my head, I looked at the lake where the paddleboarder was no longer in view and took a sip of coffee.

Today was going to be a great day.

I had a property to look at that I was interested in purchasing before it hit the market, and I had a few fixes to do in my own place, like stopping a leaky faucet in the ensuite upstairs.

So, if I knew what I needed to do today, why in God's name was I thinking about a complete stranger who had more energy than my old Australian cattle dog, Maggie? I smiled, thinking back to how quickly Maya caught on to the pet situation. I'd never paid much attention, but she was right. The house had become a shrine to my life of deceased pets.

And what did she call it? Fascinating?

She also said I was sexy and smart and . . . a bit of a grump.

I frowned harder and stood.

Why did I care?

With that last question, I made my way into my house to grab my wallet before I took off to the hardware store when my phone dinged.

I glanced at the text and couldn't help but smile.

I'm so sorry to bother you, and I'm completely mortified that I have to write this to you, but the tub seems plugged. It won't drain. Is there a trick?

My frown deepened. Why would there be a trick to draining a tub?

I wrote back.

No trick. Did you put something in there besides water?

She quickly wrote back.

Like what?
I smiled and typed.

I don't know what your self-care looks like.

She wrote back with a laughing emoji.

Self-care? I just wanted to get clean, so I added some lavender sea salts, and that was it. They dissolved fully before I even got in the tub. Promise!

I clenched my jaw and tried to push the image of her stepping into the tub right out of my mind. This was strictly professional.

I typed a quick message back.

I'll be over to unclog your pipes shortly.

The moment I sent the message, a fierce heat ran through me. What in God's name kind of text did I just send to Maya? I closed my eyes and shook my head, groaning. I stretched my arms and let out a deep breath as I typed back.

Not your pipes. The pipes. I'm only going to unclog

the tub.

Within seconds, a text from Maya came over.

What else would you be unclogging?

And waiting just enough to make me extremely uncomfortable, Maya sent another text.

Kidding. While my pipes are a little rusty, I know you meant the tub.

With a little winky emoji.

I felt a smile creep onto my lips, and I knew Maya would be pleased that she'd made me smile again.

"Alright, Rusty . . ." I stopped myself and looked behind me when it hit me that Rusty wasn't here any longer. My constant pal of eleven years was no longer eagerly waiting for me to leave the house so he could crawl into my bed and nap. My Irish setter, who'd been with me since the beginning of my life crumbling into a massive pile of rubble, was gone.

Forever.

I cleared my throat and shook my head.

"Damn dog," I muttered, wiping a tear away. "It's

been three months, and I still think he's here."

Closing the front door softly, I walked to the Jeep and wondered if I'd ever get over Rusty. He was like my child, even more so than the pets I'd grown up with.

There was just something about him. We were kindred spirits, full of mischief and a carefree middle finger salute when the time called for it.

And I'd say the last several years of my life had definitely asked for that response.

I glanced in my rearview mirror and reversed out of my driveway as I tried to shake off the emptiness of Rusty's absence.

The balmy air tangled my hair as I drove to my rental with the top off. Nothing beat a Wisconsin summer. The air was clear. The skies were brilliant blue and stretched as far as the eye could see, and the sunsets...

Man, the sunsets were out of this world. Usually, because a storm was about to cross the North and the skies would blaze.

I pulled into the rental and turned off the car right when a mosquito landed on my neck. I smacked it hard and chuckled.

The summers were great apart from the skeeters.

The door opened, and Maya gave a quick wave as she

came outside. Her pink dress stopped right above her knees, and the full skirt accentuated her hips-waist-boob ratio in an awesome way.

Just seeing her made my entire body respond in a way that it shouldn't. Sure, I was like any other male around who could see that Maya was beautiful, but it took more than beauty to ever make me notice. And the one time I did, it all got taken from me.

Damn.

Why did seeing Maya bring up all these feelings?

And Rusty?

I hadn't talked to him in weeks.

"Hey, stranger. I swear I'm not an unruly and bothersome renter." Her lips pursed into a cute pout as her eyes sizzled into me.

I cleared my throat and grabbed the toolbox I kept behind my seat.

"We'll see about that," I teased gruffly, and her eyes narrowed on me as she came to greet me.

"Oh, yeah?" she asked. "You don't take my word for it?"

I scratched my chin and looked over her shoulder to the house behind her. "Nope. I've been burned enough times by houseguests to know better."

"Ouch." She put her index finger in the air and made a searing noise.

Could she get any cuter?

I smiled, and so did she.

"I knew I could get you to crack one today."

"Believe it or not, I'm not crotchety."

"Whatever you say there, Cash." She glanced over her shoulder. "I like your toolbox. It looks nifty."

My brows rose. "Nifty?"

She smiled again, and I shook my head as I followed her to the house. "I'm really sorry the tub isn't draining, though. I take pride in making sure my homes are up to par. I'll be taking a night off your rent for the hassle."

She stopped in her tracks right when we'd made it inside and spun around. "Don't even think about doing that. It's not your fault. These things happen."

Regardless, the final charge would have it deducted.

"Okay, well. It's just upstairs, as you know. I'll be in the kitchen deciding whether I want to finally call back my ex or not."

The way she snarled the word ex made me glad I wouldn't be the one on the other end of that call.

I gave a quick nod and started toward the upstairs. When I'd reached the primary bedroom where the ensuite was located, I kept my head down. I just wanted to get to the tub, fix it, drain it, and get out of here.

As I made my way into the bathroom, I spotted a red lace thong peeking out from under a flannel nightshirt.

Exactly what I was trying to avoid seeing.

Of course, she'd wear sexy underwear under her everyday clothes.

Why?

Just to make my imagination go crazy.

I rolled my eyes and knelt by the tub filled with water and donned a pair of gloves from my toolbox. As I started messing with the drain, I spotted something white tucked underneath the drain. I leaned in for a closer look through the water. It looked like tissue.

As I began pulling, tissue started disintegrating between my fingers. It was like someone had stuffed a whole wad of toilet paper or facial tissue into the drain. The more I pulled out, the more the water drained. By the time the tub sat empty, I'd managed to pull an entire clump of tissue from the drain. I tossed it into the trash and turned the tub water on again to make sure it continued to drain normally.

"That should do it," I muttered to myself, pulling off the gloves to wash my hands.

Would Maya have stuffed tissue to plug the tub? But

why? I glanced at myself in the mirror and laughed.

Because you're such a stud, Cash.

Realizing how absolutely ridiculous that idea sounded, I started toward the stairs when I heard Maya sniffle.

And then another sniffle before she blew her nose and sniffled some more.

Oh, no. She was crying.

My mind raced to the guy she called Rob, and I suddenly wanted to meet the ex so I could take care of business. There was never a reason to make a woman cry.

Ever.

When I got to the base of the stairs, she blew her nose harder than the last time, and I let out a grunt. I wasn't exactly the best at dealing with crying women, but the thought of pretending I didn't hear her wasn't something I was willing to do.

Plus, I needed to let her know the problem had been fixed.

I set my toolbox by the front door and made my way down the hallway toward the kitchen, where I saw Maya turn toward the kitchen window that faced the lake.

It was a beautiful view, and seeing Maya enjoying it between tears gave me some sort of weird comfort. At least she had a nice place to recover from her breakup.

I tapped the counter lightly with my knuckles. "Hey, Maya. It's all fixed. I'll be getting out of your hair now."

She turned and smiled with sticky tears staining her cheeks, and I knew I wasn't going anywhere.

Chapter Five

Maya

I swore I'd never shed another tear over Rob, and here I was, snotting all over the place in front of one of the sexiest men alive who'd just dropped everything to help me with a plumbing issue. It didn't help that Cash's T-shirt tugged just right across his broad shoulders, and for some reason, his khaki shorts gripped his waist just enough to make every step interesting in the front.

Reaching for a paper towel, I tore a chunk off and wiped my nose.

"I'm so sorry." I swallowed down a mixture of mortification and grief. Or maybe it was torment. I felt tormented by Rob.

"Uh, hey. I don't know what's going on, but I'm more than happy to lend an ear." Cash's normal gruff tone had a sensitive touch to it. "Or a shoulder. I have really broad shoulders."

I snickered and nodded. "Yes, you do. They're something to be proud of."

Cash smiled and nodded. "You doing okay? Dumb question. Obviously not."

I smiled and folded my arms over my chest. "I'm doing okay. Just not used to standing up for myself, I suppose."

Cash bit his bottom lip and glanced out the window toward the lake. "You shouldn't have to stand up for yourself, Maya. No one should put you in that kind of situation."

His words hit home and made me question all my years of schooling and professional career.

Cash was right, more so than he could ever know.

Ever since I was a kid, I had felt an overwhelming need to stand up for either myself or my sisters. It was what happened when you had addicts for parents. It was probably why I became a therapist and why I'd made it my mission to make therapy easier to obtain.

Yet, here I stood, thoroughly screwed up.

I frowned and shrugged. "Thank you, and now if I could get my inner child to hear that, I'd be set." I drew a deep breath and turned around to stare at the lake. "I've spent more money than you can imagine on therapy and degrees to still put myself in situations where I need to stand up for myself."

A few seconds of silence hung in the air, but I felt him listening, even if it was to nothing.

"What is it you do for a living?" he asked as I turned around slowly to face him.

"Believe it or not, I'm a therapist." I chuckled, suddenly feeling like my secret had been revealed. I was a failure as a therapist because I couldn't even get my own life together.

He smiled, and it nearly melted me. "I believe it. You're kind and perceptive. You're smart, and you have amazing observation skills."

"Yeah? You think so?"

"Absolutely. Within minutes of walking into this house, you knew I had issues."

I chuckled and shook my head. "I hadn't really thought of my observations as issues."

"I'm a grown man who can't let go of my pets." His brow arched into a sexy smirk. "That's got to be some sort of fodder for analyzing mental health conditions."

Shaking my head, our eyes connected, and it felt like every cell in my body electrified with hope.

Hope for what? I had no idea. I slid my suddenly moist palms down the skirt of my dress and hoped for the best.

"I just think you're sentimental and sweet," I promised.

"Even if I'm a grump?"

"Jury is still out on that assessment." I winked at him, feeling less embarrassed. "But I must tell you that you have impeccable taste in wallpaper and décor."

Cash's beautiful smile stayed on his lips as I finally let out the breath I'd been holding deep inside that had felt trapped between my ribs.

"Was it Rob who made you cry?" he asked, his smile turning tender.

"He said some nasty things. Some things that scared me, actually." I straightened, thinking back to his parting words. *I'll make you pay in more ways than you can imagine. I'll expose you for the fraud you are, and that's if I don't bury you alive first.*

Cash studied my features, and I knew it wouldn't be easy to hide the truth from him, but I was embarrassed.

Embarrassed that I'd let myself fall into this kind of abusive relationship. Embarrassed that I almost married the man who dealt the verbal blows. And embarrassed that I'd cried over a man who enjoyed hurting me.

I looked into Cash's eyes and squared my shoulders. No, I wouldn't be telling Cash what Rob had told me.

Buttercup Lake was about starting over to get a fresh perspective on life. My attorneys would handle Rob and the business side of that catastrophe. I would handle the doomed relationship.

"So, I'm guessing you won't answer his next call or text?" Cash asked.

"Definitely not." I shook my head. "I actually took the bait. He sounded somewhat rational in the last text and voicemail, so I thought I'd give him a call. But the truth of the matter is that he just wants my business."

"Which is therapy?" Cash clarified.

"A little more than that." I cleared my throat and cocked my head at this near stranger, wondering why I could speak so freely with him.

I mean, the view didn't hurt as I looked at him and spoke, but there was definitely more to it than that.

My cheeks blushed, and I looked down at the floor when I realized what it was.

Cash made me feel safe.

"I, umm . . . I developed an app for therapy that lets people access a licensed therapist anytime they need. Mental health doesn't just wait for Monday mornings at eight o'clock."

Cash folded his arms across his broad chest and didn't

take his gaze away from me. "No, the brain doesn't wait for office hours."

I nodded, seeing a glimmer of something surface behind his gaze.

"Things tend to go to hell in a handbasket around Saturday night at around eleven, judging by the cars in the bar parking lots," he added.

"Exactly. When we need a little extra encouragement or someone to listen or guide us, it might be on off-hours. So, my app has done really well filling that void, and Rob wants to take it all away from me." I sighed, leaning against the kitchen counter.

"He sounds like a real jerk." His jaw ticked, and I hid a smile.

I nodded. "He's been that way since I met him, but I just kept thinking it was me."

Cash furrowed his brows. "You kept thinking that you were the jerk or that you were making him the jerk?"

When he said it that way, I chuckled. "I guess that I was the one making him be a jerk."

"Impossible." He let his arms hang down. "Anyone who lugs around polka dot luggage can't be a jerk, especially when the bags are red."

"Well, thank you for that."

He patted my shoulder like a member of a soccer team, giving one of his players a pep talk. "Hey, how about we go get some ice cream? It'll be my treat for messing with your morning."

My stomach knotted into a tight little bow of doubt and uncertainty, and his gaze fell slightly.

"Or another time," he added. "You've had a rough morning."

I glanced at the clock and brought my eyes back to Cash. "No, I'm not going to let my ex ruin a perfectly good ice cream invitation. I'll let my attorneys handle everything."

"Did you block him?" he asked.

"You can do that?"

He nodded. "You should be able to."

"Have you ever had to block people?"

Cash bit his bottom lip. "Once."

"Really?" Now, I was intrigued. He didn't look like he'd ever need to block someone. Cash looked more like the 'handle it once and for all' kind of guy. "Who'd you have to block?"

"Nah." He dismissed the question, but I wouldn't take my eyes off him. "Fine. A woman who rented one of my bungalows on the southend of the lake developed a crush."

I eyed him closely. "Did you give her any reason to?"

"You've met me. Do I look like I give off a come-hither look?"

I shrugged. "Beats me. I don't know if you're always like this to everyone or if I'm just the lucky one."

He choked a little on his breath and shook his head. "Everyone. So, when she wouldn't stop coming by my house . . ."

My eyes widened. "Your house?"

Cash nodded and scratched his chin. "I had to let her down easily."

"Wait. What are you talking about? Did you sleep with her, and then she came back for more, or where are we going with this story?"

Cash laughed. "We shouldn't be going anywhere with this story."

I grinned and hopped up on the balls of my feet a little. "But we are."

"Fine. No. I didn't sleep with her. She propositioned me several times. Flirted even harder. I tried to let her down gently."

"Tsk. Tsk." I shook my head. "But she just needed some big, old Cash lovin'."

Cash shook his head. "That's not my style."

I caught his gaze and saw a flicker of sadness coast

through his eyes, so I nodded. "If it makes you feel any better, I'm not going to be knocking on your door for nookie anytime soon."

He frowned and laughed. "I'm not sure that does, actually."

I rolled my eyes and shook my head. "Thanks again for fixing the tub. What do you think happened?" I saw that he looked extremely uncomfortable.

"A whole bunch of toilet or bath tissue had been stuck down the drain."

Surprise rippled through me. "Seriously?"

He nodded. "Yeah. I don't know how that could have happened, but I'm not kidding when I say the houseguests can be a little unruly at times."

"I guess so."

"What's weird, though, is that I had checked the tub before you arrived, and it drained fine."

"Well, thanks for helping." My mind drifted to my sister yesterday. She'd gone upstairs and claimed she needed to rest for a little bit, but . . .

I pushed the thought out of my mind. That would be crazy with a capital C. She wouldn't stuff something down the drain.

Would she?

Nah.

Although Carter Locke also went upstairs after my sister, it wasn't like it was easy for a guy in his nineties with a walker to navigate the stairs.

But he did.

I bit my bottom lip and realized I'd suddenly swallowed the delusion pill.

"You think our get-together got a little rowdy, and the guests started stuffing drains?" I teased.

Cash's laugh roared to life as he shook his head. "It's your family. You tell me."

"Speaking of, after the ice cream, would you mind dropping me off at my sister's store?"

Cash smiled. "Not at all."

"Thanks. She was going to come by and pick me up, but this would save a trip."

"Sure thing."

I grabbed my purse and smiled at Cash, realizing that I'd completely forgotten about my ex's nasty call.

"Distraction is a good thing," I hummed.

"It can be." He winked at me, and a little flutter of excitement tried to rev up, but I quickly stomped it. "And you are quite the distraction."

I rolled my eyes as we walked out of the kitchen, and

he picked up his toolbox by the front door. "You're not nearly as cranky as you were yesterday."

"Give me time. I'll go back to my ways."

"I don't know. I think it just might be my joyful spirit that spits snot everywhere and talks about her ex that got you out of your funk." I grinned.

"I'm not in a funk." He frowned. "But maybe it's you talking about yourself in the third person?"

I snorted. "Yeah?"

"Just because I don't look like a clown all the time, grinning ear to ear, doesn't mean I'm in a funk." He glanced down at my sandals and smiled for some reason.

"If you're going to use a clown analogy, I'd say you're more *Pennywise*, if anything," I muttered under my breath.

"I heard that, and thank you. And is your toe okay? It looks like it's triple the size of most toes."

I rolled my eyes. "Wasn't meant to be a compliment, and my toe is fine. I'd thank you for unclogging my pipes, but I wouldn't want you to think I'm going to be your next stalker throwing innuendos your way."

Cash's low, grumbly laughter filled the foyer as he opened the door for me, and I wasn't sure if getting ice cream was a good idea, after all.

"Maya, something tells me I couldn't pay you to stalk me, so I'm sure I'm safe." I walked under his arm as he held the door. "Like you told your sister, what I have to offer is next-level, and you aren't ready for that."

Chapter Six

Cash

On day two of Maya staying in one of my properties, I was already walking in unchartered territory. It wasn't like attractive women hadn't stayed at my B&Bs before, but something about Maya just threw me for a loop.

She was so layered and complex, didn't mind showing a little emotion or putting me in my place.

And I couldn't get the woman out of my mind.

We'd picked up some ice cream, and I'd dropped her off at her sister's earlier today. That should have been it, but as I stood staring at the next property that I was about to add to my collection, all I could think about was the way Maya demolished her peppermint ice cream. It was the most alluring thing I'd seen in a long time.

Honestly, I'd never seen anything like it. She used up

all thirty napkins she'd picked up and still had a sticky mess puddled on her chin. Granted, it was three scoops, and the temp outside had already hit ninety with the humidity at about seventy, so things just melted.

But still, it was a sight to behold.

"What do you think?" my realtor asked, coming up behind me after we'd toured the inside.

"I think it's a great median price point for vacationers. I have some high-end rentals and some inexpensive rentals, but this kind of hits the best of both worlds. The square footage would meet the needs of a family more than my larger properties, and while it's on the lake, it's overgrown and needs some work to access it." I took a few steps back and looked at the bright white vinyl siding and faded blue trim. "The place needs work. That's for sure. I probably have a good six months of projects before I can get it up and running."

My realtor nodded and stood next to me. "You can't beat the price, and you don't have to worry about going to market and getting outbid."

I laughed. "That's where you come in, Marcus. I don't worry about those scenarios. You do."

Marcus grinned at me and smiled. "True, and it's been that way for over a decade."

My cousin Marcus had been my realtor since he'd

graduated college and realized he missed Buttercup Lake. So, he took his real estate exams and moved back home.

"Do you want me to give you the bad news before or after you make the offer?" Marcus flashed his typical salesperson look.

"What do you mean, bad news?" I folded my arms and frowned.

My cousin chuckled. "I knew your good mood wouldn't last very long. It never does."

"Spill it."

"Since it's an estate sale, the family selling it has one provision."

"Not too unusual." I nodded. "What? They want to be able to stay in it once a year?"

He shook his head. "No. It's a bit more of a commitment than that."

My brows rose. "Commitment?"

"They live overseas."

I nodded, waiting for the drama king to spit out the detail that could spoil my afternoon.

"The house comes with a dog."

"Huh?" I shook my head. "What do you mean, comes with a dog? Marcy didn't have a dog."

Buttercup Lake was a small town, and I knew enough

about the woman who'd lived here up until a few years ago to know she didn't have any animals.

"Well, Marcy adopted a dog before she moved into assisted living about three years ago. Her children can't take the dog, and they don't want it to wind up in a shelter . . . or worse."

My cousin knew the *or worse* would get me.

"Damn it." I shook my head. "I knew this deal was too good to be true."

"What are you talking about, Cash? You love dogs. And you just lost Rusty. Maybe it's meant to be."

I scowled at my cousin. "Rusty was special. He was irreplaceable. He was like my child."

The balmy breeze washed over us as I stared at the house in front of me. "Who has the dog now?"

Marcus rocked on his heels and glanced in my direction and mumbled.

"What did you say?" I asked.

"I do," he repeated.

"You want this deal to happen, right?" I asked. "Then you keep the dog, and I'll keep the house."

"It's not like that, Cash. My lifestyle isn't fit for a dog. I'm a bachelor. I'm not around enough to keep her happy."

My brows rose sharply. "I'm a bachelor too."

"Yeah, but you don't do anything besides work, eat, and stare at the lake behind your house." My cousin stepped away from me as if I were going to bite him.

I laughed, nodding my head. "I can't argue with that much. What kind of dog are we talking about? Newfoundland? Australian sheepdog? German shorthair? Labrador?"

He nodded and took a few steps toward me again. "Close. She's a teacup Pomeranian."

I froze as dread threaded through every thought and word combination I had.

After a few seconds of silence, my cousin shifted his weight from one foot to the other. "She's so small. You might not even remember you have a dog half the time."

I clicked my tongue and shook my head. "Deal is dead."

"Then apparently ... so is little Chewie." My cousin's expression fell.

I narrowed my eyes at him. "You wouldn't let that happen."

"It's not up to me. I don't own their dog. I'm just babysitting."

I grunted and kicked the dirt with my hiking boots. "You said it was a girl?"

71

A smug smile dripped from his lips. "Yup."

"And her name is Chewie?"

"Chewbacca is on her papers."

"After the hairy guy from *Star Wars*?"

"Technically, Chewbacca is a Wookie, but yeah."

"Unbelievable." I shook my head. "Why's she named that? Marcy doesn't seem like the type who was a *Star Wars* fan."

"Huge, actually, and Chewie's fur is apricot. It kind of fits. She's adorable and almost potty trained."

My brows arched in surprise. "Way to sell me. If she's three years old, why isn't she completely potty trained?"

He shrugged. "I didn't raise her. I don't know."

I let out a groan, knowing what was about to happen to my life. I'd gotten into a routine with Rusty, and without Rusty, I'd been fumbling my way from day to day, making the best of things while trying not to think the worst about things.

It wasn't going well.

I rested my hands on my cousin's shoulders and gave them a firm squeeze while looking at the house. But getting a wild orange fluffball wasn't exactly going to be smooth sailing, either.

"Fine. I'll take the house and the dog."

"But?" he asked tentatively.

I shook my head. "No buts . . . other than I want to close in two weeks. I'm going to need every single day before winter hits to work on this place."

"Great. I'll let them know. It shouldn't be a problem. In fact, they'll probably be relieved that it's behind them." My cousin stepped out of my reach and turned to face me. "So, you said that you had to drop off someone before our appointment."

I gave a quick nod. "I did say that."

"Did you finally take my advice?" His brows waggled, and I grunted my answer.

"Then who'd you have to drop off in the morning?"

"A tenant."

"Yeah?"

I averted my eyes away from Marcus and back to the house. I knew what he was thinking and wasn't going to fall into his trap.

"Does the tenant happen to be a she?"

"What are you getting at?"

"Just curious why you're hanging out with a guest at one of your rentals. That's all. Was there an issue with her pipes or something?"

I studied my cousin as paranoia crept in. He couldn't

be in on it, right?

Or was he?

Was that clog not as innocent as it appeared?

Had the Sunshine Breakfast Club infiltrated my own family?

I eyed him suspiciously. "Are you sleeping with someone from the Sunshine Breakfast Club?"

He frowned. "Why would you ask that?"

I shook my head. "No reason. Listen, just get me the papers to sign, and let's get rolling."

"Awesome."

I turned to my Jeep, and my cousin started up again. "Hey, when are you coming to get Chewie?"

Might as well get it over with.

"How about now?" I hollered over my shoulder. "I should probably let Chewie start to settle in."

My cousin didn't answer, but when I got in my Jeep, he gave a thumbs-up sign as he climbed into his truck.

I glanced at the house once more and let out a deep breath, wondering if this was the sign I'd been waiting for.

Probably not.

The truth was that I wasn't waiting for any sign.

I already knew I'd been lucky enough to have love once. I didn't need to test the waters again.

This house and this dog would be distraction enough while Maya was in town, and I could just get back to the life I understood.

And a therapist?

I shook my head and pulled out of the long driveway that had been overgrown on each side, making it nearly impossible to stay on the gravel.

The one thing I didn't need was anyone psychoanalyzing me.

I was screwed up.

I knew it.

But I didn't need to change.

I didn't need to be analyzed.

I'd done plenty of that myself.

"Chewie," I muttered. "What the hell did I get myself into?"

I followed Marcus to his house and noticed an extra car in his driveway. He hopped out of the car after I pulled in behind him and dashed up to my side of the Jeep.

"I'll just go in and grab her and some of the stuff I ordered."

I noticed the front door to his house was open, and I couldn't help but smile when I saw who had come into view. "Interesting. Don't you think?"

My cousin chuckled, glancing back at the woman holding an orange fluffball. "I didn't know she'd still be here."

"What's her name?" I waved at the redhead who was leaning on the doorframe, waiting for my cousin.

"Anita," he said through clenched teeth. "It's nothing serious. She knows it. I know it."

"Whatever you say, Bro." I snickered and shook my head. "Is she going to be okay with you giving the dog away?"

My cousin rolled his eyes, and I knew this was killing him. He loved to flip everyone else crap about dating but could never handle the heat on his own.

The redhead looked excited to see Marcus as he climbed the steps to his house and reached for Chewie as he went inside.

Within seconds, my mind drifted back to Maya. Apparently, there was no peace with her in town. What I needed to do was get the dog and go straight home. Forget about Maya and her giant toe and pray that I didn't run into her again for the rest of her trip.

Which was unlikely.

But still a lofty goal.

If I stayed near my house and only went out sparingly, I should increase my chances of not running into her just enough to stay sane.

Although, I should stop by the hardware store and see if the adjoining gift shop inside had any pet toys or if the farm store had any special dog food for this small breed.

As I watched my cousin manhandle the tiny pup and a bag stuffed with a tiny pink dog bed and food, I knew that what Marcus had waiting inside for him was something I never had and something I never wanted.

Even when I was in my twenties, I wasn't the dude looking for one-night stands.

What I'd always wanted was what my parents had.

A family.

Long-term.

All boots in, ready to face whatever life threw at us.

But that wasn't in the cards, and I wasn't the kind of guy who could have meaningless encounters just for the chase of pleasure.

And Maya would be merely that.

Chapter Seven

Maya

"This is beautiful," I told my sister, who had a pair of overalls on and an orange tee poking out underneath. She beamed with pride as we stared at the indoor construction site that was promising to turn into an antique store. Pancake was chewing on a bone twice the size of her little canine self over by a temporary wall.

I'd helped Grace move in about thirty boxes of things she'd ordered that were filled with custom signage to decorate the store with fun sayings for categories. The premise of her store was great. The space had been divided into a dozen or so smaller stores where she'd get a commission from other people's items that sold, plus a rental fee for each space.

Grace frowned at me and looked around at the pile of lumber and half-framed walls before turning her attention back to me.

"I wouldn't call it beautiful, but it's getting there." She bit her lip and tried not to laugh for some reason.

"What's so funny?" My hands slid to my hips.

"You just seem to be in a very good mood since I last saw you. That's all." She slid her gaze to the one area in the store that had been completed—the front. Plastic sheathing rippled from the slightest breeze, protecting the finished product from the rest of the work.

"It's called Buttercup Lake. Something about this place just makes a person feel better."

"Are you sure it's not *someone*?"

I thought back to Cash coming to my rescue this morning and smiled. "Positive."

"Don't you think it's weird that you had to call him for maintenance already?"

"Well, he certainly seemed puzzled by it, but it happens. He can't predict what the last vacationers were up to."

My sister smirked with a twinkle in her eye. "Totally."

"What aren't you telling me?"

She clapped her hands and pretended to dust them off. "Nothing at all. But hey, since you're going to be here for the foreseeable future, wanna come to the Sunshine Breakfast

Club with me?"

"I heard about that club. Since when did you become a book club type of gal?"

"What's that supposed to mean?"

I chuckled. "I don't know. You were always into the boys, and I was into the books."

She laughed and held up her finger. "I was into one boy."

"That turned into two," I corrected since she didn't marry the first one. But she had recently rekindled things with boy number one in a surprising move.

"It's not just about books. We chat, we eat, we eat some more, and then we chat, and finally, we talk about the latest read. It's a lot of fun. Most of the meetings are in the morning so people can get to work, but sometimes there are night meetings." She walked over to a large purse slumped next to Pancake and pulled out a book. "I picked up two copies of this month's read in case you wanted to join."

"Suspicious," I muttered.

Grace rolled her eyes and put up her hands in jest. "Ooh, real suspicious. Asking her sister to join a book club. It has *shenanigans* stamped all over it."

I chuckled. "Fine. But only because you bought this for me. I have an entire library of books waiting for me."

"I know. Izzy hasn't stopped talking about how cool your vacation place is."

"I love it. I don't know how I'm going to drag myself away."

"Who says you have to?"

I grinned. "You do remember I run a company, right?"

"Have you not heard of remote work?"

Not only did I know all about it, but working remotely was a big hot button between Rob and me. I had no issue with our employees, mostly therapists, working from home. After all, the entire principle of my company was allowing people access to therapy remotely. Yet, he wanted to see everyone's body in a seat twenty-four hours a day. Thankfully, the local labor laws gave them breaks. My jaw clenched, and the familiar headache rolled down my neck to my spine.

"You okay? I didn't mean to strike a nerve."

I shivered for absolutely no reason, considering there wasn't an ounce of air-conditioning drifting through the place.

"Totally fine. Just funny that you mentioned remote work. Rob hated the concept. In fact, I'm surprised he hasn't thrown a conniption that I'm all the way in Wisconsin." I thought back to all the ignored messages and texts from him. "Actually, maybe he is throwing one, and that's why he won't stop calling."

"The phone hasn't rung much since you got here."

"That's because I blocked him." I smiled. "Thanks to Cash."

Grace pressed her lips into a concerned smile. "I always thought your ex was a controlling person."

"That's an understatement." I shrugged, thinking back to all the red flags over the years. Yet, I was the one who got stood up at the altar, or in my case, the courthouse steps.

"So, let me get this straight. He stood you up, but now he's calling and texting you?"

I let out a deep breath, yet it felt like I still had a ton of air left to exhale. "Yup."

"It sounds really complicated."

I nodded, sliding my damp palms down my dress. Why did my body physically react to the thought of Rob? And I didn't mean in a fun, fluttery, butterfly type of way.

"There was a reason I didn't want to bother explaining it over the phone." I shrugged. "The situation is just really messed up, and since I let him get so involved with the business, things are even worse. The word complicated doesn't even give credit to the layers of muck I have brought onto myself."

"Don't blame yourself. There were two people in this

union. You aren't the bad guy." Grace nodded sympathetically, but I knew I hadn't given her much to go on. I just didn't want her to worry about me. She lost her husband. She has a daughter to raise. She just moved back to Buttercup Lake. I didn't need to add my drama to her life.

"Thankfully, I have a lot of attorneys working on my behalf who assure me that everything will turn out fine, but I know Rob. He won't make it easy."

She rolled her eyes. "Why do men have to be so complicated?"

I chuckled, looking at Pancake, who was now snoozing on top of her bone. "I don't know, but it makes me really leery of love again." I shook my head. "Rob tainted love for me. No doubt about it. The concept leaves me with an icky feeling in my stomach."

Grace grabbed my hand and gave it a quick squeeze. "Don't let that weasel take away from you something that you are so good at giving." She let go. "So, how about Cash? Does he leave with you an icky feeling in your tummy?"

I pointed my index finger at her and chuckled. "I know what you're up to, and it's not going to happen. I doubt I'll even see Cash the rest of the time I'm here. But no, he does not leave me with any kind of creepy feeling. When I look at him, it's more like I see a mission in the making."

Grace's brows rose.

"You know, because he's so cranky. I like to see him smile."

Grace stayed silent and hummed while she reached for her purse. "On that note, I think I need an iced tea, or I'm going to melt, and I promised Pancake a new toy."

Pancake's ears lifted, and her head slowly moved to assess the situation.

"Thank you for helping me today," Grace added, flicking her gaze in my direction.

I smiled. "I didn't do much other than move some boxes, but you're welcome."

Grace whistled at Pancake, who reluctantly moved toward her. Grace's phone buzzed, and she glanced at the screen with a wild look in her eyes.

"Jackson just sext you or something?" I teased. "You look crazed."

She rolled her eyes. "Please."

I snickered, and a snort popped out. "You're telling me that you're dating a man who is often on the road, and you've never sexted?"

Grace's cheeks flamed red. "I wouldn't even know where to start."

"Seriously? Come on. You've got to live a little."

This time, Grace snickered. "And you're telling me that sexting will do that for me?"

"I have an idea," I teased. "Hand me the phone one time, and I'll send a crazy text to Jackson, and then I'll hand the phone back to you."

Grace started toward the door with Pancake and me following behind. "That sounds about as great of an idea as when you told me that Grandma Millie and Grandpa Renny would never know you threw a party as long as I was the one who cleaned the entire house."

"And then strategically left all the evidence for them to find that pointed to me?" I smiled at the memory. "You were always such a goody-two-shoes."

"I was not. I was completely wild."

My brow arched. "How so?"

"I was always sneaking out to be with Jackson."

"I suppose that's wild."

The moment we stepped outside, the warm heat wafted over us, and I suddenly felt like I was in Hawaii.

"All I need is sand beneath my toes, and I'd think I'm in Hawaii," I hummed, following behind a lagging Pancake.

"Sounds like you and I need a date at Buttercup Lake." She turned and stopped, glancing down at my sandals, and gasped.

"What? Is there a bug on me? What?"

"Your toe is like a Frankenstein toe." Grace bent over like the mother she was to Izzy and hissed. "That's getting worse by the minute, Maya. You should see someone."

"They'll just tell me not to walk on it."

"Or they'll bandage it properly and give you some crutches so it has a chance to stop swelling."

"And ruin my vacation? I don't think so." I smiled lovingly at Grace. She could never turn off her mom mode, which was something I'd always adored, especially since our parents were anything but.

Grace laughed as Pancake licked my toe. "You're so stubborn."

"From what I remember, it runs in the family."

Grace straightened. "Fine. We'll talk more about this once I get my beverage. I'm dying of thirst."

I nodded and happily followed Grace down to Buttercup Java, where the sign hung proudly. "Boy, Buttercup Lake has really changed."

"Can you believe it?" Grace laughed. "I remember when the big deal was that the ice cream shop opened for summer, and we'd have to get our groceries at the same place Grandma got gas. Speaking of, she'll be coming back home tomorrow."

A giddy feeling rolled through me. "I can't wait to see her."

Grace opened the door, and the sweet smells of chocolate and coffee permeated the air.

"I think I just found my new favorite place in town," I told Grace, spotting Izzy behind the counter. "So, this is where Izzy works? That's fantastic."

"And she loves it." Pancake walked right in with Grace, and I smiled.

"Dogs are allowed?"

"Pancake is special. Abby lets her in because of Izzy."

My brow arched. "Are you sure it's Pancake who is super special and not Izzy?"

Grace chuckled. "Pancake is almost the town mascot, and Izzy is probably her talent manager."

"Who is Abby?" I asked.

"Buttercup Java's owner. She's so sweet. You'll love her."

"Hey, Aunt Maya," Izzy said, waving in my direction. "Want to try my favorite drink?"

Happiness flooded through me as that word lingered in my mind.

Aunt.

Growing up, we'd never had a strong family unit that

included our parents. Grandma Millie and Grandpa Renny were our one stable and present force in our lives every single summer. It was the best time of my life and the worst because we always had to leave.

None of my sisters wanted to tell Grandma and Grandpa about how bad it was with our parents because we worried about where we'd wind up. Why it didn't occur to us that Grandma Millie and Grandpa Renny would have been the first to line up to take us in, I didn't know.

But it was because of that lack of a parental unit and solid foundation of family that I think I treasured the idea of family a little more. It was also why I'd put up with Rob so much. I wanted to wish things right for the sake of the imaginary family I'd dreamed of, which I know was completely delusional because the man was incapable of empathy or growth.

"I can't wait to try your favorite drink." I grinned. "Does it contain caffeine, or are you too young to have the serious stuff?"

Izzy chuckled. "I'm fifteen. Of course, I can have coffee."

"If her vice in life is caffeine, I'll happily support her," Grace whispered, and I chuckled as I made my way to the counter.

The coffee shop was adorned with everything related to coffee. Behind the counter, a rustic wall of stained pieces of wood was the perfect backdrop for shelves that held various glass jars filled to the brim with coffee beans. A beautiful wood carving of a giant coffee bean took center stage, which was flanked on either side with the menu written in colorful chalk.

"What do you want, Sis?" I asked Grace, who was staring at her phone again.

She smiled and looked at her daughter. "The usual. Put our drinks on my tab."

I chuckled. "You have a tab?"

A perky woman wiping down a counter grinned. "Your sister sure does. I think she solely supports Buttercup Java. I'm Abby, by the way."

"Nice to meet you. I'm Maya, but you must be psychic."

Abby chuckled. "Not psychic, but you have a very excited niece about you being here."

Grace nodded but added, "I'm addicted to their coconut tea right now only because my daughter works here, and it happens to be the best stuff on the planet."

I grinned and shook my head. "You know, there's this thing called a debit card. You don't have to carry a balance here."

"Which I used nonstop in Chicago, but half the time here, I don't even have my purse because I've been at the lake or am wandering the local boutiques."

"Are you telling me you have tabs all up and down this town?"

"It's a perk of being a local."

Izzy grinned. "I hope you love this drink. It should give you enough caffeine to last until ten o'clock tonight."

She slid an iced tea to her mom and an iced cup to me with a swirl of whipped cream on top.

"I'm in love with this drink already," I promised, taking the iced coffee. "With that amount of whipped cream, I'm already in heaven."

An incredible mixture of coffee, chocolate, and raspberry swirled around my tongue, and I shut my eyes in ecstasy.

"Amazing," I announced to my niece, opening my eyes. "Just so yummy."

"I knew you'd love it."

"Okay, off to get Pancake a toy. She's itching for one."

I glanced down at Pancake, who'd already stretched out next to Grace.

"Are you sure you don't want to grab a table and hang out here? Pancake looks like she could care less about—"

Grace grabbed my free hand and pulled me to the door with Pancake next to us. "Nonsense. I know what my girl needs."

As I nearly tumbled out the door, I looked back at Izzy and waved with a quick thank you before the door shut behind us.

"Where are we headed?" I asked.

"Across the street and down a block. Not too far. The hardware store is like one of the cute ones, where the entire front half is full of gifts like kitchen towels, fancy aprons, and pet things. Basically, anything you can imagine."

I nodded in amusement, surprised that my sister had found her happy place in a hardware store, or was it just Buttercup Lake in general? Everything about this small town dazzled Grace. I mean, I could kind of see it. I took another sip of my coffee, devouring the raspberry flavor.

I'd always loved Buttercup Lake when I was younger. The summers were magical, and the few times I'd managed to visit Grandma and Grandpa in recent years, I still enjoyed the simpler life. But I had no idea this town was bubbling up an entirely new main street and shopping district. It was a regular tourist town.

"Voila," Grace announced as we made our way to the cute hardware store with cement platters in front overflowing with hot pink petunias.

The automatic doors clapped open, and I followed Grace and Pancake into the air-conditioned store, where one of the cashiers waved at Grace.

"Hey, Bea," my sister called back.

Another cashier, about my age, waved at us. He was cute and kind of looked like a surfer lost in the middle of Wisconsin. "Who do you have with you?" he asked Grace.

"My sister, Maya. She's single, Jack," she called back.

I noticed the woman wink at my sister right before I tried to kick her and wound up tripping over my two feet to avoid killing Pancake.

In the last bid for survival, I reached for whatever was in front of me as my life went into slow motion, and a rack of towels and floral aprons collapsed on top of me as I hit the ground with a hard whack.

"Oh, my God," Grace muttered, dashing to my rescue with Pancake waddling over to me to lick the spilled drink.

"Chocolate. Stop," a man hollered from nowhere as he leaped over the towels and swept Pancake into his clutches next to a bright orange puppy in his other arm.

My eyes met his, and I couldn't believe who was in front of me, clinging to two dogs and staring at me sprawled out on the floor.

I looked away.

He was quite agile.

"I'm fine. Thank you for asking," I muttered to Cash as Grace tried to hold in her laughter and I pulled my dress back down over my lady bits.

Jack dashed over, and Cash scowled at him.

"I've got her," Cash growled at Jack.

"Whatever, man," Jack said, wandering away.

My toe throbbed, but it was nothing compared to the embarrassment flooding through me.

Cash smirked when I brought my gaze back to him. He set the dogs down away from the chocolate drink and scooped me off the floor before I had a chance to object.

When his eyes locked on mine, my mind went dizzy with excitement and annoyance, especially when his smirk turned into a smile.

"Are you okay?" he asked with his gruff voice that made my knees nearly knock.

I let out a deep breath and laughed. "Define okay."

Chapter Eight

Cash

This woman was going to be the death of me. All I wanted was to get back to my quiet and solitary life with my new orange fruitcake.

I only needed to grab a few things for Chewie before that could happen, and without fail, the one woman I needed to avoid happened to show up at the hardware store.

What were the odds?

I was beginning to realize pretty good if a person was in the center of the Sunshine Breakfast Club's bullseye.

No.

I was being completely ridiculous.

Being at the hardware store was purely a coincidence. Buttercup Lake was merely a small town with very few shopping options.

But I knew Grace was part of the book club.

And that would mean my cousin really was in on this whole thing, along with Chewie.

I shook my head and glanced at the bait, which was sitting in my recliner, staring at me with woeful eyes.

It had been four days of hiding out at my house, enjoying the lake, and dodging all requests to meet up with anyone so I didn't suddenly get slammed with a cutie-meet on my schedule . . . or was it meet-cutie? Whatever the hell it was.

I growled, and Chewie lifted her head and slightly cocked it in confusion.

These last four days had been near bliss with Chewie. She was far more trained than my cousin had let on. She hadn't peed once in the house. The only weird thing was that she fetched my dirty socks and underwear and dragged them down the hall for me to find and put in the laundry basket.

Rusty never cared whether I left my dirty clothes on my bedroom floor.

And neither did Freya.

"Freya," I whispered, shaking my head.

I hadn't said her name aloud for so long I couldn't even remember.

Rusty had been Freya's idea so we could practice raising a child without screwing up a real one first, or so she'd told me.

But the truth was that it got us one step closer to living together and one step closer to becoming married.

And then.

Gone.

Rusty and I were left to pick up the pieces, and yet, I still couldn't find most of mine.

Tears pricked my eyes, and I swore under my breath as I wiped them away and onto my jeans. It had been years since she'd passed away.

Maybe sitting here at the house for four days hadn't been a great idea.

I wasn't exactly a hermit. I didn't mind people from a distance, like a casual hi at the grocery store or a quick chat over breakfast before I went to work on a house.

This sitting and relaxing thing wasn't good for my psyche.

My parents had called earlier this morning and left a message. I should at least call them back to make sure they didn't need something.

Although they rarely did. If anything, it was me needing them to watch Rusty for a day or two while I went into the city or something.

I shook my head and patted my orange addition. I at

least had to show off Chewie to my parents. I think they missed Rusty as much as I had.

As I picked up my phone to call my parents, it buzzed with a number I didn't recognize.

When I answered, I was pleasantly surprised to hear Millie Bailey on the other end of the line until she spoke.

"Hello there, Cash. We have a bit of a predicament," she chortled.

Millie was Maya's grandmother, who'd lived in Buttercup Lake her entire life.

"We?" I asked.

"Yes. My granddaughter was trying to help a chipmunk, and needless to say, it didn't go so well."

My heart raced. "Is she hurt? Does she need a doctor?"

"I don't know yet. I just need your help getting her unstuck."

A shriek rang over the phone, and I grabbed my wallet and keys.

The noise came from Maya.

I looked over at Chewie. "Be a good girl and only pee on the pad by the slider," I told Chewie as I dashed to my garage.

"Pardon me?" Millie chirped.

"Sorry. I wasn't talking to you. I should've muted myself. I'm on my way." I hung up and glanced at Chewie once more, and the orange cotton ball looked like she was about to do something just to spite me. I think she got used to me being home, so I scooped her up to take with me.

My pulse pounded as I hopped in my Jeep, placed Chewie next to me, and pulled out of the garage at the speed of light.

Maya hadn't been the most graceful woman I'd met. She'd already ruined her toe more than once and managed to dump an entire retail unit on herself.

But the house?

What could possibly go wrong?

Unless this was a trap.

By the club.

"Okay, Cash. Now you're starting to sound really crazy," I mumbled, glancing at Chewie. "We'll just pretend I'm talking to you. How's that?"

Chewie put her chin on her minuscule paws and sighed.

As I turned down the street to the rental Maya was staying in, I saw Millie's car. The front door was wide open, presumably waiting for me.

I hopped out of the Jeep, grabbed Chewie, and dashed

to the door.

"Did she fall down the stairs? Get locked in the library?" I shouted when I crossed the threshold, hearing a couple more shrieks.

Millie appeared down the hallway and almost had a gleeful look spreading across her mouth.

She clapped her hands. "You brought company."

I nodded. "She's a new addition. Where's Maya?"

"She's in the kitchen." Millie pointed behind her.

"You said she's stuck."

"And I didn't lie." Millie grinned as I made my way past her to see the rear end of Maya sticking out of the dumbwaiter opening.

"Oh, no."

"Call the fire department," Maya shrieked.

Did this woman not believe in pants?

Her bright yellow dress had flipped over her rear, exposing a lacy white thong barely visible to the human eye as her legs flailed in all directions.

"I'm better than the fire department," I assured her, walking over to her wiggling bum while the other half of her was stuck in the wall. "This secret will be safe with me. The fire department, however, would not be able to keep this rescue to themselves."

Millie chuckled. "He has a point, Maya. By Monday's breakfast at the diner, it would be everywhere."

I handed Chewie to Millie and took a deep breath as Maya groaned.

Maya's grandma waggled her brows at me. "She has a nice rump, doesn't she, Cash? She gets it from me."

My blood went cold, but I pushed the images away.

The questions I had rolling through my mind wouldn't stop coming, but I kept them inside and tried not to laugh as Maya's legs weakened with defeat.

"Fine. Just get me out of this contraption and help me save the chipmunk."

I glanced at Millie, who seemed completely unworried while getting a kick out of things.

"The chipmunk?" I asked, coming alongside Maya's bottom half.

"Yes. He looked injured, so I caught him and thought I could let him rest in the dumbwaiter while I called the rescue service."

The overall urge to smack her bum was crushing, so I stared at her swollen big toe to keep myself distracted. "You tried to store a chipmunk in the dumbwaiter?"

"Yeah." Her body started to relax, and her voice muffled into calculated mortification. "But I didn't know he could fit through the tiny crack between the shelf and the pully system."

I scratched my chin.

Millie laughed. "Such an interesting predicament."

I drew a breath and pulled down the fabric of Maya's dress and glanced at her grandmother, wondering why she hadn't done that before I arrived. Millie averted her gaze, and I shook my head.

"Are you hurt?" I asked, ducking closer to the opening she filled.

"Apart from my pride?" She let out a deep sigh. "No, but I can see you did a great job refurbishing the dumbwaiter to its original condition."

"Can you see the chipmunk?" I asked.

"I raised the dumbwaiter up so I could try to fish her out, so she's completely in my view."

I glanced at Millie. "Would you mind going downstairs and making sure the little rodent can't push her way out the bottom door?"

Millie's gaze lit up as she squeezed Chewie. "My pleasure."

I held in a chuckle and shook my head. I couldn't even imagine what Millie thought would happen to her granddaughter when she left us alone. But I couldn't blame this on the club. This was purely Maya.

"Okay, so I want you to forget about the Chipmunk," I told her in a soothing voice.

"I can't forget about Chippy. She's my spirit animal."

I held in a chuckle. "Now, that I believe."

A somewhat spastic and tiny little beast with a twitchy tail and big eyes sounded kind of like the Maya I knew.

"Hey, now. That's no way to get to second base," Maya teased.

"I think with the view I had when I rolled in here, I've already hit a home run."

She chuckled, which made her hips wiggle a bit.

"From the looks of it, you're completely hinged over, right? So, you can see straight down the chute."

"Mmm-hmm."

"Wow. That took some doing."

"I do yoga."

"Apparently." I bit my bottom lip and shook my head.

I was a professional.

I cracked my fingers and cocked my head from side to side before shrugging my shoulders.

"Okay, I'm going to slide my hands along your hips and help bend you back out of the hole."

"What about Chippy?" she asked, sounding panicked.

"First, I rescue you, and then I rescue Chippy."

She huffed. "I don't need rescuing."

Millie's voice shot up the chute. "Like hell, you don't."

Maya chuckled as I edged in closer. "Okay, fine. Maybe at this particular juncture, I need a lending hand."

"Or two," Millie shouted again.

I smiled to myself and shook my head, wishing the view wasn't going to come to an end. "Okay. I'm going to come in slowly with my hands."

The moment I touched her, I felt her body stiffen and then soften. "You have big hands."

"Thanks," I said gruffly, knowing Millie was memorizing every interaction between Maya and me.

"I swear I didn't do this on purpose."

"I don't think you could replicate this if you tried," I said gently, wiggling my hands up her waist. "Can you roll your shoulders over a little?" I tugged a little.

"Like this?"

The moment her words hit the air, I pulled her out and fell backward with her landing on top of me. She shot up instantly and dusted herself off while also tugging on her skirt.

"Thank you." Her cheeks flushed as she ran her palms

over her dark hair that now stood on its edge from static. "Now, what about Chippy?"

As if on cue, I heard a ferocious bark, and Millie squealed as something smacked.

"Oh, no." I darted past Maya and dashed down the basement stairs to see Chewie barking her head off with the chipmunk in a prone position, praying for its life, while Millie tried desperately to hold onto my four-pound pointer.

Maya dashed right behind me, nearly shoving me over when she saw her grandma, my dog, and her rescue chipmunk in a Wisconsin standoff.

Chewie quieted her barks while Chippy—I mean, the chipmunk—played possum.

"You said the chipmunk was injured?" I asked.

"It tangled with the hose when I tried to water the plants Millie brought over."

I turned to Millie with her familiar eye twinkle, and she shrugged. "Who knows how long Maya will be here in town? She needs something to make this place feel like home."

Maya continued, "I'm only going to be here for a little while, Grandma. Anyway, her tail got tangled, and she made this horrible noise. Next thing I know, her tail is sideways."

I turned around and bent down to look at the

chipmunk who had one eye permanently placed on Chewie. The little rodent was as flat as a pancake, and its breathing was rapid.

The tail had a definite crook in it, but I highly doubted it had to do with the hose. I stood up.

As I readied myself, I heard a man's voice tumble down the stairs.

"Millie, I came as fast as I could. Where's your granddaughter? Where's the chipmunk?"

My gaze flashed to the sound to see plucky Jack darting toward us with some sort of animal cage and a medic bag.

I turned to Millie. "What the hell is he doing here?"

She feigned innocence. "I didn't know how long it might take you to get here, so I called in backup."

"I never need a backup," I grumbled, glaring at Jack.

He always had some dopey grin on his face, and today was no different.

Jack looked at me and nodded, setting the down the crate. "Makes sense since I am a volunteer EMT."

Maya chuckled. "Thank you for coming over."

What did she mean, *thank you*? I was enough.

"I have it handled, Jack. You can go back to surfing the waves of Buttercup Lake."

His brows rose. "The lake doesn't have waves, Cash."

"Right. That's the joke." I grunted something nobody heard and snuck a look in Maya's direction. She didn't seem to be overly enthused about Jack, but what if she was good at hiding it? Maybe her grandma was playing us against each other.

"We've got it," I told Jack and patted his back extra hard.

He wheezed and picked up the crate. "Okay. I'm off to pick up a shift at the hardware store."

"You do that," I snapped unexpectedly.

"Thanks again," Maya called out.

I frowned at Maya, who was already busy studying her grandma.

"How did Chippy get out of that contraption anyway, Grandma Millie?" Maya glanced at her grandma, waiting for an answer. "She was in the dumbwaiter protected from the dog." Maya glanced at me. "That is a dog, right?"

"For your information, Chewie's life was on the line. I saved her, and she's a teacup Pomeranian," I explained, realizing my tone was still aggressive. So, I added a smile.

"Good hunting dog, obviously." Maya grinned, making my pulse race.

I really liked Maya's sense of humor.

"Obviously," I said, a little gruffer than I intended.

Walking over to a closet where I usually stored cleaning products, I opened the door and found a cardboard box and a pink pair of rubber kitchen gloves.

"Grandma, you didn't answer my question," Maya teased. "How did Chippy get out?"

"I couldn't hear you two very well, so I had to open the cabinet door."

Maya snickered while I walked past them. "Why would you need to hear us?"

Her grandma ignored her granddaughter and instead asked me if I needed any help.

Chewie had finally calmed down, but one sudden move from Chippy, and I might need to call a medic if Millie got run over.

"How about you all go upstairs and keep Chewie calm?" I knelt down, and Maya nodded.

"Sounds good to me," she muttered, nearly pulling Millie with her.

"Don't you think you should help him?" Millie whispered, and we both shouted no, scaring Chippy.

When I heard the door close upstairs, I glanced at the chipmunk. It was awfully cute, but I knew they could carry all kinds of diseases out in the Northwoods. I snapped on the gloves and slowly moved toward the chipmunk.

"Here, Chippy, Chippy," I sang.

The tail shot straight up and twitched as I called her name again.

Just as she bolted, I slid the sideways box in front of her and flapped the box shut. Feverish scratching turned to a sudden acceptance.

No scratches.

No bites.

A complete success.

As I marched myself up the stairs, feeling somewhat heroic, I opened the door to see Maya crying and her grandma rubbing her back.

Chapter Nine

Maya

"What the hell happened?" Cash asked, holding the box's flaps down as he opened the door. "I was only alone for a minute."

I sniffled and shook my head. "Sorry. Nothing. I'm good."

My gaze flicked to my grandma's, pleading with her to stay quiet.

This news hurt. It dug deep.

"Her jerk of a boyfriend, which is a term I use loosely, filed a complaint against her." Grandma Millie clenched her jaw shut and shook her head. "He's trying to take everything from her."

The box started moving as scratching inside became frantic. Cash looked like he didn't care if there were a sasquatch in the box. All he wanted to do was listen.

I could see it in his eyes.

Which was exactly why I didn't want him to know. I wasn't his burden and would never put that on him. I was too messed up on many levels.

I wiped away the tears. "I'm totally fine. It's fine. I have attorneys for this kind of thing. I was almost expecting it. It's just a different thing when it happens."

He straightened and looked in the box as Chewie's eyes lit up. "Let me take care of this, and I'll be right back."

Cash dashed out the front door, and I spun around to my grandma as she shoved the orange puffball into my hands.

"I need to go. My boyfriend is waiting for me. Jack Sr. and I are going to catch the early bird supper at two different places today. If our timing is right, we won't be able to roll home tonight."

My heart raced, and I shook my head frantically. "No. Don't go."

Grandma Millie twisted her lips into a contemplative expression, and for a brief moment, I believed she might actually stay.

Until the front door swung open and Cash stepped back inside.

On a normal day, I might notice just how good-looking he was in his tight jeans and open-front flannel shirt layered over a tee, but not right now.

Right now, I had bigger things to worry about, like how long I should wallow. When I should talk myself into going back to North Carolina to fight this head-on.

I squared my shoulders as a tiny wet tongue smacked my chin.

"She likes you," Cash said, smiling.

"Okay, you two. Off I go," Millie hummed as she patted my wrist and left in a flash.

Cash pointed over his shoulder. "Listen, I can take off if you want, or I can stay and lend an ear. Really, whatever."

Cash's green eyes steadied on mine with an intensity that made my insides squeeze. He adjusted a leather band on his wrist and watched me, waiting for an answer I was slow to give.

"I don't want to be a bother. Seriously, my problems aren't your problems."

"*Well*," he joked, and I couldn't help but laugh.

"Okay, so maybe sometimes my problems become your problems." No matter how much I knew I should rip my gaze from his, I couldn't. The erratic feelings running through me made no sense. On the one hand, I wanted him to run over to me and tell me everything was going to be fine, and on the other hand, I wanted him to give a quick nod and head out the door.

"So, should I stay? Or should I go?" he prompted.

He looked at his dog and smiled. "She really likes you."

I grinned. "I'm a rather likable person on a normal day, but you haven't really seen me on any normal days."

Cash nodded and let out a deep breath. "Normal days are overrated."

"I don't know about that." I handed him the lightweight pup with one hand, and Chewie licked one of Cash's pink rubber gloves, which I just now noticed. "Pink is a good color on you."

"I thought so." Cash's eyes studied me.

"Have you eaten dinner yet?" I asked, suddenly not wanting to be alone. "I know it's kind of early."

"All this rescuing has made me famished."

I nodded, unsure of what I'd just done to myself. "I bet. Want a beer?"

"Thought you'd never ask."

I wandered into the kitchen and opened the fridge. "I'm really sorry about the dumbwaiter and all."

"Don't be. You make my life really . . ."

I turned around, handing him a beer. "Really what?"

"Interesting."

I chuckled. "Sorry about that. Most people like Buttercup Lake so things aren't so interesting."

His eyes stayed on mine. "I'm not one of them."

I swallowed away the wave of excitement that rose from my belly.

Cash let his dog down. "That's Chewie, by the way."

"Chewie?" I blurted out for no reason.

He nodded. "She came with the name. Her owner passed away, but she was apparently a huge *Star Wars* fan. So, her official name is Chewbacca."

"You know the saying, right?" I smirked.

Cash shook his head. "No. What?"

"A Wookie in the sheets and a Jedi in the streets makes for the best partner." I covered my mouth as he watched me carefully before a smile slipped over his beautiful lips.

I giggled. "I'm so sorry. I shouldn't talk that way about your dog."

Cash's eyes stayed on me. "I've only had her a few days. I don't really know what her habits are like out there in the streets. She does seem a little freaky, though."

I tore my eyes away from his and opened a beer for myself. I took a sip and squinted. I'd always shied away from most things that had a habit of altering one's mood since my parents overindulged in anything and everything they could.

But today, this beer hit the spot.

Almost.

"Do you think Chippy will be okay?" I asked, still feeling awful about her tail and the hose.

"I think Chippy already had that injury. I don't think it was the hose," he assured me, taking a step closer.

A bright moment appeared on my otherwise wonky day. "Really?"

"But she's doing just fine and scurried across the yard."

"Probably to bitch to her husband about the crazy lady who moved in. What was I thinking?" I shook my head, feeling my chest tighten. "Why would I bring in a wild animal?"

The sensation of a baby panic attack had become familiar since being stood up by Rob. But I knew deep in my heart that the feeling wasn't from being stood up. It was from my inability to stand up for myself. I should have been the one who didn't show up a long time ago.

I tried not to focus on the irony of doling out advice to others for a living when I was still on the sidelines of my own life.

"Nice ale," Cash said, taking another drink.

My shoulders relaxed slightly, and I took in a steady breath, trying not to look like I was about to fall down the crazy chute of inept decisions.

"Glad you like it," I said, taking another sip. "It's a bit tangy."

Cash nodded with his eyes still on me. "Hey, if you're too worn out from everything today—"

"No. I'd love company. Unless you have plans."

Chewie went to the slider, and Cash whipped out a leash from his back pocket. "That's my cue."

"You're such a good Daddy," I teased.

He grinned and opened the glass slider to let the dog outside. I followed them both and felt the warm air cascade over my arms and legs.

"I've missed Buttercup Lake," I said softly. The sunshine teased a glistening ripple of sapphire through the water as a canoer paddled by.

"I hear that a lot," he said as Chewie did her business. "It's a special place."

"It certainly wooed my sister." I thought back to Grace and how confused and empty she'd told me she felt before heading here earlier this year.

Kind of like my current state.

Cash turned around and faced me. "Think lake life

might ever woo you?"

I hadn't been expecting the question. "Truthfully, I feel like I've been on the run since getting dumped at the altar. Today, I feel like it's time to stop and fight back for me, but I'm not sure I can do that from here."

A flicker of disappointment wavered through Cash's gaze, but it was gone almost instantly. Had I imagined it?

"I don't know if you've noticed, but I've been smiling more since you've been around," he offered as he scooped Chewie into his arms.

I couldn't hide my own smile as I watched Cash confidently walk into the house with his teacup dog.

"Even if you did have to hoist me out of the wall?" I teased, following him inside.

"Especially then." He set Chewie on the couch in the family room and noticed the book my sister gave me to read.

"Have you read that yet?" he asked, pointing at the large paperback.

"Just started it, but I need to get a move on since I'm headed to the Sunshine Breakfast Club."

His eyes widened in near horror. "You're going?"

"Uh-huh. Is there something I should know?"

"Besides the fact that it's a cover for what the club truly is." His voice lowered, as did his head, while he glanced around the room like we were being recorded. "I don't know if you truly want in."

I chuckled and glanced around the room, ducking my head too. "Is there something I don't know about it?"

"It's a ruse. They might read a book now and again, but their main goal in life is to set people up."

"Like to fail?"

Cash laughed. "Worse."

"What could be worse than failure?"

"Somehow, the members seem to enjoy setting up potential . . ." He stopped and sucked on his bottom lip while he thought about how best to approach things, but the wait was killing me.

What was the Sunshine Breakfast Club?

He let out a deep breath, and his voice stayed low. "They try to make potential matches. You know, like they're some matchmaking service of the Northwoods. They're everywhere when you least expect them. They have spies all over town."

I looked over at Chewie and then back at Cash. "Should I buy you both tinfoil hats or is one sufficient?"

His smile widened, and a devilish look in his eyes made my tummy feel like I was parachuting. "You know the club had something to do with your sister and Jackson, right?"

"I heard a little bit about that, but it was more their history than anything."

Cash looked surprised. "You think?"

I nodded. "Yeah. Taking two strangers and smooshing them together is a lot harder than setting up first loves."

"If you say so."

I narrowed my eyes on Cash. "What are you saying?"

Cash ran his fingers through his dark hair. "Nothing. Let's eat. I'm starved."

"I can make tacos, spaghetti, or nachos," I offered.

"How about I order in tacos, nachos, and anything else you want from Puerto's?"

"What do you mean, order in?" I asked. "Don't tell me Buttercup Lake has delivery too."

He smiled and nodded. "Oh, yeah. We're big time now."

I looked around the family room at Chewie and Cash and couldn't help but marvel at how natural this felt and how unnatural Rob and I had always felt.

Part of this easy feeling was undoubtedly knowing that nothing would come of Cash and me.

"You know what? After today's news, I'll gladly take you up on that offer, and if I don't scare you away after tonight's meal, I'll get the next one."

Cash nodded, pulling out his phone. "I have them on speed dial."

"Oh, yeah? Is it a place you take your hot dates?"

He smirked with confidence oozing from him. "From the book club, you mean?"

"I'm sure you seldom have lonely weekends," I said wryly.

A guy this hot didn't just stay in and twiddle his thumbs on a Friday night.

He winked. "Then you don't know me well."

A woman at the restaurant picked up on his speaker phone immediately and recognized his number. "Hey, Cash. Want your usual?"

"I'm upping my game tonight with two number four combination plates. And let's do some mini tacos for an appetizer."

"You still want your extra side of beans?" the woman asked.

Cash glanced at me and scowled. "No, I'm fine. Thank you, though."

I held in a snicker and shrugged. "Don't hold back on the beans on account of me, Cash."

He flicked me a funny look as he filled them in on the

correct delivery address and hung up.

I dashed to the kitchen and quickly pulled out some of the plates that Cash kept for his guests and put them on the dining room table. I shoved back the curtains so the lake came into view. Grandma Millie had brought over a bouquet of daisies and hydrangeas, which I grabbed from the kitchen and brought into the dining room as Cash walked in.

"Wow. You're certainly classing up the joint." He leaned against the wall and studied me as I fluttered into the kitchen to retrieve some more beers and utensils and take a deep breath.

The beer I'd polished off had played a funny trick on me. Cash was even more attractive, and it was as if all my Rob problems had drifted away. I suddenly didn't want to think about the lawsuit hanging out there or the man who wanted to rip everything away from me.

Just the thought of eating takeout with Cash sounded absolutely refreshing.

I spun around with two beers and forks in my hand when Cash came up behind me. He smelled so sweet and spicy, kind of like his beer had mixed with a pine tree out back.

"Need any help?" His tone sounded super broody, or maybe it was that he was only a few inches away and I was swimming in everything Cash.

I brought my gaze up to his and regrouped, handing him the beer and forks.

"You are a little buzzy bee." He laughed.

"Yeah? How so?" I called into the dining room as I sipped some water.

"You just never stop going, just buzzing everywhere, getting things done, rescuing injured chipmunks, making the table extra."

"Extra?" I walked into the dining room. "Extra what?"

Cash chuckled. "It's what the kids say. You know, you're *extra*."

"Am I that old that I don't have any idea what you're talking about?"

He held his hands up as I snuck by. "I said no such thing."

My breasts accidentally rubbed against his chest, and I swore I heard his breath catch in the back of his throat.

The doorbell rang, and Cash somehow catapulted to the front door. I kind of liked that I had that power over him. It had been a long time since I'd felt like I had anything to offer the opposite sex, and granted, boobs weren't exactly how I valued myself, but it still felt good to know he noticed.

Before I even had a chance to say thank you to the driver, Cash had brought the takeout bags into the dining room, and that was when my phone buzzed. I expected the text to be from one of my sisters, but it was from an unknown number, and all it read was *Let the games begin.*

"Smells delicious," I said tightly.

"Another perk about living in a small town is that your food arrives warm." Cash cocked his head slightly when he saw the phone in my hand. "Everything okay?"

I nodded, swallowing down my disappointment. I'd been enjoying tonight. I'd turned my day around with the help of Cash.

And then this.

I didn't want to be dramatic, so I just slid my phone to Cash, and he read the text. "So, he got a different number so he could taunt you?"

"Apparently." I sighed. "Just one more thing to forward to the lawyers."

Cash nodded, but he didn't say much.

I took a bite of beans and let out a happy moan of delight as he shook his head. "That's a sound I could get used to."

"All bark and no bite," I teased, feeling a little more like myself with every passing second.

"You're just a drifter passing through, remember?"

"That's my plan, and I'm sticking to it." I stared at him happily, memorizing the small lines around his eyes that showed happiness and a bit of sorrow underneath. His green eyes seized with something unexpected. Was he thinking about a kiss?

He smiled as I happily studied him.

"You're right. I do make you smile a lot more."

"Actually, I'm just smiling because I stole all your beans, and you didn't even put up a fight."

I looked down at my plate.

"I'm a mess, Cash. The bean heist proves it. Rob has me so confused and . . ." I dipped my fork into the refried beans. "And my life is like a burning dumpster of—"

"Don't let him do that to you," Cash interrupted. His voice lowered to a timbre that made my insides squeeze with something I hadn't expected at this moment.

"Do what?" I asked softly.

"Take away your fun. Take away *you*. Your spirit lights up the room." Cash's jaw tightened as he shook his head. "He's getting inside your head, but you have the power to kick him out."

I didn't understand what changed in the air between us, but it felt like an electrical current was zipping between us at an unstoppable rate.

"And I'm the one who's supposed to be giving the advice," I said softly, realizing Cash's gaze stayed on mine as if every word I uttered mattered. "I am worth it, dammit."

Cash's eyes dropped to my mouth, and I swallowed down the lump in my throat. I felt like I needed to repeat that ten more times, and I might start to believe it, but right now, the way Cash was looking at me made me feel like I was more than okay.

He tore his gaze away from my lips and picked up a fork, stirring the beans and rice. The quiet between us was something different this time. We were both stuck in our worlds with no apparent way out.

Chapter Ten

Cash

If I could wring that little twerp's neck, I would. I actually had no idea what this guy looked like, but I pictured him like a bug to be squashed. Who did he think he was?

Maya had polished off the last mini taco, scraped her plate clean, and licked her fork.

I admired this woman more and more each day.

"Wanna head out back and enjoy the mosquitos' homeland?" I teased, hoping to bring a smile to her lips.

Her gaze connected with mine, and I saw the familiar spark that made me wonder if being alone for the rest of my life was truly the best game plan.

I'd vowed it after losing Freya.

"I think that's exactly what I need." She stood as I started to reach for the plates. "Ah, leave them there. I'll take care of them later."

"Are you sure?"

She grabbed my hand and pulled me out of the dining room in response. Chewie was licking her paws on the couch, not having moved a muscle.

The moment we stepped outside onto the back patio, I took a deep breath in and felt the warm air fill my lungs.

"I always loved these Wisconsin summer nights." She let go of my hand and made her way to one of the chairs and took a seat.

I sat next to her. "I'm sure it's beautiful in North Carolina."

She lolled her head toward me while resting it on the back of the chair. "It's a beautiful place too. I should probably go back home early with this latest revelation."

The words stung a wound I didn't know had opened. "Still thinking that's the best move?"

Maya let out a low, delicate hum and shook her head slowly as she focused on the lake. "I don't know. It's almost like any move I make will be the wrong one. The good news is that my team knows I'm on vacation for two weeks, regardless. I'd planned on working remotely for the remainder, but we'll see."

"Exactly. You've almost used up one week. Just play

it by ear." I nodded, not wanting the panic to register on my face.

It was hard to believe Maya had been in Buttercup Lake for one entire week already, and I had spent the last several days hiding from her.

Why?

If it hadn't been for Chippy, I would have missed this.

Whatever *this* was.

Not to mention, Jack would have swept in as the hero, and that could never happen on my watch. He was like one of those bros, the kind who kissed his muscles and cheated on his girlfriends. However, Jack looked like an angel compared to Rob.

Maya turned her attention back to me. "The crazy part is that since I started my company, I have never taken a vacation. Rob didn't believe in that. He thought it made my employees think less of me if I were to take time away."

This guy sounded like a real piece of work.

"I don't think I really fought it because the business was so young, and I was pouring everything I had into it."

"But there will be nothing left of you to pour into it if you don't find a little time for yourself."

She smiled and nodded. "Truer words."

As I watched the sun's evening rays slide across

Maya's arms, I thought about what it would be like to run my lips across her softness.

I looked away and let out a sigh.

"That was a heavy sigh," she said, laughing. "Have I depressed you too?"

"Quite the opposite." I stood and walked toward the sandy beach that stretched along the lake.

Picking up a pebble, I skimmed it across the glassy surface as Maya came up behind me. There were so many questions I had for her, and yet, it wasn't my place. We were merely two barely-more-than strangers passing through life. She'd be going back home to the Carolinas, and I'd stay here with Chewie, my new companion.

She stood next to me and sucked in a deep breath. "No mosquitos yet."

I chuckled and nodded. "Just be patient. They're waiting for us to let our guard down."

"You're a bit of a psychologist yourself," Maya joked.

"Only when it has to do with wildlife." I turned to her, and there was nothing I wanted more than to kiss her. I soaked in her beauty, her smile, the lake.

But I couldn't ignore the sadness behind her eyes.

"What I don't understand," I said softly, brushing

away some loose hair from her cheek, "is if he is the one who stood you up on your wedding day, why is he still tormenting you?"

It was Maya's turn to let out a heavy breath as she crossed her arms in a solo hug.

"Control," she said simply.

I waited a few seconds, and she shivered, even though the evening air was balmy.

I draped my arm over her shoulders, and she stepped into my embrace.

"Rob thought that he'd ditch me at the altar, go to work on Monday, and torment me in person, tell me all the reasons he couldn't possibly marry me until I changed. Then the cycle would start all over."

Her body flinched under mine as she recalled the memories.

"This isn't the first time you've been left at the altar?" Now I really wanted to pummel this guy.

She chuckled and shook her head. "No, not at the altar. That's a new one. But with every step in our long and very tedious relationship, there were gigantic hurdles and even more enormous letdowns. He knew I wanted a family and hung an engagement over my head based on how well I behaved."

Shock registered through me.

This kind of abuse was ruthless.

Maya went rigid under my arm, but she dug in deeper somehow. "He'd taunt me about how terrible I'd be as a mom or how horrible of a boss I was to my employees. He loved to point out to me my parents' own failures and how I was doomed to repeat them. Yet, I stayed in the cycle until I just couldn't."

"The guy did you a favor by not showing up." I hugged her.

"He just didn't expect me to stop the cycle." She shook her head. "And that's the part that is killing him inside. He's always wanted the last say, the last action, the last . . ."

"Maybe you shouldn't go back there, Maya. You said yourself that you can work remotely, and you've even wanted your employees to have that option."

The thought of her flying back to North Carolina, where he could dig his claws into her again, made my chest tighten. Maya didn't deserve this. She deserved the world and every chipmunk in it.

She nodded. "Our lease at headquarters is up in ten months. It would be a huge cost saver if we just set everyone up at their homes."

Maya stepped away from me and let her arms dangle

by her side. "Thank you."

I shook my head. "For what?"

"For talking me down from a ledge I didn't know I was on. Life doesn't have to be black and white. It never has been, so I don't know how I got myself into a relationship where my partner believed it was."

I ran my palm over my chin and nodded. "Love is a curious thing."

"I hate to say it, but I'm not even sure I was in love with Rob. He was just there." She bit her lip and turned toward the lake. "Forty is only a hop, skip, and a jump away, and I'm not even sure I've ever been in love."

Her words caused my throat to tighten, which forced me to clear it. She glanced over at me.

"Have you been in love?"

I nodded. "I have."

Maya didn't press me with any questions. She just heard me and started back toward the house as I took in her silhouette and thought about the idea of love.

I'd had it once and figured it had been enough to last a lifetime, but as I watched Maya wandering up the grass, I wondered why I was so determined to imprison myself.

But I knew.

And it was a secret I'd never let see the light of day.

Maya spun around and waved. "Want another beer?"

"Sure. I can always walk home."

She laughed. "Don't be ridiculous. This is your house. You can crash on the couch with Chewie, and if you're really nice, I'll let you have one of your guest rooms."

I chuckled and walked up toward the house.

By the time I'd sat down, she had brought out two beers and slumped in the chair next to me.

"This place is good for the soul." She turned to look at me. "Or maybe it's you."

I grinned.

"Did you know I started an internal game?"

"Yeah?"

"Every time I can get you to smile, I get a point."

"How many points do you have?"

"After today, I'm at about twenty."

"Oh, come on." I laughed. "I've definitely smiled more than twenty times."

"I don't know. You're pretty stingy."

I took a sip of beer at the same time she did, except she kept chugging.

When she was done, she set the half-full beer on the ground and kicked out her legs. "I haven't done that in years."

"Which part?"

"Pounded a beer."

"Technically, since it doesn't look to be empty, you didn't pound it."

"Are you the Frat Boy Police or something?"

I chuckled. "Just sayin'."

She reached for the beer and polished it off. "Fine. Just you watch. Crazy Maya is on the way."

"Haven't Chippy and I already met her?"

She shot up from the chair and put her hand on her hip. "Not even close."

My eyes widened as she skipped to the grass and put both hands in the air like she was a cheerleader, and the next thing I knew, she was doing a line of cartwheels across the grass.

Dress be damned.

Legs up in the air.

Arms up in the air.

Legs up in the air.

Just watching her was making me dizzy, and I couldn't imagine it was doing great things for the carbonation in her stomach.

On the last cartwheel, she jumped up.

"Ta-da." She beamed with exuberance and didn't look like any of the bubbles or beans were coming to revisit, so I stood up and clapped, trying to shove the thoughts out of my head surrounding her apparent flexibility.

"Bet you didn't see that coming." She jogged over to me.

"Not at all." I watched her bound in front of me.

And before I realized what had happened, I pulled her into me.

I brought her face up with my finger as she smiled with dopey-looking eyes.

The sweetness of her lips was intoxicating, and the little moan of unexpected pleasure made my groin almost uncomfortable with need. Her tongue danced with mine— sweeping, twirling, moving. Her breaths quickened with anticipation as she skimmed her hands underneath my shirt, and I softly nipped her bottom lip with my mouth.

She tasted so good.

Maya's hand slowly dipped below the waistband of my pants, and I sucked in a hiss of anticipation as her fingers ran along my treasure trail, never quite making it to where I'd hoped.

But it was her decision, and at least I'd let myself escape my head for the first time in years.

Chapter Eleven

Maya

"Wait a second." Grace's hands flew into the air. "You made out with Cash, and then he slept on the couch?"

"Yup." I popped the P for extra effect.

"The woman who told me I should be sexting my man is having her man sleep on the couch."

My eyes widened, and I glanced around the community center.

"He's not my man," I whispered.

She cocked her head and rolled her eyes. "Cash Knox doesn't go around with strange women."

"I'm not strange."

Grace chuckled. "You know what I mean."

"Don't tell a soul. Do you promise me? Especially not Grandma."

Grace's gaze filled with mischief. "Why? Are you

afraid she'll tell everyone like she did about you and the chipmunk?"

"Wait. What?" I slammed my hands on my book. "You know about that?"

Grace laughed and nodded, glancing around the room where the book club was meeting. "I'm sure she only told me."

"What are the odds?" I snorted, and Grace looked horrified. "You still haven't gotten over the snorting?"

I scowled at her as Grandma Millie came into the room.

"So, what did you think about the book so far?" my sister asked.

"To be perfectly honest, it kind of hits home."

"Really," Grace said flatly. A little too flat. "I guess there could be some similarities."

I flipped through the first half of the book. "Hmm. Lady gets stranded at the altar."

"Yeah, but hers was a remote wedding."

I ignored my sister. "And the guy is a complete monster, stalking her and making her life miserable."

Grace shrugged as several of the members came into the room with platters of breakfast items. "Odd."

I nodded. "It is odd that this is the book for this month.

Anyway, I like the heroine's resilience. I just hope she doesn't go crawling back to the dirtbag."

Grace flinched and shuddered. "Me too. That would be horrible."

Grandma Millie walked along the table where the breakfast items had been placed just as a woman with a giant stuffed animal walked in. She set it down along with a big carton of coffee on the table and spun around, waving.

It was Abby.

And behind her, a gigantic stuffed chipmunk leaned against the baked goods.

Grace couldn't help but chuckle as Grandma Millie turned and winked at me.

"That woman cannot keep a secret. Is she trying to get me to run from Buttercup Lake?"

Grace squeezed me. "Just the opposite. Grandma is trying to make it feel like home."

Home.

The only time I'd truly experienced that feeling growing up was with my grandparents. I'd tried recreating it repeatedly since I'd become an adult. I even played house with Rob, hoping the sensation would resurface.

It hadn't.

But being back in Buttercup Lake had started to stir

something inside me.

I just wasn't sure I was ready for it.

Or for Cash.

And certainly not the kiss.

Yet, here I sat next to my sister at seven o'clock in the morning to talk about a book with the Sunshine Breakfast Club at Buttercup Lake.

One might wonder how it was so easy to wake up so early after a couple of beers and a sensational kiss from Cash.

Well, I never fell asleep last night.

I just tossed and turned and contemplated staying, going, kissing him again, never seeing him again.

Like I'd confessed a million times to anyone who'd listen . . .

I was a mess.

Besides, he seemed like the type of guy who needed a woman who'd go hike in the woods and put a deer over her shoulders for dinner. He was all man and certainly only enjoyed rough and tumble activities, and I wasn't a rough and tumble kind of gal.

Abby walked over with Grandma Millie.

"Fresh coffee has arrived." Abby pointed behind her.

I chuckled and shook my head. "That's not all that arrived."

"I couldn't help myself. When Millie told me what happened and then I spotted this stuffed animal at the hardware store, I just had to get it."

I grinned and shook my head. "Of course you did."

Abby pulled a chair closer as Millie sat next to Grace. "It's yours. You can take it home."

"Thanks," I said wryly.

"In all seriousness, did you actually get stuck in a wall, and Cash had to pull you out?"

"Yup." I nodded. "Gracefulness does not run in our family in spite of Grace's name."

Abby chuckled, clutching her book on her lap. "Hey, Grace. Did you ever tell your sister about Jackson having to dig that thing out of your butt?"

My eyes widened as I turned and gaped at my sister. "Pardon me?"

Grace rolled her eyes. "Don't try to deflect your purchase of a chipmunk," she told Abby.

"You can't leave me hanging," I protested.

"It was a splinter. Completely innocent." Grace held up her hands.

Grandma Millie chimed in with a tsk-tsk and a wiggle of her finger. "Not when you hear Jackson Jr. tell it."

"Seriously?" Grace huffed. "When have you heard

him tell it, Grandma?"

"Many times." My grandma didn't look a day over sixty-five even though she was over eighty. But her perfectly styled white hair, hoop earrings, sparkle in her eyes, and matching hot-pink outfit told a different narrative. She always declared that a person was only as old as they felt and so far, she still felt young.

"Okay, everyone." A woman stood from the circle of chairs. "We should start by introducing Grace's sister to everyone."

Not expecting the introduction, I froze and stared at the group of women all staring back at me. I raised my hand and did a quick wave. As if a wave of dominos took hold, each woman smiled before the next.

"Welcome back to Buttercup Lake," the woman continued. "I'm Bonnie. I kind of head up this whole reading club."

I nodded, seeing the kindness rest behind her gaze.

"Thanks for having me." I slid my hands over my book and prayed that was all the intro I'd need to do.

Bonnie smiled and ducked her head. "Okay, let's chat about our heroine who seems to have one bad luck event after another."

Grandma Millie popped up. "I don't think it's bad

luck. I think this woman got tricked by this man, fell in love while hoping to escape her past, and now she's stuck."

Bonnie nodded and looked surprised as several of the women agreed with quick nods.

"And it's going to take something big to smack her on the side of the head and make her wake up."

I suddenly wasn't sure whether my grandma was talking about the heroine or me.

"And if this scumbag thinks he can take advantage of Anastasia . . ." she continued.

Phew, that was the character's name.

"I'd like to see him try. In fact, I welcome him to the lake."

Bonnie cleared her throat and glanced at Grace and me while Grandma Millie looked revved up and ready for a brawl.

"That's an interesting perspective," Bonnie said, walking over to get a cup of coffee, which seemed like a great idea.

I set my book on my chair, walked over to the table, and filled up a cup for myself too. Had the plastic wrap been taken off all the breakfast goodies, I would have piled up a plate.

"The real question is will Anastasia save herself, or

will she roll over and blindly trust the man?" Grandma Millie sighed. "That's what I worry about."

"I think the character development has shown that Anastasia is a strong lady. She won't roll over. She'll fight," my sister assured Grandma Millie.

I took a sip of the hot coffee and listened as several other women gave their two cents about the character development, but my mind wandered to Cash.

He was quite the distraction from everything back home. He was a great listener and an even better kisser.

Sure, he had the occasional grumpy streak, but I wasn't always rainbows and sunshine. Well, I had been until recently, which was what got me into this predicament in the first place. I always pretended it would get better and forced myself to forget the bad and remember the good.

"How'd that work out?" I muttered, and all eyes turned to me. "I meant for Anastasia."

Grace's brows rose as I sat back down.

"Okay, let's grab some food, and we can get back to discussions," Bonnie exclaimed, eyeing Grandma Millie.

I leaned over to my sister. "What's that all about?"

Grace's puzzled expression was phony, or I was getting paranoid.

Like Cash.

"What's what all about?" she asked, standing. "Want any food?"

My phone buzzed, and I saw a call had come in from my law firm. Setting the coffee down, I attempted to scroll to the voicemail and accidentally hit okay on speaker.

"Rob has locked the employees out," the man's voice boomed into the room. "Maya, if you could call us back, that would be great. We will get this handled, but we need a call back. I think he's about to lose his counsel between the texts he's sending you and the emails—"

My fingers finally found the right button to quiet the message, but my hands were shaking as I put my phone down.

Of course, he'd do something to make a scene, create a reason to get me back to North Carolina, to control me and the situation.

My only saving grace was that no one except my project coordinator knew that I was in Wisconsin.

I glanced at the huge pile of pastries Grace had on her plate as she came over.

"What was that all about? It didn't sound good."

I shook my head. "It's not, but I need to duck out and call my attorney back."

She tried to hand me the plate, but I was suddenly not hungry.

"I can take you back to your house," she offered as Grandma Millie scurried over.

"You need to crush that man like the little cockroach he is," my grandma nearly hissed. "No one treats a Bailey girl like that and gets away with it."

I let out a defeated sigh and stood. "I hope you're right, but I'm going to step out and make some calls."

My sister and grandma nodded their heads as I made my way out of the room and into the main hall of the community center.

My entire body felt hollow and broken. I shook my head as I pushed open the door leading outside.

Maybe it wasn't the sensation of feeling broken. I'd say more beat down, and the fight hadn't even begun.

I found a nice birch tree to sit under that offered the perfect amount of shade as I dialed my attorney's number.

My hands no longer shook, but I felt like I was going to get sick.

As soon as I was done with the attorneys, I'd need to draft a memo to my employees. I'd hoped to keep everything quiet, but Rob obviously wanted to make it messy and public. I hadn't checked my work inbox since I woke up thinking that life was under control and moving forward. Who knew that by seven o'clock in the morning, Rob would wreak havoc?

I scrunched my eyes closed as the receptionist picked up, and I asked for my lawyer. Within seconds, the calm voice of reason greeted me.

"I'm sorry to interrupt your much-needed vacation," my attorney said.

"I'm glad you did. I joined a book club, and this morning was the first meeting." I laughed. "Who knew I couldn't make it through without Rob adding some drama?"

"He does have a certain theatrical flair."

"Do I need to fly out today? I'm not sure if I'll be able to get a flight out until—"

"Not at all," my attorney assured me. "I've drafted a memo that you can send to the employees. They all have the capability to work from home, I assume?"

"Yup. Every single one of them." I watched a cardinal hop on the ground before flying to a nearby shrub. "How can he do this?"

"Well, he can't. But he did. Legally, we can get the doors open immediately, but I think it's in everyone's best interests to have your employees work from home while we make certain this doesn't happen again."

I nodded as if my attorney could see me and let out a sigh.

"Don't let this get you down, Maya. This guy, at the

most, will walk with a small settlement. But nothing else."

I snickered. "How small can we make it?"

My attorney chuckled. "The memo should be in your inbox. I'd send it out company-wide this morning. I also have a letter that is being sent to Rob and his legal team. I'm sure they aren't thrilled with his latest antics. I didn't mean to alarm you with my voicemail, but this situation needs to be dealt with swiftly."

"Totally understand. But you're sure I should stay away?"

"Absolutely. I think this is far more personal than business, and we don't need to complicate matters."

A little relief wiggled its way into my chest, but it still felt tight and uncomfortable.

"I'll be in touch if I need anything else."

"Okay, thanks."

My attorney gave a quick goodbye and hung up just as I saw a familiar Jeep roll into the parking lot. I glanced back at the row of windows where the book club met and noticed some movement near the blinds.

Suspicious.

Cash pulled into a parking spot across from me and hopped out of the Jeep with Chewie in hand.

Trying to pull myself together, I stood, dusted myself

off, and walked toward Cash as he turned to smile at me.

"A smile? For me? So early in the morning?" I teased.

His eyes connected with mine, and suddenly, nothing seemed as important.

Chapter Twelve

Cash

I'd just finished prepping a house for new vacationers when I received the call from Grace. She didn't say much other than they were at the community center for the Sunshine Breakfast Club and that Maya had received some stressful news and needed a ride. At first, I assumed it was a setup, but judging by Maya's pacing under a birch tree in the parking lot, maybe I was wrong.

Maybe she really did need help.

"Hey there," I said, smiling at Maya.

She was just as gorgeous as I remembered, and since the kiss, I'd done a lot of remembering. She had pulled back her hair into a messy bun, and she wore a pair of denim shorts and an oversized pink sweatshirt that hung off her shoulder. A hot-pink bra strap was a bit of a distraction.

"What are you doing here, stranger?" she asked,

making her way over.

She scratched Chewie's head and continued to look at me.

The feeling this woman could hand me from just a glance was disarming. I'd never experienced so much emotion from a set of eyes before.

"Your sister called and said you needed a ride." I eyed her cautiously. "And that you got some bad news?"

Maya looked over my shoulder to the building and smiled. "She did, did she?"

I nodded slowly, realizing my first hunch had been correct.

"Well, I can't say I'm mad about seeing your grumpy self."

My brows rose, and I shook my head. "I showed up with a smile. In fact, I've been smiling since the other night."

And I was still trying to figure out how to give her the cute meeting she wanted or meeting cute or whatever the heck she was talking about. I needed to Google it.

Maya bit her bottom lip before letting out a small sigh. "I probably shouldn't have."

"Shouldn't have kissed me?"

She let out a deep breath while it felt like all the air had been sucked out of my lungs. Did she regret our kiss? Was she getting back with Rob?

"You doing okay, Maya?" I asked as Chewie wiggled to get into Maya's arms.

She held out her hands, and Chewie jumped to her.

"Geez. I thought we shared something special." I glanced at Chewie.

"No, Cash. We did. It's just—"

I chuckled. "I was talking about Chewie."

Maya chuckled and rolled her eyes before nuzzling the orange furball. "Of course you were."

"Seriously, though. Do you want to go somewhere to talk? Maybe over breakfast? I just finished up for the day, so my schedule is clear."

Her brows shot up. "It's not even nine o'clock in the morning."

"The next batch of houseguests requested an early arrival, so I got up at four and just finished up prepping for their stay."

A flicker of something darted through her gaze before she glanced over my shoulder again.

"Yeah, let's get some breakfast. I think we have an audience otherwise." She held up a finger. "But let me grab one thing."

I nodded and climbed back in the Jeep, setting Chewie

on the passenger seat. Within a minute or two, Maya came bounding out with an oversized, stuffed chipmunk.

Laughter spilled through the air as she opened the door, lifted Chewie from the seat, and set her and the stuffed animal on her lap.

"So, I take it that word got around?" I chuckled a bit more.

"Yes, this was from Abby at the coffee shop. So I'm sure the entire Main Street knows about me being stuck in a wall."

I grinned and shook my head. "So much for discreetness. Just be glad I got you out before Jack showed up."

She giggled and scratched Chewie's ear, who in return let her minuscule tongue hang out panting. "What's up between you and Jack?"

I shrugged. "Nothing. He's just not the greatest guy."

"Oh, is that all?" She smirked.

"He likes to love 'em and leave 'em."

"And you don't?" she asked.

I drew a breath. "I don't get 'em in the first place. Anyway, I'm gonna drop Chewie off, and then we'll head off to breakfast. Is that okay?"

She rested her head on the seat and smiled, turning to

look at me. "Absolutely. I can finally see where the grumpy hermit lives."

I grinned and turned onto the main road to my house. "I'll take that title over the suspected serial killer."

She snickered, and a snort popped out. "In all fairness, that was Becky who brought it up, and she assured me that you aren't one. So, there's that."

As the wind skimmed the topless Jeep, silence fell between us. I snuck a couple of looks at Maya, who looked deep in thought, staring out the window as she hugged Chewie and her chipmunk. When I pulled into the long driveway leading to my house, it looked like she had come to and glanced in my direction.

"So, this is your abode?"

I laughed. "Well, once we get through the trees. I upgraded from a tent a few years ago."

Her eyes widened. "Seriously?"

I didn't answer and continued winding through the pine trees until my log home came into view. It sat on Buttercup Lake and had a lot of property. If I were smart, I'd rent this one out and stay in one of my smaller rentals, but there was something about this place that brought me peace.

I'd designed it years ago but only built it two years ago.

"This is magnificent, Cash. Wow. Really something." She looked over at me and shook her head. "I'm in shock."

I turned back to look at my home with fresh eyes. I'd lost Rusty here, and since losing him, I felt like a piece of happiness had vanished along with him.

But she was right.

"Thanks. I designed it myself. The log home company had some doubts about timing, but they finished it six months before the winter hit, and I spent the winter finishing the inside." I pulled in front of the wraparound porch and turned off the Jeep before I reached for Chewie.

The orange fluffball gave a little growl of annoyance as I held her close and walked up to my front door and opened it.

Setting her down softly, I whispered, "Be good and don't pee in the house. Or only pee on the pisser mat by the slider."

Chewie didn't bother listening. She was already halfway down the hall before I even closed the door.

When I spotted Maya in the Jeep, she was looking at her phone.

"Everything okay?" I asked, climbing back in the Jeep.

"Yes and no." She set her phone on her lap. "I had to

deal with a Rob special this morning. I'm just reviewing the letters my attorney sent. I have to send one out to my employees."

"Oh, no. That doesn't sound good. Are you sure about breakfast? I don't want to screw things up for you."

Maya's eyes settled on mine, and a warm smile spread across her beautiful lips. "Cash, I have to be honest. Right now, you are the highlight of my day." She looked down at the chipmunk. "And well, this too."

I smiled and nodded. "You might lose a signal on the stretch back into town. Do you want to stay put while you send the email to your employees?"

She nodded. "That would be great."

I rested my head on the seat and thought about everything Maya had to deal with between her ex and her business, and I was sure I didn't even know half of it. Yet, she was still pleasant. She still had a sparkle in her eye and a bounce in her step.

Don't do it, Cash, I thought to myself. *She's going to go back to the Carolinas. It's temporary.*

"Okay, all set. Thanks for letting me get that out." She glanced at me. "Would have been the topper to send the email and have it get lost somewhere in space."

I nodded and started the Jeep. "You ready for some

food for the soul?"

"You have no idea. And please pardon me in advance because I just might order everything on the menu."

"Go for it."

We pulled onto the road, and the lanky pines swayed gently in the breeze as we made our way back to town. It was a beautiful end-of-summer day, the kind we lived for and embraced before winter hit. However, I was one of those guys who loved the Wisconsin winters. I glanced at Maya and wondered if she'd like the weather.

"You were one of the campers, right?" I asked, remembering the rumors about the Bailey sisters. I was older than all of them, so I missed most of the gossip. But I did know enough to know that they spent the summers with their grandparents, and there were some issues at home, wherever that had been.

"A summer girl." She grinned, glancing at me. "My sisters and I would come for the summers, so we were the summer girls."

I grinned. "Too bad I was too old for summer camp."

She chuckled. "Why's that, Cash? You might have had a crush on me?"

A low growl of affirmation rolled off my lips as I turned onto the main street of town. "No doubt about that,

Maya."

"Really?" she prompted, almost surprised. "You seem like you'd be into someone who adores hiking, fishing, and camping for weeks on end."

I found a parking spot on the street, parallel parked, and then turned to face her. "Really?"

"Yup." Her brows furrowed. "I must confess that I love nature, but I'm not very good at hiking, and fishing involves things that I don't usually like to touch."

"What about camping?"

"I like showers. Daily. Daily showers." She shuddered. "I can't imagine living with myself after day three of no showers. Just ick."

I nodded, noticing her gaze stayed on mine as if she were waiting for some affirmation or something.

"I'm not much for hiking, but I don't mind a good walk through the woods. I only like ice-fishing because I have a great hut to hang out in and drink and eat. And I'm not much for camping unless my Winnebago is hooked behind my pickup truck."

The look on Maya's face was priceless, almost like I took the wind right out of her sails.

"What?" I teased gruffly. "Were those the reasons you came up with as to why you couldn't give me another kiss?"

A blush crept up her cheeks as she unbuckled. "Maybe."

Without thinking, I moved closer and slid my hand around her waist and pulled her a little closer as my eyes dipped to her mouth.

Maya drew a breath and slowly licked her lips as my other hand moved to the nape of her neck.

I leaned over the center console as she slowly closed her eyes.

There was no backing out as my lips touched down to hers. A frenzied need ripped through me as I felt the softness of her skin under my hands, smelled the sweet smell of her, and tasted Maya's even sweeter taste.

She parted her lips, and my tongue met hers as she melted into me. It felt like time stopped as our kisses deepened.

I'd always been guarded around town, but at this moment with Maya, I didn't care.

I wanted to kiss her forever.

The need only grew when she moved her small hand to my chest, and she let out another little moan as her other hand slid through my hair. The hardness rising was nearly painful, and I had no idea how'd I'd get through the damn breakfast.

Maya softly nipped my lip and giggled as she slowly pulled away from me, dropping her hands from me and straightening in her seat.

"Wow. I wasn't expecting that," she said softly. "I'm . . . I'm sorry."

"Sorry?" I asked. Surprise registered over my face. "Never apologize for kissing me."

I shifted in my seat, attempting to wrangle my erection so she wouldn't see it.

Her gaze dropped to my crotch.

Too late.

A smile touched her lips.

"Well, that's an interesting development," she teased, bringing her gaze back to mine.

Damn it. I should never have taken the top off this Jeep. What I would do to her if I could in the backseat.

"Maya, it's pretty difficult to stay calm when you're around," I confessed. "And I know I need to be better at it. You're going through a lot, and I need to do better at respecting—"

Her mouth came back to mine instantly as she slid her hand up my jaw while drawing the other behind my neck.

This was like a fantasy come true. Maya's mouth

covered mine, her lips parted, and the kiss intensified ten times over from the last.

A low, muffled growl tangled with our kiss, but I couldn't help it. She was intoxicating. I needed her. I wanted her, all of her.

My hand moved along her side as her body trembled from my touch. She let out a soft hum and, again, pulled away.

Which was good.

We were in the middle of Buttercup Lake in a Jeep with no top.

This could only go so far.

Right?

I opened my eyes to see her studying me, her lips pinkened and swollen from our kisses.

"You're a complicated guy, Cash." She smiled and nodded. "I think it's time we grab some breakfast."

I laughed, adjusting myself when she got out of the Jeep. "Whatever you say, Maya. You seem to be full of good ideas this morning."

Chapter Thirteen

Maya

Okay, so I didn't expect to lose control with Cash Knox.

Sure, the man was what sex dreams were made of, and I knew this because I took a class based on precisely that when I was obtaining my psychology degree.

But he took it to an entirely different level.

Just sitting across from him at breakfast made my panties nearly melt with his smoldering looks and brooding expressions. And believe it or not, what I seemed to be drawn to, even more, was the bit of grumpy that presented itself now and again. It was kind of like he was fighting the goodness of the world while trying desperately to embrace the bad. Except around Buttercup Lake, it was pretty hard to find the bad.

Unless you were like me and kept receiving calls from an attorney or an ex.

And the countless emails I received from employees based on everything that had transpired this morning.

But I'd made it a priority not to talk about me or my problems with Cash at breakfast. I just quickly answered the emails and went back to us. I didn't want to seem like a Debbie Downer or look like the hot mess I knew I truly was. So, we kept to safe topics like the Buttercup Lake Lodge, which he promised to take me to, or the corn maze that was going to open up in about two weeks at Spring Lake Farms.

I'd mentioned to him that I'd planned on going to Buttercup Lake today to get some swimming and sunning in, and he quickly looked like a puppy dog ready for an invite.

So, here we were.

Cash walked over to a large umbrella propped in the sand close to the water and turned around.

"This one work for you?" He opened up two beach chairs with a shake of his hands.

I held onto my beach hat and nodded. "Perfect."

He put them on the sand and smiled as my eyes skimmed his beautiful body. He quickly tugged his shirt over his head and tossed it on the chair.

"Want me to go grab some snacks at the shack, or do you want to go for a swim?" He checked his phone. "I think enough time has passed since breakfast."

I chuckled. "Considering I ate an entire eggs Benedict, two waffles, three sausage links, and four pieces of bacon, I'm pretty sure I'd still sink to the bottom of the lake."

Cash stood, glancing toward the glistening lake, and nodded. "Yeah, we should probably give ourselves a little more time."

I drew a deep breath, feeling the warm, sweet air fill my lungs. "Boy, did I miss Buttercup Lake."

Families were sprinkled across the sandy beach. Several kids floated on tubes in the lake, and several lifeguards watched over the water. I spread out a striped towel on my chair and sat down while Cash did the same.

We'd stopped at both of our places to grab items for the impromptu beach day.

"It's a special place." He kicked out his lean, muscular legs and closed his eyes as he rested his head on the plastic beach chair. "I can't imagine living anywhere else."

My stomach clenched from his words. Just one more reason this couldn't be. He was happy where he lived, and I was happy where I lived.

If you subtracted my ex, which I wasn't actually sure a person could do—legally—anyway, where I lived was really pleasant. I smiled at my dark humor and watched the sunlight dance across the lake. When I snuck another look at Cash, his eyes were still closed, so I took advantage of the time and let my gaze wander down his broad chest and thin waist, where the ripples of muscles led the way to his waistband and a treasure trail that made my pulse race.

He cleared his throat, and my gaze flicked to his.

Immediately, my cheeks blushed with embarrassment, and fire ran across my skin. I waved my face quickly and laughed. "Whew, it's hot out here."

"Yeah?" His brows rose in amusement.

"Yup." I sprang from my chair and placed my hands on my hips as I pretended to stare at the lake when all I could think about was Cash.

And the heat running through me wasn't lessening, and I didn't want to become a sweaty mess.

Without another thought, I unbuttoned my shorts and pulled off my sweatshirt to reveal the white and black bikini I'd slipped on back at the house while he waited patiently in the Jeep and I went back and forth a million times on which suit to wear.

Even though I was solidly in my thirties, a therapist, and usually confident, I suddenly scared myself into a frenzy of worry since I wasn't a five-foot-seven, svelte woman. I barely topped out at five feet tall, and I had lots of curves that left little to the imagination. And if I had cellulite, I'd never know because I refused to look at the back of myself in a mirror.

So, again, I was a wonderful example of being a complete mess while attempting to guide others through their lives.

But after I folded and tossed my stuff in my bag, the silence was killing me. I slowly turned around to see Cash taking me in, all of me. I buried my enlarged toe in the sand so I didn't pull him out of his fantasy.

The heat in his eyes made every single worry slip away, and I swallowed down every insecurity that didn't matter.

"Maya, I know we've only shared a couple of kisses-—"

I held up three fingers. "That last one was officially two."

His smile widened, but the smoldering look in his gaze remained. "Three kisses," he corrected. "But the thought of not kissing you again makes me nearly lose my mind."

I bit my lip since I had a feeling it might drive him crazier and smiled. "Then maybe we can share a fourth."

"I sure as hell hope so." He smiled and put his hands behind his head. "I really do."

Feeling a little loopy, I sat down and let out a happy

sigh. "Cash, when I heard my attorney's voicemail and spoke with him, I thought my day was really going to suck."

He turned to look at me but didn't say anything as he lowered his arms. The touch of a smile disappeared as he readied to listen.

"But you have made this one of the best days." I smiled. "Ever."

"Ever?" He looked shocked. "I mean, the breakfast was fantastic . . ."

I grinned, interrupting, "It was, but I wasn't just talking about the food."

"Oh, yeah?" His eyes filled with mischief. "Then what?"

"You're really good at conversation."

"Is that it?"

I shrugged, teasing.

Cash tipped his chin in laughter. "I am a good listener."

"You are." I let my hand dangle, and he reached for it, tangling our fingers.

"I know your life is really complicated, Maya." He turned his head to look at me. "But I'm here however you want me to be. Whether it's just someone to talk to or someone to make out with . . . I'm your man."

I chuckled, nodding. "I appreciate that. It's hard to find that kind of relationship."

He kept my hand in his and turned to watch the lake as warmth spread through me.

"Maybe it's time to go into the lake." I put my head against the beach chair and let out a sigh. "But if I get a stomachache, you have to promise to give me CPR."

"For a stomachache?"

"Mmm-hmm." I squeezed his hand.

"Maya, you have to be the best guest in the history of vacation rentals."

I chuckled and felt the tension rise in my chest.

It was true. I was merely just a guest in this awesome town. I didn't live here. I was only vacationing. I'd go back to my life, and Cash would continue his here at Buttercup Lake.

"Thank you. I take pride in that."

He kept his hand clutched over mine as he stood and lifted me into him. He bent down and whispered in my ear something I couldn't decipher, but instead of asking him to repeat it, I just let my imagination run wild.

And the next thing I knew, he picked me up and hoisted me over his shoulder as he jogged through the sand.

"Just know I do get scared of things brushing my legs in the lake."

"Do you need CPR for that, too?" he teased as he got us to the water.

But instead of throwing me into the lake, he slid my body down the front of his, letting my legs slip into the water slowly. When my feet touched the bottom of the sandy lake, I looked into his eyes, seeing something stirring within him.

"I never expected this," he said softly as the lap of the lake washed against us.

"Me neither, and I'm not even sure what *this* is." The lifeguard blew a few bleeps on his whistle as a couple of boys were too rowdy about ten feet away from us.

"Do you think Chewie will ever forgive you for not bringing her to the lake?"

The sunlight sprinkled across Cash's green eyes, leaving golden flecks in their wake. "By all accounts, she hates water, so she should forgive me."

"How exactly did you wind up with her?"

"She was part of a deal. I wanted a house, but she came with it. Her owner had passed away."

"That's sad."

He nodded. "So, the poor thing got stuck with me."

I winked at him, taking a step back. "You're not so bad, you know."

"You don't think?"

Without wasting another second of Wisconsin sunshine, I splashed a huge wave of water at him, soaking him completely. His dark hair hung in his face, and he quickly returned the favor, drenching me in the process.

"Not on my watch, buddy." I turned around and leaped into the water, kicking up water with my feet as I swam toward a bobbing red rope.

When I reached my destination, I spun around while holding on with one arm, but I didn't see Cash.

It wasn't until I turned back that I saw his head bob in front of me under the red rope.

"Hey, you're not following the rules," I teased, swatting at his glistening shoulders.

Could he not get any sexier? I laughed and shook my head.

He scowled. "What?"

"It's just funny."

"What? That I don't follow lake rules?"

"No, that you look like some Greek God springing from the Ionian Sea."

He swam under the red rope and popped up next to me, pushing his dark, wet hair away from his face.

"I could say the same about you, Maya Goddess."

I chuckled and shook my head. "I don't know how

you do it."

"Do what?"

"Make me forget about everything back home and all the stuff haunting me."

Cash smiled and shrugged. "I must not do that good of a job because it just snuck in your head."

"It hasn't for a long time, though. When I'm at the house, it's literally all I obsess about. This is huge progress."

"I contend that it's not me. It's Buttercup Lake." His brows rose slowly. "And she's luring you with her beauty and calmness."

I bobbed toward him, kicking underneath me, and looped my arms around his neck.

Surprise washed over his features as I looked into his eyes. "Will you be my distraction, Cash?"

His seductive eyes flashed with an intensity that only made me bolder. "I promise I won't bite. Hard."

Cash laughed, and I couldn't help but grin as he pulled me into him harder. "I will abso-freaking-lutely be your distraction as often as you want."

"Good," I said, trying to bat away all the uncertainty and worries nipping at me. "Then it's settled. I vow to have an abso-freaking-lutely amazing time for as long as I stay."

"If memory serves me right, that's until the end of

October." He bopped me on the end of my nose with his index finger, and I chuckled.

"My attorney told me it would be better if I stayed away and to inform the employees that they are currently encouraged to work from home through the end of the year."

Cash nodded. "I'm sure they'll love that."

"I know I will." I pressed my lips together and let my body fall away from his as the water caught me.

Arms wide, I kicked underneath me to stay afloat and let out a big sigh when I spotted something forming on the beach.

"Should I be concerned that at least a quarter of the Sunshine Breakfast Club is congregated on the beach looking this way, including my grandma and sister?"

Cash let out a low chuckle. "I'd be more concerned if they weren't."

Chapter Fourteen

Cash

A distraction.

I could handle being her distraction. What warm-blooded male would turn that down?

She was sexy as hell, smarter than any of my family members combined, and had a spunk about her that made the Energizer Bunny look like he ran out of juice. The woman never stopped.

But I hadn't really been with a woman since Freya.

My Freya.

Rusty.

I cleared my throat and sliced a tomato on a cutting board in my kitchen.

This was fine. Everything would be fine. It wasn't like spending time with Maya would turn into something serious. She only rented the place until October, when another family would move in, and this wasn't ever approached in a serious fashion.

She just needed a distraction.

And I would be that guy.

Freya's beautiful smile entered my mind, and the way she'd stroke my arm or tug on my ear to bring me back when I got distracted. Her beautiful red hair cascaded down her back to her waist, and she'd always get the strands stuck under her when sleeping. I'd never met a woman who got tangled in her own hair.

Until possibly Maya.

The thought made me smile as I glanced through the kitchen window at the lake.

Just a distraction.

That was all I could handle, anyway.

Obviously, since this many years after Freya passed away, and I was still thinking about her, missing her, I wasn't ready for anything serious.

At first, I wondered if I should mention Freya to Maya, but there was no future with Maya. We both knew it, and she was already going through so much.

It was probably why I looked appealing. To an outsider, I had nothing to hold me back or tie me down. I was a single guy who flipped and rented vacation rentals.

I wanted to believe that, but I didn't.

And therein lies the problem.

Maya was a professional mind reader for a living. She picked up on the fact that I was a softie in my core, that I had an unhealthy attachment to all things that come into my life, and that I wasn't actually born to be as harsh as I appeared.

Freya had always seen that too.

I let out a sigh and slapped the tomato slices on my sandwich and tossed a tiny bite to Chewie, who had impatiently waited for her reward. The tiny pink tongue of the furball poked out as she took the tomato, and I got the familiar feeling that she wanted to know how I was going to make it up to her for making her wait so long. She had a real ego, this one. I plopped another small bite of tomato near her and chuckled.

I took my sandwich and coffee outside and pulled a chair toward me when my phone rang.

It was my younger brother, Hunter.

I picked up the phone. "What?"

He laughed. "Good morning to you too."

"Sorry. I mean, hi," I grumbled before taking a bite of my sandwich.

"I didn't mean to interrupt your breakfast. What are you having?"

"Turkey sandwich."

"For breakfast?"

"I ran out of eggs."

This was what annoyed me about people, relatives included. They were all so nosy.

"Okay. Pardon me for living. So, I'm headed out for a camping trip next weekend, and I was wondering if I could borrow you and the camper."

"Why me?" I asked.

"I just might have someone I'd like you to meet."

I nearly coughed on my sandwich. Hunter had been playing the field since sixth grade, and he'd happily continued the tradition down in Madison where he had a successful bar.

"You're seeing someone?" I choked out.

"God, no. Not for me. For you."

"No," I snapped quickly.

"It's been too long. You're a relationship kind of guy." He stopped for a second. "I think I found the one for you."

"There isn't *the one*," I growled back.

"Listen, Mom and Dad are worried about you. They said you've barely left your house this summer until recently, and you're just sinking all your time into your properties."

"What of it? Why aren't they worried about you and

all the flings you're having down in Madison? That's not healthy either."

"But it's fun." He chuckled. "Plus, I'm ten years younger than you, and I didn't have my heart shattered like you did. I haven't given up on love. I just don't believe it's for me, just like Beckett."

I took another bite of my sandwich. "You can have the camper, but I can't come."

"Why?" he challenged.

"No reason."

"With you, there's always a reason."

"I have some guests coming to one of the rentals next weekend for a wedding and another guest that seems to need my help quite frequently," I explained. "It's just better if I'm around."

"You mean chipmunk lady?"

I nearly fell off my chair. "How'd you hear about that?"

"Mom and Dad."

I rolled my eyes.

Right.

They lived here too, as did my sister, Evie—sort of. She was obtaining her doctorate in nursing at Marquette and would bounce between here and there during the summer.

Although I'd noticed this summer, she'd done a lot less bouncing back to Buttercup Lake. But she was even younger than Hunter, so I guess that turned all eyes onto me since my older brother had already declared he'd be a bachelor for life and was currently in Italy living his best life.

Why Italy? No one knew.

I groaned. "Her name is Maya."

"So, there's a someone?"

"No someone," I assured him. "She's just having a real rough go of things, and I want to ensure that I'm around if she needs me."

"How very hospitable of you," Hunter chided. "Do you take it out of her deposit?"

"Seriously. She has no intention of staying in Wisconsin."

"How do you know?"

"I just know."

A few seconds of silence sat between my brother and me, so I polished off my sandwich.

"Well, I'm dating a woman named Brielle—"

"As in dating?" I interrupted.

My brother didn't date.

"I'm seeing her casually, but I thought it would be fun to take her up north. She's originally from Chicago and hasn't been to the Northwoods."

"Well, have at it. Camper is all yours."

"How about you bring Maya?"

"It's not like that."

"What's it like, then?"

"A distraction for her," I muttered.

I narrowed my eyes on the lake and noticed two someones just sitting on a paddleboard in front of my house. I craned my neck and strained my eyes to make out who I thought might be Maya's niece and a boy.

"What the . . .?"

"Huh?" Hunter asked.

"Nothing. I just . . . Wait a second. You *knew* about Maya."

"You mean that you made out with her in the middle of downtown before a breakfast out or that you were getting frisky in the lake waters? Yeah. I know about her."

I slapped my forehead. "Dear God. It's not like that."

"Which part? Were you not trading spit in your Jeep?"

"How old are you?"

"Old enough to know when it's right . . . Oh, is it right."

A thought occurred to me.

Maybe if I just let the book club see that there wasn't a possibility with Maya, they'd leave us in peace. I gave a quick wave to Maya's niece, and they quickly paddled away.

"Fine. I'll ask Maya and see if she'd be up for it." If I can persuade my brother to report back to my parents that Maya and I have no future, then maybe it will trickle back to the meddling book club, and I can go back to living my life.

"Great. Let me know today." His voice went up an octave.

"Today? Why today?"

"So I can reserve the camp spot."

"Fine."

"Good." And my bother hung up.

I stood up and stretched, wondering if I should just tell my brother she wasn't interested or if I should give her the option. She said she hated camping, so the odds were in my favor that she'd decline.

And she had a lot of work things going on that probably made being near cell service crucial.

I stared at my phone and thought about calling, paced a few steps, and shoved my phone back into my pocket.

Walking into the house, I saw Chewie already sleeping on her bed by the fireplace.

That was a first. She usually liked the couch.

"Adios, Chewie. I'll be back after I get rejected by a beautiful woman."

She didn't bother paying attention, so I grabbed my wallet and keys and headed out the door.

By the time I pulled down the street to her house, I had thought about just driving by and forgetting about the whole thing.

The time at the lake was special. Kissing her in the Jeep was spectacular. Pulling her out of the wall was even better.

But I didn't want this invitation to blow the carefree whatever this was out of the water. I gripped the steering wheel and let out a deep breath. I was nothing more than a good distraction.

Maybe she was the same for me.

I turned into the drive and saw the front door open, and my heart raced when she stepped outside, nearly oblivious that I'd pulled in front of the house. She rubbed her cheek with a tissue, and my chest tightened.

Not again. It had better not be that asshole of an ex torturing her.

I hopped out of the Jeep as Maya's eyes met mine.

"Hey, Cash," she said weakly, followed by a sniffle. "I swear I don't spend all my time crying."

I smiled and nodded, walking toward her. "No, you also make out with near strangers in front of diners, play tickle in lakes, and get stuck in walls."

Her eyes stayed on mine, and her frown tipped up into a smile.

It was the most beautiful smile I'd seen. "You're no stranger. It might not be the meet-cute I was thinking, but you're definitely no stranger."

I really needed to look that up online.

When I reached her on the front step, I wrapped my arms around her and pulled her in, kissing the top of her head. "What's up? What happened?"

I took a step back to give her some space, but I was fighting the urge to keep her in my arms all day. I wanted to take away whatever pain was haunting her.

My only fear was that the tears were based on heartache for her ex and that she just was in denial.

"I swear I'm not a nut case. I swear it," she teased.

I wiped away a stray tear that made its way to her chin. "I'd never think it."

She let out a deep sigh and stuffed the tissue into her pocket. "Seeing you makes me feel better. I don't know why."

"Well, I've heard I'm modeled after a Greek god." I tipped my chin up toward the sky and positioned my arms upward. "That would do it for anyone."

Maya giggled. "That might be it. And you're funny when you're not busy being grumpy."

I smiled. "So, what happened today? He already shut your office down. What else could he do?"

"It's more what he hasn't done today."

"Which is?" I prompted.

"It's been silent from him. His attorneys haven't received anything back from him. He hasn't acknowledged receipt of letters, emails, nothing."

"Are you worried about him?"

She shook her head frantically. "No. Not at all. I'm worried the silence means he's plotting something else."

My brows furrowed. "Like what?"

"I have no idea. But he always thinks he's above the law."

I nodded, feeling the rawness of anger nipping at me. "And he doesn't know you're here in Wisconsin, right?"

"No. I never told him, and I've kept it under wraps. He does know my sister is here, but he also knows my other sister is in New Mexico. He might figure out that I want to be closer to relatives."

I nodded. "I'll let Nate know to be on the lookout. Do you have any photos of your ex?"

"Who's Nate?"

"A police friend I have."

Maya sniffled and nodded. "Okay. I can send it to you now."

She pulled out her phone and scrolled through some photos and picked a couple to send to me. My phone buzzed, and I resisted the temptation to look at the photos immediately, even though my curiosity was killing me. This guy sounded like a complete dirtbag, and I couldn't fathom how Maya wound up with him.

"And then, to make matters worse, I stubbed my bad toe again, and it's even worse and dark purple."

I looked down at her toe and hopped backward in shock.

"You need to get that thing looked at, Maya. It looks like it's about to fall off."

She snorted, and I bent down to get a better look. "I've done a lot of things to myself over the years with hammers and drills, but this looks worse than all of those accidents."

"Thanks for that." She snickered. "That's why I called Grandma Millie to pick me up. There's a clinic the next town over."

I nodded and scratched my chin. With all of their

plotting and planning, I was surprised that I didn't somehow get the call to take Maya in for her appointment.

"Speaking of," she said as the gravel crunched behind me.

I spun around to see Millie and Jackson in a car that came to a stop next to mine. Millie's eyes lit up at the sight of me.

"Well, Cash," Millie said as she stepped out of the car, "I didn't expect you to be here."

Maya's brows scrunched, and she turned to me. "Actually, I didn't even ask why you stopped by."

I glanced at Millie, who was only a few feet away by now, and took a deep breath. "I'll chat with you after your visit."

"It's good to see you," Millie said, squeezing my upper arm. "Mmm. He's got a good build on him, Maya."

Maya's eyes widened, and her cheeks instantly reddened.

"Okay, Grandma Millie. We aren't all as boy crazy as you are."

Grandma Millie's boyfriend wandered up behind her and squeezed her bum, and he laughed. "She's got a one-track mind."

Maya looked like she wanted to slink away, and I

couldn't help but chuckle.

"Millie, I think you're embarrassing your granddaughter," Jackson Sr. said, placing a kiss on Millie's cheek.

"Isn't that what we're made for?" Grandma Millie looked at her granddaughter and tilted her head. "You've been crying." She turned her gaze to me. "You didn't do this. Did you?"

I put my hands up. "No, ma'am."

She winked at me. "I didn't think so."

Millie looked down at Maya's foot and flinched. "How are you even upright, Maya?"

"I can't sit for more than ten minutes. You know how that is, Grandma. I'm used to the pain."

Jackson grimaced, looking at Maya's toe, and he looked like he was about to turn green. "We need to get this woman some help quickly."

Millie nodded and motioned for Maya to follow her.

"Do you need anything from inside?" I asked. "I'll get the door."

"No. I have my license and debit in my pocket," Maya explained as she hobbled to her grandma's car.

"So, why did you stop by, Cash?" Millie asked as I dashed to help Maya into the car after locking her front door.

Something in Millie's eyes told me she already knew, and I wondered how immersed my parents were in this underground matchmaking service.

As I propped Maya's leg on the backseat of the car and Maya buckled her seatbelt, Maya's eyes locked on mine. "Yeah, why did you stop by? I've been so into my stuff I forgot to ask."

By this time, Jackson and Millie had turned around from the front seats and watched us with big grins.

Great. Fine.

Still leaning over Maya in the back, I let out a breath. "My brother called and invited me . . . us . . . camping using my trailer."

"Me? Us?" Maya's brows rose.

"Long story," I grumbled, not enjoying the audience. "But I know you don't like camping."

"In a tent. This is a different story."

Millie honked the horn, and I smacked my head on the ceiling of the car in shock.

"Then it's settled. Maya will be there."

"I haven't even told her when."

Millie honked the horn again and started the car. "Doesn't matter. I don't care if we have to wheel her into your trailer. She needs this."

And with that, Millie started reversing the car as I struggled to get out in time and shut the door.

Millie stomped on the brakes and grimaced as Jackson rolled his window down.

"I thought you were coming with us. I didn't know your back end was still sticking out of the car." She giggled and did another light tap of the horn.

I watched Maya sink into her seat as Millie reversed out of the driveway, and I prayed for their safety. I really should have driven them.

Chapter Fifteen

Maya

I stared at my black boot and groaned. This wasn't exactly what I imagined as part of a carefree getaway, and how was I supposed to enjoy the lake before it froze over?

Would the doctors have put a boot on me for merely a broken toe?

No. But I wanted to up the ante, and apparently, I'd fractured my foot somewhere along the way.

So, boot for me for the next six weeks.

The good news was that I only had to use a wheeliedoo for the next week.

"Knock, knock," my sister sang into my home. "I've brought food and drink."

I stared at the contraption that I was supposed to put my knee on and push off with my good foot and shivered. I'd already knocked over an end table with my lack of steering, and since this wasn't my house, I didn't want to ruin anything.

Especially a memorial to one of his beloved pets.

My sister appeared with three bags in one hand and a tray of drinks.

"Izzy said she'd have no problem hanging out with you the next few days, but she can't be here on Friday or Saturday night. She's going camping with Caleb."

"It's so sweet of her to spend time with her old, crippled aunt."

Grace rolled her eyes. "You're not old."

I smiled. "What's in the bag? It smells delicious, like garlic overload."

"I have the best cheese curds in the world with a side of garlic aioli. I picked them up from the restaurant at the lodge. They fry the curds perfectly, and somehow, the magical chefs knew to put garlic aioli on top. I'm addicted."

"Sounds amazing."

Grace put everything on the counter and started unloading the other bags. "I brought over cheese, salami, olives, premade salads, and some heat and eat macaroni and cheese that I'll put in the fridge for you."

"I won't be able to move by the time you're done feeding me."

She smiled and walked over with an iced latte and a

plate full of cheese curds with the aioli. "You're spoiling me. I'll never want to go back to North Carolina."

Grace smiled. "That's the plan."

I shook my head and took a sip of my latte. "Is it, though?"

She shrugged. "It would be nice. I mean, none of us have been near each other since we were kids."

I laughed and let out a sigh, thinking back to the childhood I'd managed to compartmentalize and rarely think about. But the truth was that I grew up with addicts for parents. Addicts who now lived on the streets of Seattle. My mom—and I use that term loosely—had recently been diagnosed with cancer. I wanted to say that changed something inside me, but it didn't.

I didn't suddenly have an urge to see her. I'd made my peace long ago. Grace had gone out to Washington to visit them, and it went as well as expected. My parents had no remorse and could barely remember with whom they were talking. They just wanted money to buy more drugs, from what I could decipher.

But my sisters and I survived. We made it through our battered childhood somewhat unscathed and with a resilience that often surprised me.

However, I had a feeling that a part of my upbringing

might also contribute to my handpicked selection of Rob.

I reached for a fried cheese curd and dipped it in the garlic aioli before plopping the fried goodness in my mouth. The creaminess and garlic mixture created perfection around my tongue.

"Oh, my gosh. I don't ever want to leave this town," I said with my hand covering my mouth. "This is insane."

Grace nodded in agreement. "Amazing."

She sat down and kicked her feet onto the ottoman with her own plate of curds. "So, tell me about the camping trip next weekend."

"You know about it too?"

A twinkle appeared in her eyes. "Of course. Do you think our grandma would keep that from me? I think even Nina knows."

I groaned happily. "Well, it's a good thing I have this weekend to recover. I can't imagine taking this contraption with me camping."

"The boot is going to be plenty," Grace teased, taking a sip of her tea. "So, Grandma also mentioned that you'd been crying when she picked you up for the doctor."

I sank into the couch and let out a deep sigh before eating another cheese curd. "It's been silent from Rob the last couple of days. Since he locked the employees out, actually."

"Isn't that a good thing?"

My eyes connected with Grace's, and she knew.

No, it wasn't a good thing.

"I think he's plotting his next move, and honestly, it's scaring me."

"I just can't wrap my head around a man standing you up on your wedding day—"

"Well, at the courthouse," I interrupted.

"Right, but still." She let out a concerned breath. "He stands you up and then gets upset that you didn't stick around?"

"It's all about control, Grace. I know it sounds crazy, but we've done cycles like this before. He'd do something rotten, and I'd stick around like a lost puppy dog. This time, I left."

"So he wanted you to stick around so he could mentally dump on you some more?"

I nodded. "Pretty much. He liked promising me things and then taking them away."

"That is cruel."

"And I stupidly played the game."

"Love is complicated." Grace tried to make me feel better.

"It is, but I don't think this was love. I think it was

comfortable. I found comfort in being ignored and used." I felt embarrassed for even saying it.

"Like our parents did to us," Grace said softly.

"I suppose." I looked at the lake outside and shook my head. "You know, the longer I'm a therapist, the more I realize I think I became one to help myself."

Grace nodded sympathetically.

"But it didn't work," I added.

Grace chuckled and tossed a pillow at me, narrowly missing my treasured cheese curds.

"You, Nina, and I are damn awesome women. If people knew what we faced growing up, they'd be in shock that we're still here." Grace straightened in her chair.

"I sometimes wish we'd told Grandma Millie and Grandpa Renny about how bad it was at home," I said softly. "They would have taken us in immediately."

"But we were kids. Our parents were what we knew." Grace shrugged. "We all did the best we could."

"Except for Mom and Dad," I added.

"Even them," she said, shaking her head.

"Their addictions are going to kill them."

Grace nodded. "I know. I've been mentally preparing. I don't even know if it's going to be our mother's cancer or her addiction that strikes first."

A knot formed in my throat. There were so few people I spoke about my parents with that I wasn't used to freely chatting about the people who'd shaped our lives, for better or worse.

"Have you ever mentioned everything to Cash?" Grace asked.

"About our parents?" I flinched. "God, no. We're just something casual. I asked him if he'd be my distraction while I'm in town, and he agreed."

Grace frowned. "A distraction?"

I nodded. "Yeah. It's for the best. The moment my attorneys get everything straightened out, back I go to North Carolina."

"If you say so." She shrugged. "I just can't imagine Cash agreeing to be your distraction."

"Why's that?" I asked, genuinely curious. It sounded like most men's perfect summer.

"He's been through a lot."

My brows rose slowly. "Like what?"

"It's not my place to say," she said softly. "Anyway, I'm just glad you're—"

I shook my head. "Oh, no, you don't. Now, you have to tell me what you're talking about."

"I figured he might have mentioned, seeing as much

time you're spending together and all."

I studied my sister and ate another cheese curd. It wasn't like her to keep things from me. In fact, it was the exact opposite.

"Since you feel strongly about letting him tell me, I'll quit pressing. But should I be worried?"

Grace shook her head. "Not worried, but maybe sensitive."

"I feel so bad. It's all about me whenever we're together."

"In your defense, you have a lot going on and a crazy ex out there somewhere."

I smiled and nodded. "Out there somewhere is what worries me."

Grace narrowed her gaze. "You don't think he'd come here, right?"

"I don't know." I shook my head. "I don't know why he would or what he'd get out of it."

Grace sat quietly.

"But the thought has crossed my mind. In fact, Cash forwarded his friend a photo just in case."

"His friend?"

I nodded. "The policeman."

"Ah, yes . . . Nate."

I sat sipping my latte and thought about Cash. Had I been so wrapped up in my own things that I dismissed something he was telling me, or had he kept whatever it was from me on purpose? Maybe I had made our situation too light.

Maybe there was a lot more in life that made him grumpy than I'd realized. Although, I never really saw that side since our first encounter.

"You like him, don't you?" Grace said softly.

"I don't *not* like him."

"It's okay to be into someone who isn't a crappy guy, you know."

I chuckled. "I know. I just don't want to get hurt or promise something I can't give."

Grace stretched her legs as she ate some more cheese curds. "Hasn't this town turned into something so cute?"

I nodded, smiling. "It has. It really has."

"Izzy loves having her aunt here," Grace added.

I chuckled, thinking back to the book club selection. I'd finished it last night after I got home from the doctor's office, and the similarities were uncanny.

"Cash is positive the book club is out to set us up."

Grace laughed. "*No.* Where would he get that idea?"

"I finished the book last night, and it was almost as if

my grandma and sister went on the hunt for a book that sounded exactly like my upside-down life."

"You don't say."

I nodded, taking another bite of the glorious cheese curd. "In fact, when Cash brought it all up to me, I promised to buy him a tinfoil hat. But I'm beginning to realize he might be right. You guys are trying to set us up."

"How do you know we haven't already?"

I chuckled. "Because I am my own person, and I got myself stuck in my own wall, thank you very much."

Grace smiled. "Whatever you say."

"What aren't you telling me?"

Grace threw her hands in the air. "All I'm saying is that the book club gave Jackson and me a push in the right direction on more than one occasion."

I rolled my eyes. "You guys were destined to be together."

"That wasn't how I saw it."

I studied my sister as my mind went to Cash. It felt so good being in his arms.

But I had to keep it casual. I was coming from a messy breakup. I had the absolute worst role models for what a healthy couple relationship should be like—courtesy of my parents.

"My mind is all over the place. I can't drag Cash into my world. Not now."

"Ding-dong," Cash's voice echoed down the hall.

My gaze flicked to Grace, who only smiled.

"Do you think he heard?"

She laughed. "Wouldn't be the first time."

"In the family room with my sister," I called out. "And the best cheese curds in the world."

"She must have swung by the lodge."

Cash walked into the family room with a huge bouquet of flowers and a bag. I couldn't wipe the grin away when he bent down and swiped a kiss against my cheek.

"I think that's my cue to leave," Grace said softly. "Izzy will be over tomorrow after her shift ends."

Cash looked at my boot and then at Grace. "I can take care of her."

My mouth fell open, and a smirk rested on Grace's features.

"She can be a handful," Grace told him. "I'm not sure you're up for it."

Cash laughed and turned to the kitchen, setting the flowers and bag on the kitchen counter before wandering back into the family room.

"Think of it as a concierge service. Plus, I want to get

you healed up enough to go on the camping trip with my brother and his . . ." He scratched his chin. "They aren't in a serious relationship, so I don't know what to call it."

"Sounds familiar," I teased as Grace leaned over and gave me a hug before taking my empty cheese curd container away.

"Just let me know if you need Izzy tomorrow."

I snuck a look at Cash and noticed him noticing me when my phone rang.

Something changed in the room, and I froze.

Grace looked over at me as I looked at the screen, and my entire world sank to a new low.

"Do you want me to answer it?" Cash asked.

Chapter Sixteen

Cash

I stared at Nate. "You're telling me there isn't anything we can do?"

He shook his head. "We'll keep an eye out, but within the law at this point, there is nothing that we can do. Our hands are tied."

Nate had been with our town's police department for as long as I could remember. He was a good guy, but he always saw things as right or wrong. No wiggle room, but life was full of zigzags.

"Her ex has been harassing her with texts. Now, it's calls. He gets new phones. It's escalating."

"At this point, there isn't anything I can do. If he shows up in town, that's a different story."

I scratched the back of my neck and let out a frustrated grunt. "Is there any way that we can find out where that cell is located or where he placed the call from?"

"You mean where the cell tower is located that it pinged to? Yes, but no. We need a warrant for that."

I glanced at Maya, who looked like she wanted to do some real damage. Fiery determination rested behind her gaze whenever she looked in my direction.

"Keep in touch, Cash," Nate said, nodding. "If anything changes, call me."

"Will do. We appreciate your help."

Nate gave a quick wave as he walked down the hall and shut the front door behind him.

"It's going to be fine," I promised her.

She pressed her lips into a thin line and nodded. "I know. I just can't believe I dated a guy like this."

"It happens," I said.

Her brow arched. "Does it, though?"

I chuckled, pulling out my phone to text my parents. I'd promised them I'd stop by after dinner, but those plans needed to change. My mom was all too happy to hear she was being stood up for 'Chipmunk Lady' instead.

"You don't have to stay. I'm perfectly fine. He'd probably get lost in the dark and drive into the lake, anyway."

I nodded, thinking back to the phone call.

I answered, and a sharp breath greeted me on the other

end. His only words were, *Is she there with you?*

He hung up before hearing my answer.

Unease still rested between my shoulders. Something wasn't right with that guy, but I didn't know how far he'd take it.

Maya unstrapped her leg from the boot and stretched it on the couch.

"I don't think that's how it's supposed to work," I told her, smiling.

"This is the last straw," she said, pointing at her foot. "I just need my tootsies to be free."

"One with the toes and all that." I smiled, wishing I could take away Maya's problems.

I walked over and sat at the opposite end of the couch, where her small toes stretched toward the ceiling.

There was something I'd wanted to ask, but I knew it wouldn't be an easy answer because it wasn't an easy question.

I turned and watched Maya, who looked like she was finally starting to calm down.

"I need to ask you a question, Maya."

Her eyes fastened to mine, and she nodded with a little hum.

"Was your ex ever physically—"

She shook her head frantically. "Never. He chose words as his weapon of choice."

I wished that answer made me feel better, but it didn't.

Maya continued, "Honestly, a few years ago, I never would have thought I'd be in this situation. There were red flags, for sure. He liked to be in control and things like that, but it started with the little things. The changes over time were insidious and nearly silent as they crept up on me."

"You deserve so much better, Maya. I hope you truly know that in your heart."

Her smile softened as she nodded. "Thank you. I have to remind myself that I was the idiot who picked the guy."

"And think. All you had to do was come to Buttercup Lake, and you would have found me," I teased.

"You're a pretty amazing catch." Her gentle gaze swept over me. "Someone will be very lucky to have you as a partner."

But not her.

Distraction.

"I feel the same about you." I nodded, and she turned her gaze to the window where only darkness rested beyond.

"I told my sister how I begged you to be my distraction."

My eyes caught hers, and I smiled. "You didn't have

to do much begging."

She rested her head against the cushion and smiled. "She seemed surprised."

"About us?" I laughed, thinking back to the meddling book club. "She's part of the group of orchestrators."

Maya laughed and nodded. "That she is."

"What was she surprised about?"

"That you'd do casual."

My chest tightened, and I looked away.

I wanted to explain that I only wanted to be casual because that's all she wanted.

I wanted to tell Maya that I'd try for so much more if she'd let me.

I wanted to talk to her about my life.

Before.

And how I wanted my life now.

I wanted a lot.

Until I realized that I'd probably scare Maya off. She had enough to deal with, and she certainly didn't need to think about me.

"So why would she say that?" Maya pressed. "You kind of hinted that you didn't do relationships."

"I don't," I agreed. "Or I haven't for a long time."

I brought my eyes to hers and drew a breath. "But

bumping into you did something a little unexpected to me."

She frowned and tipped her head. "What do you mean? I'm not following."

"There's no reason you would." I kicked out my legs.

"You don't have to tell me," Maya offered, seeing the discomfort settling around me.

I straightened and crossed my leg over my knee and bounced it nervously.

"I probably should."

Maya scooted her leg off the couch and propped it on the ottoman. "Slide over closer."

I chuckled. "You don't do this with your other clients, do you?"

She grinned. "You're not a client. You're a friend."

A distraction.

A friend.

I was climbing up in the world.

As I scooted over, she held up her hand. "But I have to apologize immensely."

"For what?"

"All the garlic I ate."

I laughed and shook my head. "I don't smell any garlic."

And it was true. I only smelled the sweetness I'd

come to know as Maya.

I didn't know where to begin. My worlds collided. I'd kept Freya neatly tucked away where I could think of her fondly on-demand. She was where I needed her to be, but talking aloud with someone would change that. Emotions could get involved. Misunderstandings.

"Have you been married before?" I asked Maya.

She shook her head. "No, thank God. It would have been Rob."

I nodded.

Maya shivered at the thought, but her gaze caught mine. "Have you?"

I leaned over, propping my elbows on my knees as I stared straight out the row of windows.

"Yes. Her name was Freya."

Maya's breath caught.

"She passed away the first year of our marriage."

Maya gasped and reached out to my arm, wrapping her tiny fingers around as much of it as she could.

"Cash, I'm so sorry. I had no idea." She shook her head. "I feel absolutely ridiculous about my stuff when you've been through so much."

I straightened and turned to see compassion spilling out of Maya.

But I didn't see pity.

For the first time in a long time, someone was looking at me and recognizing the sorrow of the situation, the gravity of the loss, but she wasn't pitying me.

"Two different situations," I said gruffly.

"When?" Maya asked. "When did your wife pass?"

Tears rested on the edge of Maya's bottom lids, and I smiled, realizing why Maya truly chose her profession. She had a heart of gold and enough compassion to fill the entire state. The world needed more of that.

Rob didn't, but the world did.

"Six years ago." Speaking it didn't do all the things I thought it would, but I knew it was because of who I was speaking with. "I forgot to pick up something up. She asked me to get it at the market when I was getting gas. When I got home and didn't have it, she dashed out to get the missing ingredient, but she never came back."

Maya's hand flew to her mouth as she shook her head and rubbed my back with her free hand. "I can't even imagine what you've gone through."

"Guilt. Anger. Not in any particular order." I shook my head, feeling the hollowness of the situation permeate my existence. "If I'd just remembered to pick up what she'd asked me to get, she'd still be here. Rusty survived."

"Rusty?" Maya asked softly.

"Our first dog together. A beautiful Irish setter. He went with her in the car. The police found him hovering over her. She wasn't wearing a seatbelt." I let out a heavy sigh. "He passed away a little over three months ago."

Maya nodded, rubbing my back. "There are no words."

I agreed and turned to face Maya. "So, agreeing to be your distraction seemed like a really good idea."

She cupped my hands in hers. "Do you still feel that way?"

"More than ever, Maya." I glanced toward the lake. "You've been a breath of fresh air."

And I wanted more than ever to start over. Give her a cute meeting or whatever it was she wanted. Show her that there was another way.

"I knew there was more to you than the average guy, Cash. I just didn't know it would be born from so much pain."

"But there's hope," he said, smiling. "There's always hope. That's what kept Rusty and me alive every day. We woke up and hoped for a better day. I won't lie. When I lost him, it was hard to keep hold of that hope."

Maya brushed my cheek with her hand and nodded.

"Until you bounded into my life." I smiled. "But don't

worry. I fully understand that you have your life in North Carolina. I get it. I'm purely a distraction. I know what I signed up for, but if this was all too heavy for you, I'd get that too. Just know that you deserve to be treated right."

Maya pulled herself onto my lap, straddling me with her tiny body. "Be careful with your foot."

She pressed her finger to my lips as her long hair brushed the fabric of my shirt. "Shh."

Maya's lips were so close to mine, but there was no kiss.

She slowly looped her arms around my neck and buried her head into the crook of my neck.

"You deserve to be treated right, too," she whispered. Her warm breath coated my flesh as I held her close and finally breathed.

Chapter Seventeen

Maya

Since Cash had answered the call three nights ago, I hadn't heard any more from my ex. But that didn't mean he wasn't still out there plotting his next revenge. I just didn't seem to care as much now. Cash had been an amazing nurse until I'd chased him away during the day so he could go take care of his business and I could read until the evening when he'd return. He took one of the spare bedrooms, so there wasn't any weirdness.

But there was something different between us, and I couldn't tell what had changed.

I felt closer to him but farther at the same time.

As I sat outside, stretching my legs in front of me and pretending I wasn't still wearing a boot, I thought back to that night he told me everything. My heart ached for his loss, for the pain he'd experienced, and for the future that had been stolen from him.

I also knew I didn't want to steal another future from him. As I sat with that thought for a few minutes, my phone rang, and my entire body tensed until I saw that it was my sister Nina calling me.

"I'm so glad it's you," I told her over speakerphone.

"Who else would it be? Are Grace and Grandma Millie driving you crazy?"

I chuckled. "Surprisingly, no. I think they're trying to force a love connection and are waiting in the audience with their popcorn."

"Sounds about right." She drew a breath that filled our connection with tension.

"What? What's going on?"

"Mom has passed away."

"What?" I screamed before numbness muted me.

"I'm sorry. I just found out. No thanks to our father. He's gone MIA, but the county's coroner wanted to know what to do with the body."

I hung my head in my hands and gathered my thoughts.

"Was it the cancer?"

"No, she overdosed." Nina's voice was emotionless until the last word.

"I want to say all the things a child should say, like I can't believe it and how could this happen, but all I am is angry." I'd kept it in for years.

Nina let out a sigh. "I haven't told Grace yet. I was hoping since you were there, you might be able to do it in person. I know she held the most hope for change with those two."

I ran my fingers over my eyes to wipe away the sudden dampness.

"I'm so sorry you had to get that call," I said softly.

"It had to be one of us. I just wish the circumstances were different."

"Me too." I stared across the lake where the start of Buttercup Camp sat empty. The campers had long since left for the summer. "It didn't matter how much I studied and learned about addiction. I still hurt from what they did."

"We all do, sweetie." Nina cleared her throat. "But we set our boundaries and did the best we could with what we were given."

"What did they find in Mom's system?" I asked. "I know Grace will want details."

"Well, they found a bit of everything, but what killed her was methamphetamine. She had a cardiac event."

"And Dad is nowhere to be found?"

"Nope."

"They will cremate her, and her ashes will be sent here." Nina sniffled. "But I don't know."

I knew exactly what she meant. Then what?

It wasn't like our parents had special places they visited with fond memories or cherished certain times hiking the mountains where we could sprinkle her ashes. They chose to live on the streets. Or, as I would say, as the professional that I was, the addiction chose for them.

But as a child who suffered from it, that didn't make it easier.

"I thought while you're in Buttercup Lake I'd fly up for a visit. Then I could see you both."

I chuckled. "Since when did you become a planner? But, I'd love that." I heard Cash's Jeep pull into the driveway. "I've got the place here until the end of October."

"Awesome. I'll look at my work schedule and text you guys."

"I have dinner," Cash's voice boomed through the back yard, and surely, through the speakerphone.

"Who's that?" Nina cooed.

"Oh, he's, umm." I cleared my throat as his gaze locked on mine. "He's helping me with my broken foot. He owns the property I'm renting."

"Oh, yeah?"

"Yeah."

"That's first-class service."

"It is. I'm spoiled. Talk soon. Love you, and I'm sorry you had to get that call."

"I'm sorry any of us did," she said. "Love you too."

I hung up as Cash knelt in front of me. "That didn't quite sound like Grace."

"It was my other sister, Nina."

"Where does she live?" Cash asked.

"In New Mexico." I tried to change the subject. "You're home early."

"Well, I saw BBQ Bob's food truck in front of the hardware store and had to order everything off the menu before he ran out."

"Good stuff, huh?" I smiled, but he cocked his head and studied me.

"What's wrong?"

"Nah. We've got food waiting."

I wasn't sure I could go through with telling him. I didn't want to sound cold or heartless or confused or any of the things I actually felt about my mom. I knew I should be under an oak tree bawling my eyes out, but I knew those tears wouldn't come. Not yet, anyway.

He brushed his finger under my chin before tricking me. With a quick scoop of his arms, he picked me up and carried me to the patio table where he'd set the takeout.

"Wow. It smells amazing."

He picked up a napkin from one of the bags and handed it to me. "You still have a tear on your left cheek."

I quickly grabbed the napkin and dabbed the remaining tear.

Cash started opening containers and spreading them out along the table. He opened two sodas and set one in front of me before spooning mac and cheese, coleslaw, beans, pork brisket, and a chicken leg onto my plate.

"That should start you off well." He smiled, studying me. "But I'd really like to know what happened while I was gone. Is it your ex? Do I need to call Nate?"

I let out a groan and placed my forehead in both palms. "When I say I'm a hot mess, I mean it. I come with baggage, and that baggage has small purses, bags, and organizers for all my crap."

"It can't be that bad."

I smiled and nodded. "Oh, it is."

I spooned in a couple of mouthfuls of baked beans and sat quietly eating with Cash. I didn't know how to start or what to say, so I stared at the lake.

From everything I could tell, Cash had a normal family.

I didn't.

There was nothing normal about being left home alone for weeks at a time with no food or money while our parents were on a bender. There was nothing normal about lying to case managers to protect the people who were supposed to be protecting us.

"Is there anything I can help with?" Cash tried again.

I turned my gaze to his and took a bite of chicken. "I don't want you to think I'm an awful person."

He shook his head. "I never would."

"Nina called me because she had news about my mom."

He nodded and wiped his mouth with a paper napkin. "You haven't mentioned much about your parents. You told me Rob called them failures, but it sounded like it was in a nasty comparison."

I let out a deep breath. "Yeah. He was partially right, for once. They weren't the parents that we needed growing up."

"I'm sorry."

I took a sip of soda as my bravery rose. "My parents are addicts. They live on the streets and have for most of my grown life. My home life growing up was hell until I came here to Buttercup Lake. Even my grandma didn't know what was going on at home. We wanted to protect our dad, her son."

Shock registered across Cash's face. "Wow. That wasn't something I expected."

"It always seems to surprise people, which I take as a compliment. Most of the time."

He tried again. "Is everything okay with the call?"

"Not really." I clasped my hands together and set them on my lap. "My sister called because my mom died of an overdose. My father is MIA, so the county coroner reached out to Nina."

Cash shot from his seat toward me and pulled a chair next to mine.

"I can't even imagine what you're feeling right now."

My eyes connected with his. "That's just it. I feel nothing."

"And that's your right." He nodded. "I can't imagine growing up with parents like that. Our family was close. We were a priority. I don't know how I'd feel if that hadn't been the case."

I licked my lips, feeling my throat restrict. "I feel like an awful daughter, a horrible person for not breaking down and crumpling and . . ."

Cash ran his fingers through my hair and rubbed my shoulder. "Don't worry about how you're viewed. I'm sure you experienced things I can't even fathom."

Without warning, tears began to stream down my face. Cash pulled me into his chest and rubbed the back of my head as the tears became fiercer and the sorrow dug deeper.

I was sorrowful that my parents missed out on experiencing amazing daughters.

I was hurt that my mom never remembered our birthdays.

I grieved for the parents I never had.

I broke for the pain my parents had created for themselves and what I had experienced my entire life.

The hollowness and the search for something more that they never found.

They'd always wanted it to be the next hit.

The sobs turned to softer cries as Cash gently rubbed my back.

The release felt good, needed.

But it didn't conjure a different relationship with my mom.

The tears only solidified the sadness I felt over the life she'd missed out on.

I slowly pulled away from Cash and wiped my face.

"Sorry. You can evict me at any time."

He laughed, sweeping my hair over my shoulder. "Why would I do that? You already prepaid."

I chuckled and rested my head on his chest again. "If I weren't so exhausted, I'd be embarrassed."

"You have nothing to be embarrassed about, Maya. You're an incredible woman in spite of the hardships you faced growing up."

I let out a sigh and straightened.

His gaze stayed on mine.

"Thank you for not judging me."

"You've already proven to me that you're an amazing woman, Maya."

I sniffled and looked at his chest. "I got barbeque sauce on your shirt."

He looked down and smiled. "Why, yes, you did."

"I should tell my sister in person. I hate to ask, but could you drive me to her house?"

"Absolutely." He sprang up and gathered the takeout containers. "We can come back and eat if we want to."

"I feel so bad. You stopped at this awesome BBQ spot and then—"

"Maya, seriously. We need to tell your sister, and this food is no big deal. It reheats great."

"I don't know how I'd survive this summer if I didn't run into you," I said, surprising myself.

Cash smiled and nodded. "I feel the same."

I chuckled. "You mean about my surviving?"

Cash laughed and went inside as I texted Grace to ensure she was at her house. She texted back quickly that she was and that we could come on over. She's spent the day working on her store.

By the time we reached Grace's rental, which coincidentally was also one of Cash's, I'd gotten enough nerve to tell Grace.

She'd always been the one to hold out hope for Mom and Dad, but after the last trip she made out there this summer when she learned of our mom's illness, something changed. I didn't know how this would go.

"Do you want me to stay in the Jeep?" Cash asked.

I looked at the house and drew a breath before answering. "Would you mind?"

Chapter Eighteen

Cash

Damn it. Did this woman ever catch a break?

I couldn't even comprehend what Maya and her sisters encountered growing up, but I was certain it was the complete opposite of what I experienced with my siblings. I always had a parent cheering me on from the sidelines or volunteering for field trips. I always had clothes on my back, and my parents remembered our birthdays.

Maya had spent about an hour inside with her sister, and when she came out with her red nose and even redder eyes, I wanted to do nothing more than hold her in my arms forever.

But I could sense something had changed. Whatever vulnerabilities she'd willingly shown me earlier had disappeared.

We went back to the house, ate the rest of our dinner,

played a little with Chewie, and each went to bed without saying much.

I didn't want to say anything that would hurt her. She didn't want to say anything that would make her hurt. It was as if she suddenly saw tears as a weakness, or maybe she'd cried them all out with her sister.

I really had no idea, but when I left in the morning to go check on one of my houses, she was nowhere to be seen. Usually, she'd hobble around with her knee up on the upright scooter, trying to make coffee and feed me breakfast before I left. It was nearly impossible to convince Maya to slow down.

However, this morning, the house was silent. I made her a pot of coffee for when she awoke and defrosted a pastry I found in the freezer.

I managed to grab a bagel from the coffee shop and now stood in front of my newly purchased house, which needed a lot of work to entice tourists. I'd left Chewie back with Maya in case she lifted her spirits. Hauling over a ladder, I propped it on the side of the house and climbed each step slowly until I made it to the top and scanned the shingles. Everything looked pretty solid and in good shape.

As I started back down, my phone rang. It was Nate.

Balancing carefully, I answered.

"One of the deputies said they saw someone in town

at the hardware store who looked like Rob."

My heart stopped. "Seriously?"

"Yup. Of course, I can't be sure until we have a positive ID from Maya, but my guy shot a pic. Should we stop by now?"

My heart went from stalling to a million miles an hour. "Give me about twenty minutes. I'm not home with her, and I want to be there when she sees the photo."

"Absolutely. I'll bring it over in a bit."

I climbed down the ladder, slid it closed, and carried it inside before quickly locking the door behind me.

Maya's ex had better stay the hell away from her. I shook my head in frustration. What was he doing here?

I'd gotten myself all worked up by the time I was pulling into the driveway. I scanned the property, and nothing seemed out of the ordinary. There was a good chance that if her ex was in town, he wouldn't know where she was staying since all of the rental properties were in my name. If she were at the lodge and he called the front desk, they just might give him everything he needed.

I turned off the Jeep and marched inside to see Maya sipping a cup of coffee next to the empty pastry plate.

"Good morning," I said, trying to be as cheerful as possible.

She saw right through it.

"What now?" She set the coffee cup down.

"Nate is going to be over with a photo one of the other deputies took of a guy who matched the pictures you sent them."

Her expression dropped. "You've got to be kidding me."

I shook my head and drew a breath. "I wish I were. But there's no reason he should know you're here at this house."

She nodded in agreement. "It's a good thing I already showered. I don't need to look like a complete mess in front of the police."

I shook my head. "You never could." I walked over to the coffeepot and poured myself some and took a sip.

"Hey, Cash," she said softly.

My eyes went to hers, and I saw the familiar softness flickering through. "Yeah?"

"I'm sorry if I seemed a little off yesterday after seeing my sister. I didn't mean to come off like—"

"Like a woman who lost her mom to addiction?" I shook my head and set the coffee down, bringing her into my arms. "You have nothing to apologize for."

A knock at the door interrupted what else I wanted to

tell her, but it was probably for the better.

"You stay here," I said, and she gave me a funny look.

And then she used her scooter right behind me as I made my way to the front door. I opened it up to see Nate and another deputy, Tim, behind him.

"Thanks for doing this," I told them both.

Nate gave a quick nod as we invited them in. "Would you like any coffee?"

Nate shook his head. "This ought to be quick. We've got to make our way over to the station. The rotary club is honoring Tim for his birthday today."

Maya smiled. "Well, happy birthday."

Tim grinned and tipped his hat. "Thanks."

Nate pulled out his phone and flipped to a set of photos. "Tim sent these to me."

I stood behind Maya and looked over her shoulder.

A little gasp swooshed from her lips when she saw the first photo, but she quickly flipped through the other four.

"It's him," she said softly. Disappointment filled each syllable.

I glanced at the photos and shook my head. "It certainly looks like the photos I've seen of him."

"Well, we'll be on our way, but I think that answers your question. He is here." Nate nodded. "If you need us for anything, we're only a call away."

"And there's nothing we can do?" I already knew the answer before I asked, but I thought I'd try again.

"Not unless he starts harassing or . . ." Nate drew a breath. "Just keep your phone with you."

Maya nodded, but her shoulders slumped in defeat.

When the officers left, she turned to me. "I think he's gone off the deep end."

"Let's hope not, but I'd let your attorneys know he showed up uninvited."

She wheeled her way back down the hall toward the kitchen. "Could this week get any worse?"

I chuckled to myself and followed behind her. "As a matter of fact, yes."

Maya's brown eyes locked on mine. "How?"

"This is the week we promised my brother we'd go camping."

She snickered and nodded. "I can tell you with full honesty that this is the first time I'm excited about going on a camping trip. No, actually relieved."

I nodded in agreement. "It's probably best that we leave town for a few days. Maybe not being able to find you will make your ex go back home."

Maya scooted toward the window with her knee

propped on the scooter and looked at the lake glistening in the sunshine.

Without thinking, I walked over to Maya and slid my arms over her shoulders from behind as we looked at the water together.

She held onto my hands that hung over her chest, finally letting out a deep breath. "The good news is that this is the last day of the scooter. I can start putting weight on my foot."

"There's a silver lining," I teased.

Maya hobbled around to face me, and I knew I wanted nothing more than to kiss her. So much had gone on since we last kissed that I wasn't sure if there'd ever be another one.

But I thought of her every second we weren't together.

Her beautiful dark hair.

Her soft brown eyes.

The little pucker in her lips when she'd get confused . . . or stuck in a wall.

Maya looked into my eyes, and I lost it.

"You've been through so much, and it's not over," I said gruffly. "Tell me if this isn't okay."

She blinked and nodded, and my entire body heated with the desire I'd been ignoring since I'd temporarily moved in.

My hands cupped her cheeks, and her eyes closed, waiting.

It was the most beautiful thing, seeing the anticipation and the same need I felt.

I pressed my mouth to hers. Maya's lips parted, and her tongue swirled against mine. Her sweetness surrounded me as my mouth pressed against hers. Our kisses felt like only the beginning of what was to come.

Her hands slowly moved underneath my shirt, sliding against my skin, leaving a wake of warmth where they left. I moved her slowly and kicked away the scooter.

She giggled between kisses as I cupped her butt and sat her on the counter.

Maya opened her eyes and looped her arms around my neck.

"You make me feel so special and like all my problems are manageable." She pressed her forehead against mine as my pulse quickened at her words. "I'm so confused."

But she didn't let go. She didn't push me away.

She held me.

I brushed my hands along her back, and she closed her eyes, and I knew I needed another kiss.

This time, the need outweighed any gentle touch.

My mouth pressed against hers.

Hard.

She let a little moan escape as she pulled me in closer, wrapping one leg around my waist as the other one with the boot dangled.

There was something so raw, so Maya with what was happening between us.

Maya's fingers twisted through my hair as her tongue danced with mine, feeling a rhythm of only our making.

Her breathing changed. I slid one hand down her belly, resting it on her thighs. I could feel the warmth between her legs as my breath caught in my throat. She pulled away slightly, her eyes fluttering open as she licked her lips.

She grabbed my hand and put it on her chest. "My heart is beating so fast."

I smiled, running my other hand along her hairline as her sultry gaze stayed locked on mine.

She gently nipped my bottom lip, beckoning me for more, when my phone rang. I silenced it and kissed her again.

But my phone started again.

And then it buzzed several texts.

She pressed her lips together and let out a sigh as our kiss came to an end.

"Sounds important."

"Can't imagine it is."

I stepped back, feeling my heart still pounding, when I glanced down at the text.

It was from Nate.

The guy is at Buttercup Lake Lodge. Do what you will with that info.

I looked up at Maya. Her shoulders slumped. "What's up? Everything okay?"

I glanced back down at my phone and debated whether to tell her. I shoved my phone into my back pocket and let out a deep breath.

"Everything's fine. I just have something I need to take care of."

"One of the rentals?"

I didn't answer. I couldn't lie to her.

So I said nothing and swept another kiss across her lips.

"Well, you're going to have to get me down from here, or I might break my other foot."

I chuckled, feeling her in my arms as she slid down to the floor. I moved her scooter back to her and grinned.

"Don't do anything I wouldn't."

"That doesn't really tell me much." She laughed and scooted her way to the family room. "It's officially time for some reality television. Go forth, good man. I'll see you when you get back."

I hated lying to her, but I wasn't really saying anything one way or another. I wiped my palm over my mouth and cleared my throat.

"Maybe we can pick up where we left off?"

She looked over at me and smirked. "If you're lucky."

By the time I got to my Jeep, I was fired up and ready to go. Maya's ex couldn't keep haunting her like this, and maybe it was time he had a talk with someone his own size rather than a barely five-foot female.

Grateful my parents were back in town, I dialed my dad as I backed out of the drive.

"Yello, Son." He laughed.

It was physically impossible for my dad to say hello like a normal person.

"Hey, Dad." I pulled onto the main road and let out a breath. "Are you busy?"

"Not really. I'm retired. I did just put a loaf in the oven, but—"

"Dad, I know this sounds crazy, but I'll explain when I pick you up. I'm going to need your help with something."

"Sounds like my night just got a lot more exciting."

I laughed and shook my head, still in disbelief at what I was about to do.

Chapter Nineteen

Maya

"Get a grip, girl," I whispered to myself, pacing in front of the fireplace. "You can't sleep with Cash. You've only known him a few weeks."

Chewie whined and curled back on the couch as I stared at her.

"Sorry. This isn't really a G-rated conversation." I let out a sigh and scooted again. I only had a few more hours, and I could say goodbye to this contraption.

Hopefully, Cash would be back by then, and we could start where we'd left off.

But he hadn't answered my texts since he'd left, and I was kind of starting to get worried.

I'd already reached out to my attorneys about Rob, and they were alarmed, to say the least.

Which wasn't exactly comforting, and I'd be lying if

I didn't admit that I was a little freaked out being here alone.

Since it was now dark.

I growled in frustration, but it didn't make me feel any better.

Rob had never showed a violent side, but he didn't fight nicely with words, either. He had a habit of muttering things under his breath that I often pretended to ignore.

I probably shouldn't have.

A shudder ran down my spine right when the doorbell rang.

I nearly fell off my scooter in shock, and Chewie hopped up on her four tiny feet, spinning in circles and yapping like she was a parakeet—not a dog.

I glanced at one of Cash's pet mementos that I could use as a club but shook myself out of it. I was being ridiculous.

But I grabbed it anyway and scooted toward the door. If all else failed, I could shove the scooter at Rob too.

"Who is it?" I asked, feeling a prickle down my spine.

"It's your grandmother. Who else would pop over here close to ten o'clock at night to bring you tiramisu and some of my lemonade?"

Relief never tasted so sweet.

I swung open the door, and Grandma Millie hopped back.

"You look like a fright."

Chuckling, I ushered my grandma in. "You look nice too."

She spun around as I backed my scooter up and then forward and then sideways in order to shut the door.

"You could have just asked for help."

"That makes life too easy."

Grandma Millie smiled, holding the jug and tinfoil tray of tiramisu. "I thought this might lift your spirits after getting the news about your mom."

My stomach clenched. She was Grandma Millie's daughter-in-law. I'd done an okay job of compartmentalizing her passing.

I went to grab the jug, and my grandma shook her head. "If you drive the scooter as well as you walk, I don't think either of these things will make it to the kitchen."

She glanced around as I pushed off. "I didn't see Cash's Jeep outside. I was surprised."

I propped myself against the counter in the kitchen. "He had something to take care of at another place."

"You sure it wasn't another someone?" Her white eyebrows waggled up and down.

"Grandma, he's not like that."

She chuckled. "I know. I just wanted to see if I could

get a rise out of you, and I could."

"Which means?"

"That you like this fellow. Grace and I chose well."

I looked at her. "What do you mean, Grace and you *chose* well?"

"Well, she rented her place from Cash, and she thought you two would be a perfect fit. Unfortunately, when she thought that, you were still with Rob. But then you got stranded at the altar, and life fell perfectly into place."

My brow arched. "Yes. Life has fit so perfectly into place that my life simultaneously imploded while my ex was trying to take my company and is now apparently stalking me. All the while, I have a broken foot. Remind me not to have you two put together any other magical spells."

Grandma Millie opened two different cupboards until she found the set of plates. "What is this about Rob stalking you? The messages he's sending?"

I let out a sigh. I hadn't told anyone in my family about the latest. Grandma Millie slid over a plate and fork. Taking a bite, I closed my eyes and smiled.

"This is heaven."

She waved her hands. "I'm glad you think so. Continue."

"Cash asked Nate to keep an eye out for Rob because

he kind of went off the grid. Sure enough, one of the deputies saw him at the hardware store today."

Grandma Millie looked horrified. "And Cash left you alone?"

"Well, when you put it that way . . ." I laughed nervously.

I'm sure I was overthinking things. I set down the carving of a lizard that I was certain commemorated some reptile Cash had as a kid. I hadn't even realized I was still clinging onto it like it was my lifeline.

Grandma Millie eyed the wood. "And that was your club in case I was Rob?"

"Maybe."

"Oh, baby." Grandma Millie put down her fork and hugged me closely. "You girls have not had an easy time of it, but that will all change. My love, that will all change."

Being in her arms instantly brought me back to my summers at Buttercup Lake when I'd fall off a bike, get my heart crushed by a mean boy, or deal with a bunch of nasty girls. She was always there for me.

"I wish we'd told you about our childhood. I wish we'd lived with you."

Grandma Millie gave me an extra squeeze. "There's not a day that goes by that I don't beat myself up over that.

But your parents were good storytellers."

"I prefer the term liars."

Grandma Millie pressed her lips together and took a few steps back to her tiramisu. "I don't know what I did wrong when raising your dad. It was probably best that I didn't have you girls, too."

I gasped at the insinuation. "Grandma, it wasn't you. You did everything you could to help Dad, and once he met Mom, well . . ." I shook my head. "They made their decisions to support their disease."

"Well, regardless. I'm proud of how you girls turned out. It takes grit and determination to make it out okay from the things you saw."

I nodded and smiled at Grandma Millie. "Well, unfortunately, I think my upbringing gave me horrible taste in men."

"Rob is no peach." My grandmother shook her head. "But Cash is certainly easy on the eyes. Although, I'm disappointed he's not here. Does he truly understand the seriousness of this?"

"I think so. I thought so. I'm sure he does." I nodded. "He was the one who contacted Nate and wanted the police to get involved, but nothing has happened. Just scare tactics."

Grandma Millie let out a sigh. "How are the

employees taking everything?"

"By all accounts, they still know who's in charge, but they're all working from home now. At least for the time being, it makes sense." I rubbed my temples in between taking another bite of dessert. "I'm just so upset at myself for sticking around with Rob."

My grandma scowled. "He's a control freak. You can't blame yourself. I'm sure he always put on the charm to win you back, and then his old ways came back gradually."

"Pretty much sums it up. I think that's why he's so irritated this time. He wanted the last word, wanted me to grovel, to try to win him back."

"He's no prize, dear." Grandma Millie chuckled, sliding me a glass of lemonade.

"That's an understatement."

"Well, I'm not leaving here until Cash shows up tonight. I'm sure Rob is just talking himself into a tizzy somewhere, but I'd rather be with you all the same."

I smiled at my grandma and took a sip of lemonade. "You think we could take him, right?"

She chuckled. "Don't count me out. I still do my morning stretches, my afternoon yoga, and then sex with Jackson Sr. every night." Grandma Millie cracked her neck and grinned. "I've got stamina."

I nearly spat out my drink in a snort, and Grandma Millie winked at me. "Just wait. You'll see how things get even better with time."

Clearing my throat, I was afraid to even look at my grandma. "Good to know."

"I'm serious, dear. There's nothing to be embarrassed about. I tell Izzy that all the time."

I laughed and shook my head. "And I'm sure your great-granddaughter loves hearing it."

"Speaking of . . ." Her brows raised. "Have you and Cash done the deed?"

"Grandma." I smacked her.

"Careful. I might bruise." She flashed a wry grin. "Well, have you?"

"Grandma, that is none of your business."

"So, that means you have, which makes sense since he's been staying here to help you out."

My cheeks reddened. "Grandma, it does not mean that at all. If you must know, we've only kissed."

"What is taking you so long? He's good-looking. Has a heart of a saint. He is overprotective in a good way. But he isn't here, so I'll dock him a point for that."

"It's not that simple, Grandma. I have a life waiting back in North Carolina."

My grandma stared at me without saying a word.

"It's true. My business is there. My house is there."

"And your sister is here. Your niece is here. Your incredibly spunky grandma is here. You said yourself that your business can go remote." She shrugged. "Unless you're dying to bump into Rob at the grocery store, I'd be calling a moving van like yesterday."

I sighed. "You make it sound so easy."

"Life doesn't have to be complicated," she chided. "You and your sister seem to excel at that, though."

My eyes almost popped out of my head. "Have you seen my life lately?"

Grandma Millie smiled and glanced at my scooter. "Yes, I have. It's extremely complicated."

I didn't know what to say, so I just finished off my tiramisu.

And that was when it hit me.

Cash wouldn't have left me here alone unless he knew Rob wouldn't be a problem.

"Why do you have that funny look on your face?" Grandma Millie asked, finishing her last bite.

"Because it just dawned on me why Cash isn't here."

"Yeah, why?"

I drew a breath and shook my head. "I think he knows

where Rob is."

"And?"

"I don't know . . ."

Grandma Millie rubbed her hands together. "Ooh, now it's getting good. Did you know Cash's dad was in the special forces? He's retired military."

I studied my grandma as I watched the wheels spin. She was deep in thought.

"We should try to find them," I prompted.

"I don't think that's a very good idea."

"I didn't say it was a good idea. I just thought it might be something we should do."

Grandma Millie's jaw locked, and she drew a breath. "We'll give him one more hour, and then we'll go on the hunt."

Chapter Twenty

Cash

"How long are we going to sit here? It's already past ten o'clock." My dad shifted in his chair. We were camped in the lodge's lounge, positioned to see the lobby and who went in and who went out.

"Until I spot Rob."

Daisy came over to refill my dad's cup. She bartended at the lodge and was one of the unintended targets of the Sunshine Breakfast Club. She was a sweet girl but too young for me. She also was Jackson Jr.'s cousin. The whole thing was just a bad idea, but I was grateful that she felt the same way.

She wandered back to the bar, where the infamous Jack swooped in and started to flirt with her.

Good.

Maybe he'd stay out of Maya's hair now.

"And then what?" My dad took a sip of his coffee to stay awake.

"We just need to have a chat with him." I wanted to get a sense of this guy in person and gauge his intentions and hostility.

My dad smiled. "You're really falling for this girl."

I shrugged and took a sip of my Diet Coke. "I'd do it for anyone."

"Except that you've been such a hermit for how many years? So you wouldn't know anyone to do it for."

"Point taken," I grumbled.

"My point is that this girl is special."

"She's also a tourist."

And hell, I'd love to give her some cute meet or cutesy meet or whatever she wanted. But why? Why did I care? Why did I want to impress her?

My dad wagged his finger at me. "She has roots here. She has a connection."

"Why do you know more about her than I do?"

The lobby doors opened, and a family wandered inside, their cheeks flushed from whatever adventure they'd returned from.

I glanced at my dad. "One step at a time. The first thing we need to do is to get this guy to leave Maya alone."

"And if he doesn't?"

I clenched my jaw and shook my head, knowing if the message wasn't received the first time, it most certainly would be the second.

The elevator dinged, but after sitting here for hours, I almost didn't believe my eyes.

I straightened in the chair and pointed toward the lobby. "That's him."

Rob wore a black jacket, jeans, and a ball cap. He didn't look scrawny, but he didn't look overly fit, either.

"What a jerk," I muttered, but my dad caught it.

"Okay, Cash. Don't do anything stupid. I'll come up behind you, but you've got to deal with this gentleman properly. Just get a sense of his intentions."

"He's no gentleman. You should see the texts he sends her." I left some money on the table for our drinks and stood.

My dad gave a quick nod, and he followed behind me.

"Rob," I called only about ten feet away.

He stopped and turned slowly. His gaze hardened as I approached. He glanced at my dad before returning his eyes to me.

"May I help you?" he asked with a smirk.

"Just wondering why you're here in Buttercup Lake."

"Am I not welcome?" His eyes cooled, and his phony smile widened, and I wanted to deck the guy.

"Depends on what your intentions are."

Unbeknownst to Rob, my dad was filming us. I figured we couldn't trust the guy, and I didn't need anything to be taken out of context.

"Intentions?" He grinned. "My only intentions are to enjoy the incredible weather, the beautiful lakes and rivers, and speak with my fiancée."

"She's not your fiancée."

He folded his arms and raised a brow. "But she is."

"You dumped her at her wedding, and now you're attempting to steal something that she worked to build."

"The courthouse marriage wasn't a wedding. I knew she wanted a big wedding, so I didn't show at city hall because I knew what she truly wanted."

"Yeah? How saintly. Women love to be stood up when they're about to say *I do*."

This guy was a prick and had an excuse for everything.

"I know her better than anyone. I understand what she wants in life."

His words stung. I didn't like the idea that he knew anything about Maya.

"And what is that?" I cocked my head, knowing he just wanted to torment Maya more.

"I had planned to give her the wedding of her dreams."

"Was that before or after you threatened to take everything from her?"

"Who are you?" Rob asked. He squinted his eyes. "Her bodyguard?"

My dad stepped forward, sensing the unease building. Rob still didn't notice how my dad had his phone positioned to film.

"Maya has made things clear to you through her lawyers. It's best if you leave it between them and quit harassing her."

He chuckled. "I can't possibly be harassing her since I'm engaged to her."

"You *were* engaged. You are no longer a couple. That ended when you stood her up and attempted to hijack her company. If you insist on staying in Buttercup Lake, please do not attempt to contact her. She's been through enough. Leave her alone."

"Or what?"

I smiled at Rob and gave him a hard stare. "Or nothing. The lawyers will deal with everything. And if needed, the police."

"That's what I thought. All show and no go." He shook his head and started toward the lobby doors.

"Where do you think you're going?" I asked. "It's almost eleven o'clock."

He spun around and pointed his finger at me like a trigger and winked. "Wherever I want, but don't worry. I'm not headed to see the whore."

Fury bolted through me. My dad grabbed my wrist, yanking me to my senses.

That was what this guy did. He knew the power of his words.

"Have a nice night, Rob," I muttered between gritted teeth.

My dad turned the phone off.

"It's not worth it, Cash," my dad said in a gruff voice. "But we need to get you back to the house. Maya will start to wonder. And I don't trust this guy any farther than I can throw him."

I nodded, knowing I needed to get to her before he did. "Well, let's head out. I'll drop you off at the house and get back to Maya."

My dad shook his head, and relief spread through me. "Just get to Maya's, and Mom will come to get me."

"You're feeling that uneasy too?"

"Absolutely."

My chest tightened as we made our way outside. I scanned the parking lot and didn't see any sign of Rob.

We climbed into the Jeep, and I quickly pulled out of the parking lot. Instead of heading to the house directly, I took a lot of county roads in case Rob was smart enough to try to follow us. My hunch said he wasn't, but I didn't want to take any chances.

No one pulled out after us, and I didn't see any headlights behind us.

When I pulled into the drive, my heart hammered. There was a car in the driveway.

"Shit. He got here."

My dad put his hand on my arm. "No, it's okay. That's Millie Bailey's car."

"How in the world do you know these things?"

Feeling my heart slow, I climbed out of the car as my dad followed behind me.

I tapped on the door a few times and entered the code.

"Success," I whispered to my dad. "It's just me, Maya."

Millie appeared down the hall. "There you are. Maya was worried about you."

She spotted my dad. "Nice to see you, Harold."

"You too, Millie."

They traded a knowing glance, which made it difficult to ignore.

"Millie, I hate to ask, but would you mind dropping me off at my house on the way home?" My dad's brows rose.

"Perfect idea," Millie said, looking over at me. "Cash, there's some tiramisu for you."

"No, there's not. I ate it," Maya's voice rang down the hall.

I chuckled as my dad leaned over. "Sounds like your mother."

Maya appeared from the kitchen without her scooter and smiled when she saw my dad. But I noticed she was doing a great job of ignoring me. She hobbled down the hall with her walking boot.

"I'm Maya," she said, reaching her hand out to my dad.

"Harold's the name. I'm Cash's dad." He shook her hand and took a step back, smiling.

"You have an incredible son." But her words were sharp.

My dad grinned. "We're pretty proud of him. We've been extremely blessed with all three sons and our daughter.

I've heard wonderful things about you."

Maya looked over at me, and I shrugged, trying not to smile. I could see she was really pissed.

She brought her attention back to my dad and looked as lovely as ever. "Hopefully, some of them are true."

"They're all true," Millie explained, "because I'm the one who told Harold and Nancy all about you."

Maya's brows scooped into an arch. "Nancy?"

"That's my mom," I explained.

"Anyway, off we go. It's already going to be crazy dodging the wildlife on the way home," Millie muttered. "Don't forget to finish the book for Thursday's book club."

"Yes, Grandma. It was lovely meeting you, Harold," Maya called after my dad as they went through the front door.

The moment it clicked shut and I locked the door, Maya's expression turned.

"You lied to me." Her face hardened. "And you didn't answer my texts."

Chapter Twenty-One

Maya

"For your information, an eighty-year-old great-grandma and a woman with a broken foot were about to head out the door in the dead of night to try to find you. Why? You may ask. Because you didn't answer my texts." My hands flew to my hips. "Do you know how worried I've been about you?"

Cash's eyes softened, and I could tell he was trying to hide a smile, which only infuriated me more.

"I don't like being lied to," I added, surprised at all the feelings boiling over.

He was only supposed to be a summer distraction.

"I didn't lie. Exactly."

My scowl deepened. "Really? What would you call it?"

"Leaving out some pertinent information."

251

"You went to find Rob, didn't you? That's why you left me here alone, because you knew where he was and that I'd be safe." I eyed him, unable to push down the feelings bubbling through me. I hadn't had someone in my life who cared enough to do something like this. But he should have told me.

Cash bit his bottom lip and took a deep breath.

I stared at him. "Well?"

"I didn't want to concern you."

"Concern me?" I gritted my teeth and hobbled over to my glass of lemonade. "One minute, we're making out, and the next, you get a call and fly out of here like Batman."

"Batman?" He frowned. "I thought I was more like Thor or—"

I stomped my good foot. "It's not funny, Cash. You could have gotten hurt."

"Unlikely." Cash's confidence poured off him, and I'd be lying if I didn't confess to finding it extremely attractive.

Seeing the certainty swirl in his gaze made all sorts of questions flutter to the surface. I wanted to be so angry with him for omitting facts, but the way he looked at me made me question whether it even mattered.

"How about this?" he asked, taking a step toward me.

"You call me Thor instead of Batman, and I promise I'll never omit anything to you ever again."

"I'm not sure I care to agree to that." I stared at Chewie and snuggled up to my chipmunk.

Cash's finger slid under my chin and gently lifted my face. When our eyes connected, a spark of something I could no longer deny lit through me. Maybe I didn't want him to be a distraction.

"Would you mind if we picked up where we left off?" Cash's voice deepened to a growl. "Hmm?"

I glanced at Chewie and chuckled. "Do you have a blanket to throw over her or anything?"

He smiled as his gaze stayed on mine, and he shook his head.

But I couldn't shake the thought of where Cash went tonight. He was gone for a long time. I knew him enough to know he wouldn't do anything foolish. He had his dad with him. But why did he have his dad with him?

I drew a breath and took a step back. Disappointment dashed across Cash's face.

"Before I get caught up in my emotions . . ."

Cash smirked and raised a brow.

"Would you mind telling me what happened tonight?"

"Well—"

"And I mean from the moment you got the message on your phone."

Cash leaned against the kitchen cabinet and rested an elbow against the counter. He looked irresistible with his dark hair and muscular build. Part of me wanted to imagine him putting Rob in his place, but the saner part of me knew better.

"I got a text from Nate that Rob was seen checking into Buttercup Lodge."

Just the thought annoyed me beyond no end. This was my special place, even if it was only for a couple of months.

"I figured I'd have the best chance of running into him on his first day here," he continued. "I called my dad and explained the situation, and we basically sat in the lounge until I spotted him. He was in his room a lot longer than I expected."

"Then why couldn't you answer a text?"

"I'm very acquainted with Murphy's Law. I knew the second I looked down at my phone, he'd wander through and out the lobby, and I'd miss him."

I nodded.

"Finally, he wandered off the elevator, and I caught up to him with my dad."

"Why'd you want your dad with you?"

His gaze hardened, and I blurted out what my grandma had told me. "My grandma said your dad was in the special forces. Did you need some extra muscle?"

Cash's lip curled up slightly at the revelation. "Yes, but that wasn't why I called him. Although, he would be the one I'd want by my side if shit hit the fan."

"Well, did it hit the fan?" My pulse quickened.

"No. My dad was there recording the interaction on his phone because I don't trust the weasel, but I just asked why he was here and got no clear response other than he wants to reconcile."

"Pfft." I shook my head. "Disgusting."

Cash nodded. "And I wanted to put him on notice that we knew he was here, that there are enough people who will be watching. I have no idea what he plans or planned to do. But I'll just be glad we're headed out camping soon."

"So, you didn't punch him?"

Cash chuckled. "I wanted to a couple of times, but I refrained."

I stepped toward Cash with my boot thudding with me and rested my hands on his chest. I let out a deep sigh, realizing how protected I felt for the first time in my life.

Cash smiled at me and gently kissed me. His lips were soft, but the need was running hard between us.

It was almost impossible to stand as he kissed me. I sank into him as he let out a sexy growl.

We hugged and kissed and ripped clothes off my body and his as we made our way up the stairs.

Cash scanned my nearly naked body before taking a step forward, our eyes locked on one another's. He slowly brushed his jaw along my collarbone, sending a wave of shivers through me. This was the most vulnerable I'd ever felt, but I also felt needed, wanted, and more powerful than ever before.

My pulse ran wild, and my head was dizzy with lust.

"I need you, Cash," I whispered, standing bare.

His mouth slowly opened as he peppered kisses along my bare skin, creating a frenzy of need. When my hand slid along his hard stomach, he caught my wrists in his hand, and I'd never felt so small.

"I need to taste you, Maya." He moved his fingers along my thighs and underneath the cotton of my underwear, moving into my slit as his mouth came closer to mine.

"Bed," he whispered between kisses.

I could only utter a simple yes as he picked me up and carried me over. He stretched my hands over my head as his gaze canvassed my body.

"You're the most beautiful woman, Maya. I can't wait

to be inside you."

Hearing those words made me squirm under his presence, writhing my hips to seduce him.

Cash smiled but didn't take his gaze away from mine.

Instead, he slowly moved our hands down my belly. I felt so vulnerable, but it was like I was in a spectacular trance of pleasure.

Cash leaned over me, propping himself up with one arm as his lips followed our hands over the plumpness of my thighs to the V-shape of my underwear. He pressed his mouth over the fabric, and his warm breath sent a wave of electricity through me as I let out a little moan, wanting him to do so much more.

I had no idea I could be so turned on when nothing had even really happened yet.

Just kissing.

Touching.

Cash cupped his hands over mine, twisting our fingers together as he worked my underwear to the side and guided my hands to the warmth and wetness.

His eyes connected with mine, and I saw the intense hunger behind his gaze.

He pressed softly over my hands, rubbing and creating a rhythm that made me crazy with need.

"Please stop," I said softly. "I need you inside me."

Cash stood before caging me in. "I need to be in you, baby."

He kissed me a few times, only creating a deeper frenzy inside as he caged me underneath him.

His eyes stayed on mine as my heart beat wildly in my chest. My breathing turned ragged with every passing second as I took in his spectacular chest, hard abdomen, and strong forearms that were now flexing as he pulled my underwear off.

Cash's fingers feathered inside me as he moved his body on top of mine, quickly replacing his fingers with his hardness.

"Oh, my . . ." I said softly, my back arching in bliss. He filled every part of me as he hissed in a sharp breath and moved in and out.

"You're so tight," he whispered, bringing his mouth to my ear as his fingers continued to work between my legs.

His very words threatened to send me over the edge as I wrapped my legs around his waist and we found our secret rhythm.

Cash trailed his mouth to my chest, where he teased each nipple as my hips ground into him in a fiery need.

"Please," I moaned.

He took me into his arms and brought his mouth back to mine as he pushed into me, and my entire world exploded in a pleasure I never knew possible. Every thrust created a ferocious need as my body tingled with pleasure.

The buildup was far more intense than I even knew possible. Cash's breathing turned harsh as my body clenched around him. He pushed his fingers through my hair as my hips curled into him and his hardness pulsed into me.

It was like our bodies were frozen in time as pleasure rippled through us together.

"Cash," I breathed, feeling my heart still racing.

His green eyes stayed on mine as he rolled next to me, breathing heavily and dopey with sex. I ran my fingers across a long scar scraped over his abdomen.

It snapped me out of my intoxication.

"What's this from?" I asked, not realizing the words had fallen from my lips.

Cash shook his head, but he pulled me in closer before his mouth found mine and he distracted me once more.

Chapter Twenty-Two

Cash

"Nothing about meeting Maya has been typical," I explained to my younger brother over the speakerphone. "She came into my life as a guest at one of my properties, and now I can't stop thinking about her."

"So, you're finally admitting you've got a thing for Chipmunk Lady."

"I don't think she'd be thrilled if you called her that. Her name is Maya."

"Sorry. It's a bad habit. That's what Mom calls her." Hunter laughed and let out a sigh. "Well, I'll try to be on my best behavior when I get up there."

"I'd appreciate it." I glanced at my trailer, which had been freshly washed. I'd hauled it out of my garage and spent all morning scrubbing it down. It was only two years old, but I wanted it to look nice.

"Alright. Well, text me anything you want me to bring, and I'll see you tomorrow."

Which only left me tonight to get everything just right. Maya was a romantic at heart. I could see that in her. Everything she did was with intention, and even her vision of the first encounter with a partner had an adorable name.

And tonight, I was going to make that happen. Even if we can't redo how we met, maybe tonight will change her mind about my being merely a distraction. If she wanted a darling meet, she would get one.

It also helped that I'd heard that Rob checked out of the lodge and there hadn't been any other sightings of him around the lake. He'd also resumed speaking with his attorneys because Maya had mentioned that some negotiations had started.

I didn't like that she had to waste any of her money negotiating with him, but her legal team knew best.

As I opened the door to the trailer, Chewie spun in circles, and I picked her up.

"Remember, where we are going, you could be somebody's dinner. A fox would think it hit the jackpot, and a wolf would love you as an appetizer, so you'd better listen to me. Understand?"

Chewie's eyes widened as if she heard every single

word I said.

Poor thing. I'd never think about taking a dog the size of a dessert plate out camping with me, but I didn't really have a choice. My parents were out of town and weren't coming back until after we'd be at the campsite. I didn't trust leaving Chewie with just anyone, so she was stuck with me and the great outdoors.

I closed the door behind me and put her on the floor. The trailer still smelled like new. It had pop-out sides, a gourmet kitchen, a dining room, and a cozy family room. It was a decent-sized place and thankfully had two sleeping areas. Of course, I'd be giving my brother and his girlfriend the smaller one that converted because that's what younger brothers were for, to irritate. Plus, Maya still had the boot. She needed space.

I opened the kitchen drawers to make sure all the silverware and utensils were still inside and wandered to the big bedroom to put fresh sheets on the bed.

As I shook out the flat sheet, Chewie tried to wrestle with the flannel, and the next thing I knew, she flew through the air toward a window I'd opened earlier.

I dove toward her and managed to clutch her little body in my palm before she went diving through the window and crashed outside. I spun her around with her little tongue hanging out, completely oblivious to the fact that her life had almost ended.

"This is going to be an interesting weekend," I muttered to myself.

I set Chewie in the hall and closed the door while I changed the sheets, closed the window, and made my way into the rest of the trailer. I'd finish in the morning.

As of now, I needed to head out to the lake to make sure everything had been prepared just right. Grace was going to drop off her sister for me where I'd planned our little get-together.

I set Chewie with her pink blanket on the passenger seat of the Jeep and took off.

I wanted this to be special, to be a happy surprise.

Maya had been through so much the last couple of months that the least I could do was brighten her day and give her the meet sweet she wanted.

Maya knew I was going to be at my place getting the trailer ready, and she had spent most of the afternoon with her sister at the antique store. So hopefully, the picnic at the lake would be a surprise. I reserved an area that was away from the sand so she and her boot wouldn't get stuck. I'd tried to think of everything.

But I needed to tell her how I felt.

I needed to open myself up.

Let her see my wounds.

Understand my intentions.

Show her I wasn't just a distraction.

Just the thought of tonight made my pulse soar. It could go so many different ways. She could love it, or I could scare her away.

Sleeping with Maya had only made it clearer for me. Maya's energy and spirit blew me away, but her body fit perfectly with mine.

The way she shyly came up to me in the morning like she wasn't sure we should have done what we did . . . the thought made me hard just thinking about her.

When she'd let herself be vulnerable, it was a truly beautiful thing.

And I had to tell her that.

She needed to hear from me that the last few weeks have been incredible, and maybe today, we could move forward as something other than me being a distraction.

And that was what the meet sweet was all about. Our first romantic encounter with the possibility for a future.

I rolled into the parking lot at the lake and found a spot to park. I jumped out of my Jeep and reached for a bracelet I'd found in one of the stores locally to give her. I scooped Chewie into my other hand.

When I'd made my way to the covered picnic area, I saw Grace and Maya pull into the parking lot. I scanned the table that the florist had sprinkled rose petals all over, along with a trail leading from the path to the picnic table. White LED lights hung from the ceiling, which would be perfect if we lasted until evening. Hopefully, if all she wanted in life was a distraction, I wouldn't just send her straight to the airport.

I looped Chewie's leash to the picnic bench, and she curled up on her pink blanket I'd grabbed from the Jeep.

Dinner was set to be delivered in about thirty minutes from the lodge with her favorite fried cheese curds with aioli.

I glanced toward Grace's car to see Maya walking over alone, putting her hand up to her eyes to shield the glare of the sun. She waved when she spotted me.

Everything I wanted to say disappeared from my mind when I saw her. I couldn't speak.

She was gorgeous, but she wasn't mine.

Would I scare her away with this?

I looked around and suddenly wished I'd waited until after the camping trip. Was I pushing it too far, too fast?

Maya got closer, and her walk slowed as she took in everything surrounding her. She stopped and stared at the red and pink rose petals at her feet before she slowly brought her gaze to mine.

"What?" She stopped herself. "What is going on?"

I swallowed my worry and knew I had to tell her how I felt. She needed to know. Or maybe I just needed to know how she felt.

Maya slowly stepped onto the concrete and made her way over, smiling.

"I'm worried. I'm so used to seeing your smile," she said softly. "And it has completely disappeared, only to be replaced by beautiful flowers."

I held out my arms and chuckled as she made her way toward me. She came in for a hug, pressing her head against my chest.

"So, what have you been up to?"

I smiled wider and held her close.

"Is this to celebrate that Mr. Wicked Witch of North Carolina has gone back home?" she asked, taking a step back.

"Something like that."

She stood taking everything in when her attention went to the lake. "Remember our day in the water?"

I chuckled. "I think about it every single day."

Maya rolled her eyes. "Such a guy thing to say."

"Well, having your legs wrapped around my

waist . . ." I shook my head. "Nothing like it."

"Whatever you've got going on here is quite lovely. Beautiful."

"It's all for you."

"I don't know what I did to deserve this, but thank you."

"There is so much I want to tell you." I glanced toward the water and raked my fingers through my hair before turning my eyes back to her. "I've been doing a lot of thinking, and since we slept together, I knew I had to tell you something."

Her expression dropped, and worry filled her gaze. "Should I sit down for this?"

We both took a seat, and I could see the worry etching her expression. "It's . . . listen, meeting you three weeks ago has changed my life in a lot of unexpected ways."

Maya nodded. "I can only imagine. You've got a high-maintenance guest with a crazy ex. I can't walk in a straight line without tripping over my own feet, which, might I add, is a new thing. And then I beg you to keep me distracted from the real issues going on in my life. You're definitely not getting paid enough."

I smiled, laughing. "That's not exactly how I see it."

She chuckled. "That's good, I suppose."

"What I see is a woman who has somehow managed to crack my stone exterior. You've been crumbling away the walls I built since everything happened. I haven't smiled this much or felt this good in years."

Maya looked nervous, but I kept going.

"I know I promised to be your distraction." I drew a breath and didn't let it out. "But I want to start over with you."

Her brows furrowed as she shook her head. "I don't understand."

"I remember when you talked about all the romance books you read and romcoms you've watched and how there's always this special moment between the love interests when they first meet. We never had that."

She cocked her head slightly.

"I want to be the one who shows you some sweet meet," I explained.

Maya's eyes widened, and the loudest snort startled Chewie right off her blanket.

"Sweet meat? What the heck are you talking about?" Maya grinned and shook her head.

"You know, the sweet meet from your romance books?" I tried again. "I can do that for you. That's what this is. I want this to be what you remember for how we met. I don't just want to be a distraction for your vacation. I want to see if there's something between us."

A few seconds of silence sat between us.

"So, let me have this moment with you. Let me give you the sweet meet you've always wanted," I tried again, wondering why this wasn't going as planned.

A funny look flashed across Maya's features before she finally said something. "That has to be the sweetest thing anyone has ever said to me."

"It was your idea," I explained.

A cocky smile grew on Maya's beautiful mouth. "I never asked for your sweet meat, Cash. I said a meet-cute. Not your sweet meat."

Realizing what I'd just said to her over and over again, I groaned as she tried to stifle her laughter until she just couldn't.

I smacked the picnic table and shook my head. "Dang it. I knew I should have looked it up. The meet-cute. I wanted to give you the meet-cute to remember me by."

Maya couldn't stop laughing even though she kept trying to regain composure, wiping tears from her face in between.

She stood and hobbled to the other side of the picnic table and sat on my lap, looping her arms over my neck.

"Cash, you are just full of surprises." She smiled,

making me feel like the luckiest man in the world. "The good kind of surprises."

Chapter Twenty-Three

Maya

Waking up in Cash's arms this morning was a dream. He nuzzled his whiskers along my cheek, and I chuckled before he hopped up from the bed.

"Time to shave," he said. "I'm hopping in the shower. My brother will be at my house in an hour or so."

For some reason, the idea of spending a camping trip with Cash's brother freaked me out a bit. I had no idea what he was like or what he would think of Cash and me.

I sat up and pulled the sheet up to my chin. "I hope your brother likes me."

Cash turned around and smiled. "He will love you."

When Cash turned on the shower and stepped inside, I groaned and fell back against the soft pillows.

I knew that I liked Cash. There was no doubt about that. He was all I could think about in between getting obnoxious emails from my legal team. But the idea of this turning into something more than casual panicked me.

I should know better than to get involved with someone so quickly after the horrible relationship I just got out of. Yet, there was something happening between Cash and me that I couldn't even understand. I craved him. I daydreamed about my future with him in it.

Shoving down the sheets with my big boot, I flopped out of bed and got brave. Holding my head up high, I marched right into the bathroom, seeing Cash's beautiful and very naked body as beads of water rolled down his skin with his eyes closed.

I turned right around and hopped in the other shower down the hall after unfastening myself from my boot. I'd never want to leave the shower if we started up again.

As I rinsed the last of the soap off, I heard Cash whistling downstairs, and for some reason, it made my entire day. It sounded like such a happy whistle coming from a happy guy.

I dried off, wrapped the towel around me, and picked up my boot as I wandered down the hall back to the bedroom, where I slipped on a pair of jeans and a red flannel over a white camisole. I glanced at my bag, where I'd packed jeans, shorts, multiple sweatshirts, and tees. Wisconsin weather changed every hour this time of year, and I didn't want to be caught freezing to death.

After struggling with the Velcro and straps on my boot, I made my way downstairs, where I spotted Cash holding two giant coffee mugs. He handed me one and kissed the tip of my nose.

"You look gorgeous," he said, taking a sip while looking over the top of the mug.

A smile tugged at my lips. "Yeah. You're not looking so bad yourself."

And that was an understatement. The man had a knack for looking like he had stepped out of an outdoor catalog. All he was missing was an axe propped on his shoulder. He had the smoldering smile down.

"Hunter texted that they're only thirty minutes away."

"Eek."

He laughed. "What was that?"

"Sorry. I'm kind of freaking out a lot."

Cash swept his fingers along my cheek and smiled. "Don't be."

I blew out a gust of air and grinned. "Fine. I'll pretend like I'm not freaking out a little."

"Why would you? You're smart, funny, amazing, and completely out of my league."

I chuckled, putting my coffee on the counter. "Yeah, right. You have like the perfect family. You're out of *my* league."

I reached into a bag of almonds, and Chewie came running.

Cash scowled. "What's that about?"

"It's the only way Chewie comes for me."

He shook his head. "Anyway, I'm not dating your parents. I'm dating you, and you are most definitely out of my league."

I shrugged.

"You are so wrong it hurts my heart." He set his mug down and pulled me into him. "Give yourself some credit."

I looked into his gaze and believed the words.

Cash smiled and let out a deep breath. "Which leads me to my next request."

"Uh-oh. Shoot." I grimaced, chuckling.

"My parents invited us over for dinner next Wednesday."

I froze. Things were suddenly moving fast. A camping trip with his brother and then meeting the parents.

Granted, I already met Harold briefly, but having dinner with them and trying to impress them about sent me over the edge.

That was the only plus side of dating Rob. I never had to meet his parents.

On the flip side, maybe that should have been a red flag.

I looked into Cash's eyes and saw so much hope building behind his gaze that there was no way I'd say no.

"Sounds awesome."

His right brow arched as he shook his head. "You are a terrible liar."

I giggled, letting out a deep breath. "With you by my side, I'm sure it will be totally fine."

"That's the spirit." He snapped his fingers at Chewie, who hopped off the couch and circled her way to the kitchen. "I'll get your bags in the Jeep and drive us over to the house."

"Sounds good."

He started toward the stairs and turned around. "Don't be nervous. I'm the one who should be scared of you meeting my brother. He's a mess. Basically, he drinks for a living."

I chuckled, knowing Cash mentioned his brother owned a bar in Madison.

Chewie yapped, found her leash in the basket by the door, and dragged it over.

"Good girl, Chewie. How in the world did Cash teach you that?"

She sat down with her little pink tongue dipping out of her mouth as Cash carried my bag down the stairs.

"She's a genius. That's how."

I chuckled, bending over to fasten Chewie's leash.

"Your daddy loves you," I whispered, but she looked like she didn't need to be told.

"I have to tell you, I feel a lot better leaving for our camping trip, not thinking that Rob is traipsing around Buttercup Lake."

Cash nodded, holding the door open as Chewie and I walked under his arm. "Agreed. Has everything continued to move forward?"

I nodded even though my chest tightened. "I'm at the point where I just want my people to throw money at him to make him go away, but they feel strongly that he isn't owed very much. I would rather just buy him out and go on my merry way."

Cash nodded, sliding the bag into the backseat as I hoisted myself into the front seat.

"Not to mention, you'll probably pay more in legal fees than if you'd just written the check."

"So true." I glanced at Cash as he slid into the driver's seat. "I have a confession. I probably shouldn't even say it aloud."

"What's that? You want to ravage me all weekend instead of meeting my brother for a camping trip? Me too."

I chuckled. "No, but that does sound more fun."

"What's your confession?"

"I'm falling out of love with my profession."

Cash turned on the Jeep and backed out of the drive before saying anything.

"Do you think it's because of the headache your ex has caused?"

I shrugged. "I don't know. I'd always liked the idea of helping people."

Cash nodded.

"And coming up with the idea about online therapy was a bonus. The industry has exploded, and I'm always getting offers for my company."

"Well, you've always impressed me, but wow. That's incredible."

"I always thought no way would I sell. I want to build the company and watch it grow."

Cash nodded. "And now?"

I shook my head. "Selling is kind of appealing."

"Don't let Rob steal the joy that your company has always given you."

I smiled at Cash and nodded. "You're right. I know.

I'd give it time before I did anything crazy."

"You should be so proud of what you've accomplished, and you're not even forty."

I rubbed Chewie and let out a wistful sigh. "You too."

"Except that I'm forty."

I snorted. "That's right. You're about to sign up for AARP."

"Hey, now," he teased. "Just a few more years, and I'll get to tease you too. Better watch out."

Complete happiness drifted through me as we drove to Cash's house.

"I'm excited to go glamping," I told him as we pulled into his drive.

"Is that what it's called?"

I stared at the mammoth trailer in front of us and chuckled. "Definitely glamping."

"Wait until you see the granite countertops."

"You're kidding."

He smiled and shook his head as he pulled in front of his garage.

As we climbed out of the Jeep, Cash grabbed my bag, and a car turned into his drive.

"Hunter's here."

Nerves shot through me as I watched the car slow

down, and two figures sat in the front seat.

"I can't remember who he said he was bringing, but he said they weren't serious."

"Good to know."

The car slowed, and Hunter climbed out, waving at his brother as he wandered to the other side to let his guest out of the car.

Her dark hair reached below her waist, and she was dressed in a tight beige turtleneck dress that somehow left little to the imagination. A gold belt cinched her tiny waist, and once she stood up, she was at least six inches taller than me, which wasn't hard to do. Her scarlet lipstick pursed into a smile, but the oversized black sunglasses made it impossible to see her eyes.

But I didn't need to see them to know she was drooling over Cash.

"This is Brielle, a friend of mine." Hunter smiled at us. "You must be Maya."

I nodded, suddenly feeling very underdressed in my flannel for the camping trip.

Hunter closed the car door, and Brielle pursed her lips into a scowl. "Nice to meet you."

Didn't seem like it.

"Nice to meet you too," I told her as Cash reached out

his hand to hers.

"Any friend of my brother's is a friend of mine." He gave a quick nod, but she didn't release his hand for a second, which made Cash glance awkwardly at me.

I shrugged, and she finally let go.

"How long have you been seeing each other?" I asked.

"We've known each other for years," she drawled. "But I knew better than to date him, sweetie. He's not the marrying type."

"Oh." I glanced at Cash, who looked as baffled as I felt.

Hunter went to the trunk of his car and pulled out two big bags. "Should I put them in the Winnebago?"

Cash nodded. "Go ahead. It's unlocked."

Brielle didn't try to help as Hunter walked by with their luggage, and Cash followed him inside with my bag.

Awkward.

I glanced at Brielle, who was sneering at Chewie. "What is that thing?"

"She's a teacup Pom. Her name is Chewie," I answered proudly.

Brielle's brow arched, escaping her sunglasses. "Whatever."

I smiled. "So, what do you do for a living?"

She laughed, which made me glance at the Winnebago, wishing they'd come out quickly. I didn't know it was that funny of a question.

"I married well and divorced even better."

"Ah, gotcha." I smoothed my palms over my flannel, confused about why Hunter wanted to spend time with this woman.

Although, I didn't know Hunter, so . . .

When the door opened, Cash dashed down the two small steps and walked over to me and wrapped his arms over my shoulder, kissing me just behind my ear.

I caught a withering look from Brielle, and that was with her shades on.

I hid a smile and turned to face Cash, grateful that he was so attentive in front of the ice queen.

"I'll go grab my bag, load up the freezer, and we're off." Cash smiled. "Just don't let me forget to unplug it before we take off."

"No promises."

Cash and Hunter took off toward the house, and Brielle watched me. "You guys are sweet together."

I wasn't sure if that was a compliment coming from her, so I just nodded. "Thanks."

"It must be nice living somewhere so . . ."

My brow arched. "I don't live here. I live in North Carolina. I'm only summering out here."

Brielle slid her sunglasses off. "Oh?"

I nodded. "I own a business, but I can work remotely."

"I never would have guessed."

I laughed. "Really. Was it the flannel? The boot? Or the dog?"

She narrowed her eyes and didn't answer as she sucked the tip of her sunglasses.

I'd never been happier to see Cash and Hunter emerge with a cooler full of food and a laundry basket filled with snacks.

"First stop needs to be Starbucks," Brielle announced, chuckling.

Hunter and Cash traded a look while I tried to keep in my laugh.

"There's no Starbucks around here. But we have a great coffee house we can stop at before we leave."

She shuddered.

"It's way better than Starbucks or Dunkin', in my opinion," I offered.

"It will have to do." She sighed as if the world had

just dumped all of its painful woes on her.

Cash grimaced as he unplugged the extension cord from the trailer. "Fridge is nice and cold. Hunter can put everything into the fridge, and I'll get us hitched up."

Brielle turned around and sat back in the car they'd arrived in.

I picked up Chewie and followed Cash to his pickup and climbed in.

Cash smiled at me and turned on the truck. "Had enough of Bougee Brielle?"

"It's going to be a hoot this weekend. That's for sure."

Chapter Twenty-Four

Cash

We pulled up to the campsite, and I backed into the slot as Hunter waited in his car with Brielle.

"Do you think she liked the latte she got back at Buttercup Java?" Maya asked.

I shook my head, checking the backup camera and sticking my head out the window to get it right the first time. "I would be stunned if she did."

Once I put the trailer on the pad and turned off the truck, I looked over at her and smiled. "It just reminds me of how lucky I am that we met."

Maya smiled, watching Hunter park his car on the patch of gravel in front of our campsite.

"Here's to an exciting camping trip," she quipped.

"Hopefully, not too exciting." I reached over and squeezed her hand. "We'll try to sneak away as much as possible."

She chuckled. "Promise? I just may hold you to it."

I leaned over and kissed her, instantly feeling the pull to keep her in my arms.

But my brother did a double honk of his horn, and Maya pulled away.

Just then, a fox pranced between my truck and my brother's car.

"Wait," Maya said softly, craning her neck. "Is that Brielle screaming?"

We both looked over to see Brielle's hands up to her mouth as Hunter tried to calm her down.

"Is it too late to get back home?" Maya teased.

"She's not really afraid of a fox, is she?" I glanced at Chewie. "If anyone should be afraid of a fox, it should be that thing."

Maya chuckled and nuzzled Chewie from her sleep. "I'll be holding onto you tightly."

Hunter's car door opened, and then Brielle's. I glanced at Maya and couldn't believe her beauty. It was effortless. Watching Brielle struggle in her heeled boots, I kept in my chuckle as Maya, her boot, and Chewie slid to the ground.

Brielle hightailed it to the trailer with Hunter right

behind her.

"I'll unlock it," I promised, making my way to the door. "I'd planned on unhitching everything, but hey. What do I know?"

Brielle reached over and rested her hand on my shoulder while my brother came over. "Thanks, Cash. I love that name."

Hunter shook his head. "No, you love the meaning."

She laughed. "That too."

I backed away from her grasp as the door opened, and I turned my attention to unhitching the trailer. This was going to be a long couple of days, but I couldn't for the life of me figure out why Hunter brought Brielle...

Unless it was to chase away an lingering doubts about Maya, which I didn't have.

Maya and Chewie appeared to my right. "Anything I can help with?"

I shook my head and smiled at the woman who was stealing my heart one snort at a time. "I'm just going to pull forward a bit, hook up the electricity and hoses, and we should be set."

Maya stood there watching me.

"You don't want to go in there alone?"

She shook her head. "No. Not really."

I laughed and nodded. "I don't blame you."

Voices from inside the Winnebago heightened to a level that didn't sound good. Maya's brows furrowed as she craned her neck to see through the open door. "Ooh. She sounds pissed."

I snickered. "Maybe she's not happy that I don't have an espresso machine."

"I'm going to be brave." She turned around and started toward the door. "Oh, who am I kidding? I'm just nosy."

I laughed, watching Maya gimp into the trailer with her boot. Even with only one good foot, she was more capable in the woods than Brielle.

The whole thing between my brother and Brielle was baffling. He never settled down long enough to go date someone for more than a couple of weeks, and certainly not long enough to bring someone on a trip with his family.

I hopped into the truck and pulled forward before hooking up our lifeline to civilization. By the time I got inside, Maya was preparing a tray of food for everyone, and Brielle was moping on the couch.

"Okay, so I'm just going to push this button, and both sides will slide out, so we have more living space."

Brielle slid her sunglasses off and smiled at me.

"Sounds awesome."

"Yeah. I suppose it is." I glanced at Hunter, who seemed oblivious as I pushed the button.

The trailer expanded as the dining room unfolded, and the living room became nearly the size of an apartment home's space.

"Wow. I'm officially impressed." She clapped her hands and sat back down, but she didn't take her gaze off me.

I glanced over at Maya in the kitchen, who waggled her brows in my direction. She'd obviously noticed the sudden attention I was receiving as well.

Rubbing my hands together, I walked over to Maya, leaned over her shoulder, and whispered, "What are you making?"

She curled her fingers through my hair and happily hummed. "A charcuterie board, or as my grandma calls it, cheese, crackers, and a bit of salami."

I lowered my lips to her ear. "Is the fancy woman still staring at me?"

Maya chuckled and nodded. "Yeah. At times."

Hunter wandered over and stole a piece of cheese off the platter.

"Sorry for interrupting you two lovebirds, but I'm going to take Brielle on a hike. Just wondering if you two would like to join us."

"Does she know you're taking her on a hike?" I asked, surprised.

Maya snorted, and Brielle looked over, throwing Maya daggers.

"No, but I want her to see what the Northwoods have to offer."

"Why's that?"

Hunter shrugged. "I think she just needs to see that there's something beyond the city life."

I moved closer to Hunter as Brielle groaned. "Cell service sucks out here."

"Why do you care if she does?" I whispered to my brother.

"I see potential."

That was enough for me. I didn't agree with it, and I certainly didn't see it, but far be it from me to get in the way of it.

"Maya and I'll catch the next one with you two. We'll just stay back and get everything organized, if that's okay with you, Maya."

"So okay," she spat out as fast as possible.

Hunter smiled and nodded. "Have fun."

"Oh, that reminds me." I wandered to a cabinet and

pulled out a sign. "If you see this hanging on the door, you know, stay busy."

My brother grabbed the sign and started cracking up.

"What? What's it say?" Brielle asked, looking over his shoulder.

She started to read each word very slowly, whispering it to herself.

Maya leaned over and started chuckling. "Seriously? *Don't come a-knockin' if the Winnie is a-boppin.*'"

Brielle looked confused while tears streamed down Maya's face. Hunter smacked my back and shook his head. "I'm so disappointed in your humor."

"Let's go on your first official hike, Brie," Hunter said, scooping her hand in his.

She looked horrified and immediately looked down at her boots with four-inch heels.

My brother glanced at their bedroom where her bag was stored. "You can change if you want."

Brielle nodded. "It'll just be one second."

It looked like Maya secretly couldn't wait to see what Brielle put on this time. She only had to wait a few minutes to find out when Brielle came back out in a pair of black leather leggings, a camo sequin top, and strappy sandals.

"Huh," Maya said, smiling. "Have fun, you two."

Hunter looked down at Brielle's sandals but didn't say anything. Instead, he reached for her hand as she slid her sunglasses on, and they made their way out the door.

"What the hell was that?" Maya chuckled.

"I was going to ask you the same thing."

Maya grinned. "But I think it's safe to say she's got the hots for you."

I laughed and shook my head. "Great. Two women unable to keep their hands off me."

Maya snatched a piece of cheese and rested her chin on my chest as she looked into my eyes. "Speaking of, I'm really sorry that I won't be able to hike more with this thing on."

I bent down and kissed Maya's forehead. "I'd much rather spend my time pigging out on salami and cheese and snuggling on the couch with you any day."

She lit up, and I smiled wider. "Are you positive?"

"Positive."

I opened up a cabinet and pushed a button hidden within.

"Oh, fancy." Maya grinned, watching the flatscreen move into place. "Too bad we don't have cable."

I laughed, squeezing her. "True, but we do have satellite."

Maya's brows shot up. "Are you serious?"

"Deadly."

"You really aren't into roughing it, are you?"

"And then there's this." I pulled down the chaise that now had enough room to expand from the couch since the sides had slid out.

Maya collapsed onto the chaise, and I threw a fleece blanket on her. "This is heaven."

"I'm glad you think so."

She smiled, and her eyes fastened on mine. "Do you think it's okay that Chewie is sleeping on our bed? Will she be mad that she missed out on cheese, movies, and snuggle time?"

"I'd prefer if she did." I laughed, bringing over the food.

I sat down next to Maya, who'd propped her boot in front of her.

"I have to confess something," she began.

"What?" I asked, leaning my head against the couch so I could see her. "You decided you want to sell your company and permanently move into my trailer?"

She giggled, but something shifted in her gaze, which worried me. I tried to push away the feeling as she clasped her hands over mine.

"No, but for the first time since I arrived in Wisconsin, I finally feel like I'm on vacation. Like none of my previous worries can find me here."

I smiled, seeing her gaze fall to my lips.

Electricity zipped through us as her eyes closed, and I leaned in to feel her lips against mine.

Then suddenly, all we could hear was a woman shrieking . . . or a fox. Maybe it was a fox.

Either one.

Maya broke away and glanced out a window. "What the heck?"

"Either a fox is giving birth, or Brielle ran into a wasp nest."

I was only half-kidding as the door flung open with a panting Hunter.

"What's wrong?" Maya asked, springing up from the chaise. "Where's Brielle?"

"She's stuck?" Hunter looked embarrassed.

"Stuck where?" I asked, glancing at Maya. "Will she get hurt by herself?"

"You guys couldn't have gotten more than two hundred feet. What could possibly go wrong?" Maya asked, scratching her head, trying to look out the windows to find Brielle.

"Do you have a First-Aid kit?" Hunter asked.

I nodded and reached into the overhead cabinet and handed it to him. "Do you need help?

Hunter looked at Maya. "Maybe hers."

Maya glanced at me, and I shrugged. "I'll come with you both."

Chapter Twenty-Five

Maya

The gravity of the situation was severe, yet it took everything I had not to burst into a fit of giggles. It didn't help that Cash was down the hill, trying not to howl in laughter. In fact, one of his merriments erupted, and I had to assure Brielle that it was a wolf looking for its mate.

The situation was obvious.

Brielle and Hunter had tried to get down and do the nasty, but in their haste, they didn't see that they were in a thicket of buckthorn.

Her black leggings were down around her ankles. Her sequin camo had been snagged behind her, so two upright and perky breasts stared right at me, and judging at what was front and center, the girl also went commando.

"What do we do?" Hunter asked.

He'd already attempted to grab her from the shrubs,

but Brielle seemed to be in shock and would just shoosh him away.

"You're gonna get scraped up, Hunter." I pointed behind Brielle. "But I think her best shot is if you come from behind her and push her in my direction. I can catch her."

"You're like four feet tall. How can you catch me?" She finally came back to life.

"Trust me. I've been in worse situations."

She frowned, but when she went to move a hand, one of the thorns scratched her wrist.

"I have no choice," she muttered. "I'll depend on a leprechaun if I have to."

"Be nice, would you?" Hunter asked, snapping the shrubs as he weaved in behind her.

"The first thing is to untangle her disco ball from the brush," I told Hunter.

He nodded in agreement as he came from behind and detached the fabric from the thorns.

I moved closer to Brielle and kicked my boot out front. "Who knew this would come in handy?"

Smashing down the bush that wove in between her pants, I freed her leggings and nodded at Hunter.

"On the count of three. One, two, three," I shouted as Hunter shoved his naked guest in my direction.

Her hair got tangled in the buckthorn as she fell forward and collapsed on me, naked body and all.

Hunter quickly worked to untangle her hair as I heard Cash's footsteps coming up the hill.

"Stay there, Cash. We aren't ready yet."

"Okey-dokey," he said, laughter nipping at every word.

Brielle groaned as I tried to push her upright, and Hunter helped to stabilize her.

I quickly scanned her body for any thorns sticking to her skin. "I'm really impressed with how few scratches you managed to get. That's a dangerous shrub to fall into." I took a step back and bit my bottom lip as Hunter checked out her behind.

"Do you need any help getting your pants up or . . ."

"Ope. I see one," Hunter said.

"Okay." I opened the First-Aid kit and handed him some tweezers and alcohol.

He bent over, and out of the corner of my eye, I saw Cash cracking up down the hill, glimpsing his brother bending over to fetch a thorn out of his *guest's* behind.

Brielle grunted.

"Got it." Hunter held it up as Brielle bent over and pulled her pants up in one quick motion.

We started back down the hill where Cash had been waiting.

"I think Brielle is probably thrilled you wanted to show her the Northwoods," Cash said, chuckling as he slapped his brother's back.

Hunter gave him a death stare as we made our way back to the trailer.

"Are you okay?" I asked Brielle.

She frowned and shrugged, but the look in her eyes told another story.

"I'll start the campfire," Cash said, and I nodded.

"Sounds good. Brielle, did you want something to drink?"

"Yes. Lots of it." She walked past me and marched into the trailer.

It would definitely take some time for her ego to heal. Hunter stayed with Cash outside, and I went to the kitchen where I'd left the snack tray.

"Did you want any meat or cheese? We have chips too. Those tend to make me feel better."

Brielle eyed me coolly. "Do you have any white wine?"

I smiled and nodded. "I think we do. I'll check the fridge."

Opening it up, I spotted a bottle on its side and pulled it out. Brielle was suddenly next to me and took the bottle from my hand.

"Where're the glasses?" she mumbled, looking through the kitchen. "I hate camping."

"I think they're here." I opened a cabinet and handed her a glass. "It's not a wine glass, but it should do."

Brielle opened the bottle and poured a gigantic amount of wine into the glass, and I chuckled.

She grabbed a piece of cheese and put her glass in the air. "Cheers."

"Absolutely."

"How long have you been with Hunter's brother?" she asked, warming up slightly.

"Oh. Well, we're not really. I mean . . ." I cleared my throat, unsure why I suddenly couldn't answer. "We just started seeing each other."

Her brows rose. "So, you're not serious yet? Not exclusive?"

I hadn't really thought about it yet. We were just hanging out, taking every day as it came.

"We haven't exactly hammered that out yet since I don't live here."

"In guy code, that means not exclusive." Her eyes lit

up. "Nice."

I cocked my head slightly. "Nice, what?"

She chuckled and drank her wine as if she'd just told herself a great private joke.

Her amusement with the situation left me unsettled. I reached for a chip bag and poured some into a bowl and made some ranch dip to take out to the guys.

"I'll be back. The remote for the tv is on the couch, or you can look through some books I brought."

She rolled her eyes. "I'm not into books."

My jaw dropped open, but I closed it quickly.

With chips and dip in hand, I opened the door to see the campfire burning but no sight of the guys.

I set the bowls down when I heard their voices in the woods behind the trailer. I started toward the noise to let them know about the snack when I heard Hunter.

"I just don't want to see you crushed, Cash. You were absolutely destroyed after Freya. It's only recently that you're even acting somewhat human again."

Cash grunted, but he didn't respond.

"You said she lives in North Carolina and has a thriving business. I want to see you happy, Cash. We all do, but what if it doesn't work? What if you're left even worse than before?"

"You mean when my wife was stolen from me?" Cash sounded angry. "I've been in my own personal hell since she died, Hunter. You don't know what it's like living with the guilt every single day."

"Don't blame yourself." Hunter sighed. "You have to stop doing that."

"Listen, I'm willing to take the chance with Maya. Okay? Let's just leave it at that."

"Mom, Dad, and I were so excited when we heard about Chipmunk Lady, but then it dawned on us."

A couple of twigs snapped.

"What dawned on you?"

"That she'll probably leave, and you'll be as miserable as you were before."

"Maya is the first woman to make me see clearly again. Don't you get it? She makes me happy. I haven't been happy in years, Hunter," Cash snapped. "Years. I'd just wake up, do my work, play with Rusty, and go to bed. And then Rusty died on me. So, life hasn't been spectacular for me. I don't have the luxury of pretending I've never loved before. I don't just schmooze with a bar full of people every night and go home with a different woman each night."

The pain in his voice was like a million stabs to the heart.

"I'm sorry, Cash. I wasn't trying to rev you up."

"You're not revving me up. I'm just trying to tell you that Maya has made me want to live again. She's so full of fire, and she's gorgeous and smart. The thought of waking up without her kills me."

Hunter let out a deep breath. "And that right there is what I'm worried about. When she leaves. Dad and I were there to pick you up when you fell. No one in our family knows except us three. We will always keep our word. We will never tell a soul, not even Mom . . . But I couldn't bear to see you that low again."

My heart stopped. What was he talking about?

"Maybe she won't leave. Maybe I'll go with her."

"Why don't you just keep it casual with her like I do? Wait until you know whether she's planning on sticking around."

Cash laughed wickedly. "Like you and Cruella?"

"You told me it was a distraction," Hunter tried a different approach.

My stomach clenched as the words I threw around so casually came back to haunt me.

"Things are starting to get serious. I want to see where this goes."

Hunter let out a groan. "I have a bad feeling about it.

I'm just worried that losing another woman you fall in love with would kill you. But that's it. I won't say another word about it."

The slurry of emotions sloshed in my belly as the words hung in the air. What if it wasn't just living in North Carolina that doomed us? What if it was the simple fact that I sucked at relationships because I had no good example? I shook the thoughts aside.

One step at a time.

"Thank you."

More twigs snapped, and I dashed back to the campfire just in time. Hunter and Cash stepped into the clearing, and I picked up the bowl of dip.

"I made chips and dip," I offered, avoiding Cash's gaze.

The Winnebago door swung open and crashed into the side to reveal Brielle with the empty wine bottle in her hand.

So much for the rest of us having a sip or two.

"Hunter. I'm done. I can't do the woods any longer. Take me back to the city."

The brothers traded bewildered glances, and she stomped her foot. "I want to go back now."

"We won't get back until dark," Hunter protested.

"Can't we wait until morning?"

She stepped down to the campsite. "Only if I get to sleep with him."

My eyes followed her pointing finger as she wiggled it at Cash.

I scowled and shook my head. "I don't think that would be a good idea."

Cash laughed. "Yeah. I don't think so either."

Brielle nearly tripped into the fire as she attempted to walk over to Cash, who looked like he was side galloping to get away from her. Hunter's brows rose as he chuckled, watching the events unfold around us.

"Come on, Cash. Maya said you weren't serious yet."

My hands went up to my temples and pressed on the building headache. Was this for real? After what I just heard from Cash and Hunter, I hoped he didn't hear that because that wasn't what I meant. I didn't know what I meant other than I didn't intend for drunk Brielle to discuss my relationship status.

"Okay, Brielle. We should probably wrap it up for the night," Hunter said.

She pouted and tossed the empty wine bottle to the ground, but Hunter managed to catch it before it hit the dirt.

Cash wandered over to me and whispered an apology

in my ear.

I looked into his eyes and smiled. "It's been the most entertaining camping trip I've ever been on."

Cash smiled and kissed my cheek.

"Oh, come on." Brielle stomped her foot again. "I want that. Hunter, why aren't you sweet like that?"

Cash's chest rumbled as he kept his laughter in.

"I didn't think you were into that. You always make fun of couples being sweet."

"Funny what the wine brings out in a person," Cash whispered, chuckling.

He hung his arm around my shoulders, and I clasped his hand as we continued watching the show.

"Maybe I was wrong. Maybe I want the happily-ever-after." She turned to Cash, and he hugged me harder. "When you're ready for a little more excitement, give me a call. Come on, Hunter."

Hunter opened his mouth and smacked it back down as she marched into the camper to pack.

"And then there were three?" I said softly, looking into Cash's gaze.

"Three?" Cash's brows rose.

"Chewie."

"Oh, right." He grinned. "I think I'll like it better this

way."

"I didn't exactly say we weren't serious. She caught me off guard, and I told her we hadn't been together all that long and weren't exclusive." I pressed my lips together.

Cash laughed. "We're not exclusive? Is there someone else I should know about?"

I chuckled. "I told you, I got all confused."

"So, you're not seeing anyone on the side?" he teased, shaking his head. "I didn't even pay attention to what she said."

"I'm sure you caught that she wants to be next in line," I joked.

"Well, I did catch that." He brought me in for a hug. "But there is no line."

I rested my head on his chest, feeling the gentle beats of his heart, but all I could think about were his brother's words, and I didn't know what to do.

Because I knew I couldn't promise more than I could give.

Chapter Twenty-Six

Cash

"Don't even think about trying to cram in here," Maya teased, letting the suds rinse down her body.

I laughed and shook my head. "I wouldn't even think of it. We don't need to call the volunteer fire department because two naked adults are stuck in a Winnebago shower."

Maya's little snort filled me with happiness. After Hunter and Brielle drove off, never to return, Maya and I had an amazing dinner and night.

But my brother's words continued to haunt me. He was right. My dad and Hunter saw me when I'd done something absolutely stupid, reckless . . . because I'd stopped caring. I'd forgotten that life wasn't just about me. I had a family that needed me, and I slowly got back on track, thanks to soul-searching and therapy. It was something we'd never brought up again, and yet, here he did . . . because of Maya.

"Could have happened yesterday with Brielle's mishap. Get the volunteers up here to see an eye full." She chuckled. "She had piercings in places that I had to look up. I couldn't even imagine the pain."

"Really?"

"Yup." Maya turned off the water and dried off as I wandered into the kitchen.

I could tell something had changed between Maya and me. I didn't know what, exactly. I wasn't sure if it came from all of Brielle's incessant flirting or what had happened. Maybe it was me.

Maya didn't strike me as the jealous type, but I just sensed something different, and it concerned me.

"I smell bacon. You're my hero," she sang as she wandered into the kitchen. "I hope you don't mind that I'm wearing my pink sweats."

My gaze followed along her voluptuous body, and I couldn't help but smile. "I love them."

She wiggled her hips. "Good."

This was where she normally would have popped over for a kiss, but instead, she grabbed a piece of bacon and plopped down on the couch next to Chewie.

As I cracked eggs into a bowl for a scramble, I debated whether to bring it up or just drop it. Maybe we'd get back to normal.

"So, what are our plans?" She stretched her arms toward the ceiling and kicked her legs out in front of her. "I don't want to cramp your style with this boot."

"It wouldn't matter if you were in a full-body cast. You could never cramp my style." I chuckled. "I have no style."

She smiled and glanced down at her phone, and her expression fell as a groan echoed into the family room.

"Oh, no. Is our friend back? Did he send another text?" I stirred the eggs into the skillet.

"He's demanding fifty-one percent of the company and has turned down every monetary offer we've sent."

"It's all about control."

She nodded, looking completely defeated. "He has no real claim. I'd started the company before we started dating, but he's arguing it was him who got it to this level. It could be a nasty fight."

I walked over with her breakfast plate and sat down next to her. She grabbed a piece of bacon. "I guess it can't be that bad if I'm still hungry." She flashed me a smile as she took another bite. "But the scary thing is . . . I wonder how much of a fight do I even want?"

"You shouldn't have to be in this position. I wish

there were something I could do."

"Just be here for me." Maya rubbed my knee as she polished off her piece of bacon. "Now, go grab your food."

I stood and walked over to the kitchen to grab two cups of coffee. I handed her a steaming mug and put mine down on the built-in table while I reached for my plate.

Maybe this was it. Maya was purely concerned about everything going on with her business, and rightfully so. She had more on her plate than most people. Not to mention, she'd lost her mom. Even though she didn't think it bothered her in the same way as some children, I'd be surprised if it didn't bother her more than she realized.

She let out a happy sigh. "I just needed food. I'm feeling better already. So, did Hunter let you know how the drive home went?"

I scratched my chin and shook my head. "Haven't heard a word. I'm completely baffled by that whole thing."

"Yeah. It was a curious set of adventures. Do you see your brother settling down?"

Shaking my head, I took a bite of my omelet. "He idolizes our older brother. Beckett pledged to be a bachelor for life, and Hunter wants the same."

Maya nodded slowly. "And what about you?"

"It's not in my DNA."

"What isn't?" She brought her brows together.

"Being a man-whore."

Maya giggled and nodded, polishing off her breakfast. "Good to know."

"It's true. I like relationships, and when I fall, I tend to fall hard."

"Yeah?" she asked, standing and hobbling to the kitchen where she rinsed off her plate. "And when was the last time you fell for someone?"

She turned around and leaned against the counter.

I drew a deep breath as her eyes connected with mine. "My wife. She was the last woman I dated and swore to love the rest of our lives."

Maya's smile deepened. "And you still do. I can see the love, and it's beautiful."

I brought my plate over and rinsed it in the sink, placing it on top of Maya's. I didn't know what to make of Maya's observations.

Damn it.

I felt stuck in the past, haunted by the ghosts of my own creation. I didn't want to feel the pain and rawness of loss, yet it had eaten away at me every single day since Freya's death. Rusty's death was like a swift kick to the chops for the final act.

And then I met Maya, and the next thing I knew, Chewie came into my life. It was a lot of change all at once, and I didn't do change.

I had my routine.

But Maya blew it out of the water. I looked over at her, and she was staring at the floor. I could tell she had a lot to say, but she didn't say a word.

"You don't think I'm over my wife," I said flatly.

She turned, moving her gaze to mine. "I wouldn't expect you to be, Cash. I would never expect you to be, honestly. She'll always be a part of you. The part might change over time, but there's no getting over someone you love."

"Did you love Rob?" I asked.

Maya pressed her usually full lips into a thin line and let out a deep sigh. "I am embarrassed to say that I don't think I ever did. I'm not just saying that because of present circumstances. I just never got that feeling of giddiness and rainbows and butterflies." She shrugged. "I always chalked it up to one too many romantic comedies, I guess, that love like that didn't exist."

I wanted to shout and jump and say that kind of love did exist. I'd had it with Freya, and I never thought I'd have it again. But the feeling after years of nothing was starting to erupt again. Like this morning when I rolled over in bed to see Maya's smiling face. The overwhelming swell of emotions made me kiss her as if I were about to embark on a worldwide cruise and wouldn't see her for a year.

But it had been only one night.

Eight hours where I hadn't kissed Maya, and yet that was the first thing I wanted to do.

I wasn't kidding when I told Hunter that love would make me move. It was true. Would that happen with Maya and me? Too soon to tell.

"Why'd you get so quiet? Does that make me even weirder for being in a relationship with him for so long?" She hugged herself. "For wanting to be engaged to a man I didn't actually get butterflies for?"

"It doesn't make you weird. It makes you human, Maya. Sometimes, convenience gets in the way of love."

She dropped her arms to her sides and turned to face me. "Why does it always feel like you're inside my mind? The things I'm thinking, you manage to say before I can even articulate them."

I shrugged, taking a step closer. "Same wavelength, I guess?"

Maya's lips tipped up into a perky grin. "I guess so."

"Serious question for you."

"I don't know if I can handle much more," she confessed. "Between your brother's girlfriend spread eagle in a buckthorn patch and her waiting in the wings to date you next, I can't handle too much more thinking."

I touched her cheek softly and smiled. "Fair enough."

"How serious are we talking?"

I drew a breath. "Do you get butterflies when you see me?"

A few seconds of silence traded between us, and it felt like ages.

"It's more like a stampede of angry rams are coming at me full steam, and I don't know what direction to turn."

That wasn't quite the response I expected. Scratching my chin, I reached for my mug of coffee and took a sip. "Okay. Angry rams. I can work with that."

"What about with Rob? I need a comparison."

She chuckled. "Oh, that's easy. Absolutely nothing. I never got anything fluttering or mobbing my insides. I'd just look at him and think, *huh, did I do that?*"

"I'll definitely take mine then." I smiled at her, and she looped her arms around my waist.

"Okay, I also get butterflies swarming my belly. It's just there are times when the emotions running through me are way beyond colorful winged creatures."

Maya let out a wistful sigh. "What about you? Do I give you the flutters?"

I kissed the top of Maya's head and closed my eyes as I wrapped my arms around her in return. "More like a harem of pixies in the middle of an adrenaline rush."

She stepped back and frowned. "Huh? What? Pixies?"

"Honestly, Maya. Since I picked you up at Becky's house, I haven't been able to get you out of my mind. It's not only about getting all flustered around you. It's that I can barely remember my name."

She smiled and laughed. "Is that why you couldn't remember the door code?"

"Possibly."

She bobbed her head in satisfaction. "That makes me feel . . . good."

I laughed. "I think about you all the time. While you're at the house, and I'm working on my latest project, I'm literally daydreaming about you."

Her eyes widened. "I might be doing the same."

"So, this camping trip might have been really productive."

"I'm learning a lot. That's for sure." She traced her finger along my chest and looked into my eyes. "And I appreciate your honesty. It's something I need, and on that note, I do get worried."

"About?"

"What happens when the end of October rolls around and I go back to North Carolina? And if I'm the first woman you're starting to seriously date after your wife, am I a rebound? Will I make things worse for you if I let things get too serious? All kinds of questions race through my head."

I let out a low growl of dissatisfaction and pulled her into me. "Do I seem like a guy who can't handle myself? I'll be fine if you dump my sorry ass. I might return to my evil and cynical ways, but I'll be fine."

"Oh, yeah?" she teased. "You won't be moping around Buttercup Lake?"

I laughed and shook my head. "I didn't say that. I just said I'd be fine. Fine is a relative term."

"I suppose."

"And who's to say it's you dumping me?"

"Oh, is that a challenge?"

I chuckled. "Not a very good one."

I'd survive, but I'd probably write off women for the next decade. There were too many things to love about Maya. Too many things not to fantasize about.

And within three weeks of knowing the woman, we'd

shared so much. I told her things I'd never told anyone—not my parents or even my siblings.

"Okay, fine. I'm not going to overthink things. I'm not the best at it, but I'll give it a go," Maya explained. "And you can now tell your brother to tell Brielle that we are exclusive."

I laughed and shook my head. "Is that a little seed of jealousy?"

"If she'd stuck around for another day, maybe. But I was still at stage one."

"Which is?"

"Annoyance." She looked into my eyes and smiled. "Just promise me one thing. If we don't work out, you'll be okay."

I nodded.

She hugged me tighter, and I knew I was lying. I'd probably be destroyed. Maybe my brother was right.

Chapter Twenty-Seven

Maya

"Tell me all about the camping trip." Grace eyed me as I mopped the floor in her store. Jackson wanted to do a soft opening to celebrate because he was going to be on the road when her antique store really opened in a few weeks, so we were scurrying around trying to get everything in order. Jackson also told me some secret plans for Grace and Izzy, but he wouldn't elaborate. All I knew was that we needed to stay at the store today until he swung by.

Which was a great distraction because when we'd gotten home from the camping trip, I saw two pieces of mail stuffed in the letterbox next to the door. I assumed they were for Cash, but then I saw my name.

In Rob's handwriting.

The first one read,

I hope you're enjoying your lakeside vacation.

The second one read,

I hope he's not charging you full price since you're sleeping with him.

I scanned and emailed them to my attorneys, but since there were no outright threats, there was nothing law enforcement could do. And I was determined not to let him take away the remaining joys while I was here at the lake. I didn't tell my family or Cash, and I wouldn't.

Rob was just full of it, and I knew it. He was just trying to get a response from me, but I refused to give him one.

So, this time with my sister was really needed. Izzy was opening boxes in the back, so I had a little adult time with Grace, which was nice.

"It was amazing. Apart from his brother's girlfriend falling into the buckthorn while they were trying to do it."

Grace's mouth dropped open. "It? Outside?"

I chuckled. "Believe it or not, people find all sorts of places to do the deed."

"Anyway, she wanted me to help pull her out of the

predicament, so lucky me got to see all of her lady bits. Normally, I wouldn't mind helping, but she wasn't the most pleasant human being on the planet. Anyway, they went back early."

"Oh, so you two had a lot of alone time?" She waggled her brows.

"We did." I licked my lips and thought about sharing my concerns with Grace.

"Listen, I know you're rooting for Cash and me on some level. I get the book selection. I know there've been a couple of setups."

"Never."

My brows rose. "Someone purposefully plugged my tub drain so that Cash had to come over."

Grace bent over and dusted.

"But I'm worried that once I go back to my life, things will fall apart, and I'll leave Cash more wounded than he already was before."

Grace spun around with a hand on her hip. "Why would you think that?"

"Which part?"

"That it's not going to work out?" She frowned, looking at me like I had four heads.

"Uh, because I don't live here? I have a thriving

business in North Carolina and a heck of a legal fight ahead of me for at least the next two years."

"Do you like him?"

"Of course. He's amazing. He's sexy. He's charming."

"Then what's the problem?"

I scratched my head. "Were you listening at all?"

Grace walked over and sat down on an old milk crate. "Listen, I know you're used to dysfunctional relationships and men stalking you, but Cash is an adult. Regardless of what happens or how this ends, he's going to be fine."

"I heard his brother talking to him about me while we were camping. He's worried that Cash is going to go to a dark place when I leave."

"That's what siblings do."

I chuckled and shook my head. "That's not what you're doing. You're trying to pawn me off on the first available bachelor in Buttercup Lake."

She whipped out a finger and wagged it in front of me. "First of all, there are plenty of single men we could have set you up with, but Grandma and I chose him. Do you think it's a coincidence that I gave you his number for a rental? He's special. I knew it, and Grandma knew it."

"So now you two are matchmakers?" I teased.

Grace shrugged. "We'll see how this shakes out. But the book club has a good track record. I'm a believer."

"You would be."

The bell rang, and Caleb walked into the store. As if on cue, Izzy dashed out from the back room with open arms.

"I'll be right back. I just need to use the restroom."

Grace nodded as she turned her attention to Caleb, and I wandered to the bathroom closest to the back room meant for the employees.

As I flipped on the light, I saw something dangling on the sink.

I moved closer to look at it and nearly fell over when I realized what the long, narrow piece of colorful plastic was staring back at me.

A pregnancy test.

Not just any pregnancy test.

A positive pregnancy test.

Oh, my God.

Grace was going to die. Well, not die, but she would literally spin herself into a tizzy about being a grandma.

I shook my head.

What was I thinking?

Poor Izzy. She wasn't even out of high school.

Oh, my gosh. I ran my fingers through my hair and

took in a deep breath.

I paced back and forth.

I couldn't keep this secret, but I couldn't *not* keep this secret. Did I call Izzy in or Grace?

I sat on the toilet and hung my head in confusion.

I knew Grace had explained the birds and the bees to Izzy along with anything else she could throw in the talk too. Don't do drugs, the whole bit.

"You okay in there, Aunt Maya?" Izzy tapped on the door.

This was my answer.

It was Izzy I should talk to first.

I was her aunt. This was what I was built for.

"Yeah. Just umm . . ." I flew to the door and opened it to see her looking at me with wide eyes. She looked like such a mixture of her mom and her dad. "I saw something I think you left in here."

Izzy shook her head and pushed her lips down. "I didn't leave anything in here."

I took her hand. "Izzy, it's okay to tell me. I know."

Izzy craned her neck and frowned. "Know what, Aunt Maya?"

"You know . . . that you're . . ."

"Hungry?" She looked at me.

"No. Although that would make sense."

Izzy shrugged and slipped her hand out of mine. "I seriously don't know what you're talking about."

"Fine." I stepped out of the way and pointed at the stick on the sink.

Izzy wandered over and picked it up. "What's the plus? Wait . . ."

I looked at her, and she looked at me. "It's not yours?"

She shook her head. "No way. I'm . . . just no."

My eyes widened when I realized what we happened upon. "Your mom . . ."

Izzy's hand slid to her mouth. "My mom. Jackson."

I nodded, unable to keep the smile off my lips.

"Oh, shoot. I think I left something in the bathroom," Grace called out, coming our direction.

When she made her way toward us, Izzy and I traded glances.

Grace scooted by us and picked up the stick and drew it up to her eyes as if she couldn't believe it.

"Um, congratulations?" I told Grace, who looked in a daze.

"I peed on this like a half hour ago and forgot." She put it back down and looked at her daughter. "Are you okay?"

Izzy chuckled. "Yeah. I'm great. Are you okay?"

Grace smiled. "I think so. I think I'm really okay."

Grace turned toward me, and I couldn't help it. I squealed and hugged her as Izzy did the same. We were in the midst of the best group hug in the bathroom of my sister's new antique store when Izzy's boyfriend came to find everyone.

"You guys okay?" he asked.

Izzy let go of our group first, and then I finally let go of my sister.

Grace had happy tears in her eyes and smiled at Caleb. "Girl things."

Caleb flinched and nodded before turning away.

"Are you going to tell Jackson today?" I asked.

Izzy waited for her mom's reply.

"For sure. I can't keep this from him. Especially since he's going on tour."

"I am so happy for you," I told her belly.

Grace instinctively rubbed her stomach and shook her head. "I thought something was up, but I figured, what are the odds? I'm not exactly a spring chicken."

"It only takes once," Izzy said, schooling her mom, followed by a chuckle.

"Well, back to it. Things have to be close to perfect," Grace said, wandering back to the front of the store.

I turned to Izzy, who looked to be contemplating life.

"How are you with this news?"

She smiled at me and nodded. "Really good. I was kind of worried about my mom."

"Really?"

Izzy laughed. "Yeah. I'll be going to college soon, and I was worried she'd be all sad, but I think this will be a very good distraction."

I chuckled. "That is an understatement."

We heard voices out front and came out to see Jackson and Grace. It looked like she was telling him the good news, but then she darted in our direction.

"Sorry, have to tinkle."

"Do you want us to wait here after you're done?"

Grace nodded. "I want to tell him right after I'm done here."

Izzy and I found Caleb staring at some antique yoyos.

We heard the flush of the toilet, the sink running, and then Grace throwing open the door like a mad woman. "Wish me luck."

I knew there wasn't an ounce of luck needed. They'd been in love since they were teenagers, and it was only now that the timing had been right. I thought back to Cash and wondered if our timing would ever be right.

Izzy, Caleb, and I peered at her mom from behind a

stack of boxes. Grace looked to be telling him something. She grabbed the wand from a cubby to show him, and the next thing we knew, he was spinning her around and kissing her like there was no tomorrow.

"Ah, to be in love." I smiled, making our way to the happy couple.

Izzy, Caleb, Pancake, and I walked toward Grace and Jackson.

"Should we head over to the lake before the weather says we can't?"

Jackson looked at me to see if maybe I knew, and I smiled wryly.

"Izzy and Maya both know. Clumsy me left the stick in the bathroom. Maya panicked and thought it was my daughter."

Caleb's eyes nearly popped out of his head, and we all knew everything we didn't need to know.

"Izzy and Caleb, you can ride with me," I informed them.

Grace and Jackson climbed into Jackson's truck as I wrangled the teens into Grace's car.

I parked the car and spotted Jackson pulling in with Grace. The kids and I hopped out of the car and wandered to the beach, where I spotted a few members of the Sunshine

Breakfast Club. I glanced around for Cash but didn't see him.

Izzy put Pancake down, and Grace called the pup over, lifting her into her arms. When Grace wasn't looking, I saw Jackson loop a box around Pancake's collar and whisper in her ear.

I didn't know what was going on, but I started to wonder . . .

Pancake looked up at Jackson with such big doe eyes, and Grace looked as oblivious as always.

When I spotted Grandma Millie with her boyfriend and Jackson's parents, who were sitting under cover next to Carter, it suddenly felt real. Sure, there were all of their friends gathering around for Grace's antique store celebration, but why would Jackson make us start at the beach?

And then I saw the candles and rose petals lining a path to the water.

Grace spotted them, too, when Izzy let out a low whistle.

"Jackson, this looks a bit romantic," Grace told Jackson.

The crowd started lining up as we watched Grace hold Jackson's hand as they walked toward the water.

Within seconds, Jackson got down on one knee and whistled for Pancake, who zoomed toward them. We all sucked in a deep breath and waited.

"Grace, you've taught me that my life was missing a lot. I'd barely scratched the surface of happiness, but you and Izzy made me realize what true bliss is. The thought of living another day without you being mine makes it hard to breathe."

Pancake crashed into Jackson as he held Grace's hand, and everyone chuckled, including Grace.

"Grace, will you make me the luckiest man in the world? Will you marry me?" He held Pancake up for Grace to see the ring, and the crowd melted.

Chapter Twenty-Eight

Cash

My parents called me to the house, and I stopped working on my latest rental the moment they did. They wouldn't tell me what it was about, so I thought the worst.

Hunter got into trouble?

Maybe Brielle got Hunter into trouble?

I shook my head as I did a light tap on my parents' front door and opened it.

"It's Cash," I called into the emptiness.

I walked down the hall and saw the slider open and both of my parents drinking margaritas with Millie Bailey on their patio.

This didn't look good.

"Hello, Cash," Grandma Millie stood with her own pink drink. "It's nice to see you."

"Always nice to see you, Millie," I said, giving her a

quick hug.

Grandma Millie chuckled. "He didn't just grunt at me."

I laughed. "Come on. I was never that bad."

Everyone's brows rose.

"Was I?"

My mom smiled as I bent down and kissed her cheek.

"So, you called me over. Is everything okay?"

"Take a seat," my dad said, gesturing at the bench.

"Sure. Okay. What's up?"

"Two things."

"Okay." I nodded.

"How'd the camping trip go?" my dad asked.

I laughed and kicked out my legs. "Before or after Hunter and Brielle left?"

My mom squirmed in her chair and took a sip of her drink. "That's what we thought."

"How did you know about her?"

My mom chuckled. "The horror couple stopped by on the way home from your camping trip and spent the night. Turned out she got poison ivy up her hoo-hah, and she refused to go to a doctor."

"I guess the buckthorn wasn't enough for her," I muttered.

"Thank goodness I had some Benadryl and anti-itch cream. It says not to use down there, but what was I to do? Watch her writhe in pain all night? I may not care for her, but I don't want to see her hurt."

I steepled my fingers together and leaned over. "Okay . . ."

I really didn't understand what this had to do with me or how my mom had met Brielle long enough to know she didn't like her.

My mom shuddered. "I don't know what Hunter sees in her."

"I think I do," my dad muttered.

"We kept her in a cool bath until she went to bed," my mom continued.

Millie nodded. "It's about all you can do."

"While this story has provided more than enough imagery, I'm dying to know what it has to do with me."

Millie took a sip of her drink and eyed my mom. A sudden quietness came over the patio as my father shook his head.

"Son, I don't condone your mother and Millie's actions."

"Harold, you're always an accomplice. Look how quickly you ponied up with your son to hunt down that wretched ex of Maya's." My mom laughed. "You know you love every minute of this stuff."

I eyed my mom. She hadn't even met Maya yet, and she was already Team Maya.

But that was how it was with Maya. She was incredible. The moment you met her, you wanted to know everything about her. My dad must have filled my mom in on the two-minute encounter he'd had. Plus, I'd spent the night talking about her.

I glanced at Millie. Who knew how much she'd been talking about her granddaughter?

"Okay. What stuff? What did you rope Dad into?" I asked my mom.

"Daisy." Millie sang her name instead.

I shook my head slowly. "What about Daisy? We aren't compatible."

My mom smiled. "No, you're not. But I believe that Hunter and Daisy are the next power couple."

"Power couple? Why does Buttercup Lake need a power couple?" I asked.

Giddiness rolled off Millie. "Think about it. She's a bartender. He owns a bar."

"Right. In Madison, which would be a really long commute for Daisy."

My mom laughed and nodded. "Obviously, but distance shouldn't matter when it comes to love."

"But it does." I shifted on the bench. "In fact, it's a big deal to Hunter. On the camping trip, he wouldn't shut up about how Maya and I were doomed since she'd be headed back to North Carolina soon."

"Three weeks, right?" my mom asked.

"You're certainly keeping tabs, and you haven't even met her yet."

"A lot can happen in three weeks, Cash. You gotta keep the faith."

I laughed and shook my head. "I'm fully stocked on faith, Mom. Hunter, not so much."

"Well, it just so happens that in three weeks, we're having a little soiree down at Spring Lake Farms and Apple Orchard." My mom glanced at Millie, who took over for my mom.

"And we just need you to make sure your brother makes it there."

"I'll do my best," I said, feeling all eyes on me.

"No, it needs to happen."

I let out a defeated laugh. "Fine. Hunter will be at Spring Lake Farms and Apple Orchard."

"Good." My mom nodded.

Hunter was going to hate me for this. Sure, Daisy was super cute, and any guy would be lucky to hang out with her, but a blind date? Hunter would rather be celibate.

"You said there were two things you needed to talk to me about?"

Dad stood with his empty margarita glass. "Anyone need a refill? I sure do."

Millie and my mom shook their heads.

After my dad went inside, Millie leaned forward. "You're behind schedule."

My brows shot up. "Schedule for what?"

"Oh, look! A hummingbird. She's late going south," Millie pointed out the tiny bird hovering over my mom's orange and burgundy mums. Millie had the attention span of a goldfish.

"A lot can happen in three weeks," my mom started.

"But I was hoping that you two would be farther along. We're about to start the next book tomorrow at the club, and usually, we're already feeling good about things before we move to the next."

I sat back on the bench and scowled. "The next book or the next set of victims?"

Millie laughed. "Both."

I shook my head, smiling. "What on earth are you

talking about?"

"You and Maya."

My dad walked onto the patio with his margarita and turned right back around.

"Oh, no, you don't, Dad," I said, waving him down. "You get to be out here with me."

He chuckled and let out a sigh. "Fine."

"Listen, I appreciate your concern about Maya and about me." I crossed my ankles. "But there's nothing to rush. She's got a lot going on back home, and I'm not going to put pressure on her. She just got out of a really crappy relationship. I won't be that guy making her feel like she has to rush into things."

My mom laughed. "But love doesn't abide the clock."

"We're talking love now?" I shook my head. "Dad, can I have your margarita?"

"It's a double."

I laughed and shook my head. "Never mind. I have to drive."

"Since the Sunshine Breakfast Club seems to have some sort of vested interest in my relationship, what is it that would make you happy?" I eyed Millie.

"I know my granddaughter. She's not very good at picking men."

I scowled.

"Present company excluded, of course," she added.

I couldn't believe this. I wasn't crazy. This book club was nuts.

"We have an amazing score for matchmaking."

I laughed, shaking my head.

"I hate to break it to you, but the club wasn't responsible for my connection with Maya."

Millie grinned. "How do you think you met her?"

"She rented a place from me to get away from a bad set of circumstances."

My mom flashed a wicked grin. "You think you're the only one who has vacation rentals?"

"Grace convinced Maya that she needed to rent from you," Millie added.

"Okay, fine."

"And considering how beautiful of a yard Becky and her husband have, do you think it might be an odd coincidence that they suddenly have a branch blocking the address? The limb didn't even match the tree they'd tied it to, but you didn't notice." Millie beamed. "You know, Becky could have driven Maya to her rental. She would have had it not been a plan."

I groaned. "Fine. I get it. The club has an uncanny ability to put two people together in various situations, shake them up well, and see what happens."

"Love," Millie said. "Love is what happens."

I shook my head and laughed. "If only life were so simple. I appreciate the thought. I know it all comes from a place of well-meaning, but . . ."

"You'll believe in it for your brother, but you won't believe in it for yourself?" my mom asked.

"What do you mean?"

"You're helping him to meet Daisy."

I stood and laughed, glancing at my dad. "I am not part of this conspiracy."

"Whatever you say," Millie hummed. "I just know that my granddaughter is head over heels for you."

"Yeah?"

She nodded. "She can't stop talking to Grace about you, and now that Grace got engaged . . ."

A few seconds passed.

"What? What were you going to say?"

A wicked grin spread across Millie's lips. "Well, you told us you didn't want to rush things. Didn't want to put pressure on her. I certainly don't want to hand you information that could speed anything up."

I laughed. "This little meddling book club of yours is seditious."

Millie chuckled. "It seems to work."

My mom and dad looked at each other and smiled. They'd managed to have an amazing marriage, great kids, and a retirement that they're enjoying together. Those two had always been the ones I looked up to and always would.

Maya's thoughts about her parents wedged their way into my mind. She clung to the fact that she didn't have good role models for her parents, partially blamed herself for getting into a mess with Rob, and was fearful of making the wrong choice.

But the thing about love was there weren't right or wrong choices. Love molds to both. It's what clings people together when the wrong choices have been made so they could get to the right ones.

"Cash, my granddaughter might look like the hot-mess express, but she's not."

I sat back down, my knee bobbing up and down as I thought about Millie's words.

"I know she's not. Maya is the smartest woman I've met. She's creative, expressive, and has the world in front of her."

Millie smiled and nodded. "But she also gets herself stuck in walls. That's where you come in. Rob is a wall."

Just hearing his name sent a prickle down my spine

and a tingle in my knuckles.

"I don't think she believes that she can move on with her life until things are tidied up," Millie explained. "And the legal process is slow as molasses, but Maya could easily fall into the old ways just to make things go away. I've seen it happen many times before with those two."

I hated hearing them referred to as a couple.

"Has it ever blown up like this before, though, where attorneys are involved? It feels like she's really seen his true colors," I explained. "I don't get the feeling that she's going back to him."

"What if that was because she met you?" my mom offered.

"Well, I'm pretty great. I get that, but I highly doubt I had anything to do with it."

"I'd just hate for my granddaughter to go back to North Carolina and have Rob manipulate her into thinking all this legal stuff would go away if she'd just try him again."

My stomach knotted. "She wouldn't."

Millie pursed her lips together and shrugged. "Hope not."

"We've said all we can say, but I'm glad we can count on you to get Hunter to your parents' soiree in a few weeks."

"What's the date, and I'll do my best?"

"October thirtieth," my mom told me.

"That's the day before Maya is checking out."

"Huh. Who knew?" My mom smiled at me.

"Think about what we said," Millie tried again. "Maybe a little push in the right direction isn't all bad."

I stood and looked at my dad, who hadn't said another word.

My phone buzzed, and I slid it out of my pocket.

My first attempt at apple cider donuts. I think you'll be impressed.

A picture slid over next, and the cinnamon sugar made my stomach growl.

I smiled, thinking back to the many mishaps of Maya. Honestly, I was surprised that she wasn't the one stuck in the buckthorn with poison ivy up her hoo-hah. But she was smarter than that. We would have taken precautions. I smiled wider.

"Something's got you smiling over there." My gaze flashed to Millie's, and I knew I certainly wasn't going to tell her what was on my mind.

"Maya made some donuts. It's time for me to take off anyway."

341

My parents and Millie all traded excited looks, and I rolled my eyes.

"Don't get your hopes up. She's been clear that she's leaving at the end of the month."

Millie rolled her eyes, and my dad stood up to walk me out.

When we'd made it to the foyer, he reached up and rubbed my shoulder.

"I just want to check in with you."

I glanced up at him. "About what?"

"Things. How you're coping? How you might cope if she leaves?"

I groaned and closed my eyes. "Did Hunter put you up to this when he was here?"

My dad frowned. "No. Of course not. I'm just concerned. It's not like you're dating a woman a town over, and by the looks of things, you're really falling hard."

I wiped my brows and blew air out of my mouth while trying to regroup.

"I'm fine. I will be fine." I stared at my dad. "You and Hunter found me at a low point, and it will never happen again."

"What if it does, and what if we aren't there to find you?"

I gritted my teeth, hating that they looked at me as if I were wounded and needed to be coddled. I was a grown man who'd felt more loss and guilt than they could fathom.

My dad squeezed my shoulder. "Son, I know you're braver than most men, tougher than most. But I know a level of the pain you feel. I went as low as you went."

Surprise filled me as I eyed my dad. "How? When?"

"When I lost my best friend from childhood. We were on a mission together in Afghanistan. He was picking up the slack for me, and I made it home. He didn't." My dad brought me in for a hug, but I knew he needed it more than me. He sniffed and continued to embrace me. "I didn't even tell your mom everything. I couldn't."

He took a step back, and he nodded at me. "I am always a phone call away."

For the first time in a long time, I felt understood. My father was the bravest man I'd ever encountered, and he even knew what it was like to see only darkness.

"You've always been my hero, Dad." I smiled and shook my head. "And now you're like a god."

My dad shook his head. "I'm just a lucky man to have you kids and your mother."

And I left the house knowing I needed to do what was best for me, even if I didn't know what that was.

Chapter Twenty-Nine

Maya

"How'd the house go today?" I asked Cash when he walked into the kitchen.

Most of my day had consisted of trading texts with Grace about wedding venues and reading over documents from my attorney. In between that, I tried to come up with a plan for the inevitable—the moment three weeks from now when I'd have to tell Cash goodbye.

I'd received another letter from Rob that just said *Hi!* But I had no intention of telling Cash. I was exhausted from the drama I'd managed to coat myself in. I wanted it to just be us tonight.

Cash set down a bag of groceries and smiled. "It went well until my parents called."

"Everything okay?"

Cash grunted and shrugged with a smile.

"Uh-oh. Are the grunts coming back?"

Cash chuckled and stretched his arms toward me.

I gladly took the invite and looped my arms around his waist.

"You know what I realized today?" I asked him.

"What's that?" His green eyes steadied on mine.

"You don't actually have to stay here any longer. Rob's been back in North Carolina for a while now."

He smirked. "Damn. I was hoping you didn't put two and two together."

I laughed and took a step back. "Notice anything?"

I spun around without my boot.

"You're supposed to have it on for another three weeks." His brows rose.

"Grace took me to physical therapy at the doctor's office, and they checked with the doctor, who said that I seem to be healing really well, and as long as I don't do anything crazy and keep up with my exercises, I can have the boot off for most of the day."

Surprise darted across his expression. "Nice. That will make the corn maze a lot easier. I had visions of you and your boot getting stuck in the mud."

I rolled my eyes. "Tell me about your parents."

He stalled for a few seconds before answering by

pulling my hands into his. "They met Brielle and Hunter on the way out of town."

I was shocked. "From the camping trip?"

"Turns out it wasn't only buckthorn Brielle got into during their sexcapade." Cash chuckled. "She had a bad case of poison ivy . . . *down there* . . . so Hunter stopped off at my parents', and she spent the night in a cool bath."

My hands went to my mouth. "No way."

Cash nodded. "And my mom doesn't seem to be very impressed."

"Well, trying to explain how you got poison ivy there probably doesn't do well for potential daughter-in-law relations."

Cash shuddered and opened the grocery bag. "Definitely not a potential daughter-in-law with Brielle."

I chuckled. "I don't know. If it doesn't work out between you and me, she seemed pretty game."

Cash put down the hot dog buns and stared at me. "It's going to work out with us."

Seeing the seriousness in his eyes made my stomach gnarl into a giant ball.

"I was only teasing."

Cash smiled and nodded. "I know. It's just . . ."

I walked over and slid my arms over his shoulders.

"It's just what?"

"It's nothing." His voice lowered.

He emptied out the rest of the grocery bags and wandered over to Chewie for pets.

I'd obviously struck a nerve.

Maybe we were getting too serious, too fast.

We'd been on a permanent vacation nearly since I'd gotten to town. Granted, I'd loved every second of it, but maybe it was making things too real.

Making the unattainable seem reachable.

"I didn't mean to make light of us." I drew a deep breath and collapsed next to Chewie.

"I know. It's totally fine." He sat down and propped his feet on the ottoman and stretched.

It was hard not to lean over and start rubbing my hands along his broad chest and go down the path of hopping into bed early.

But that was what he did to me. All I had to do was be near him, and I suddenly wanted to climb on his lap.

"What?" His brows arched. He sounded like the grump I'd first met.

"Nothing." I folded my arms over my chest. "Two can play that game."

A smile touched his lips, but it dropped when he saw

me looking at him.

"So, what about Brielle and Hunter?"

"My parents and your grandmother apparently feel it would be a good idea to set up my brother and Daisy."

"What?" I squealed. "Are you serious?"

"It's all part of the book club, I'm telling you."

I chuckled and shook my head. "Granted, I do believe there have been some major coincidences, and Grace has joked about their meddling, but I've gone to two meetings, and I didn't find any evidence."

Cash laughed and shook his head. "Even when they called me to pick you up from the book club? Grace could have driven you home."

I knew he was right, but it was kind of fun seeing his feathers get ruffled. It was part of what made me fall for Cash in the first place.

"You're like an old man boxed up inside a super sexy body."

"Oh, yeah?" He grinned and looked at Chewie. "She thinks I'm an old man."

"In a super sexy body," I added.

Cash's eyes connected with mine, and he rested his head on the couch.

"I need to go down south to pick up some stuff for my

new property. It's just easier for me to take the utility trailer, but I'll probably spend the night. Are you okay with staying overnight alone?"

His words froze me in place. I wanted to tell him about Rob, but I was so sick of him and his games. I hated how they were becoming a part of what Cash and I shared.

And they were merely words. He wouldn't come back here. He'd decided to cause pain in the only place left to hurt—my pocketbook.

"Totally fine," I assured him, pushing away the unease slowly creeping into my veins.

He flipped on some music and smiled, closing his eyes. "There is something so effortless about being with you."

I had to agree.

Sliding my hand to his, I let out a sigh as he sat up. I turned to look at him.

Our eyes met, and I smiled. "Do you think it's going to work when I leave in three weeks?"

Something darted behind his gaze. "If we want it to."

"That sounds easy, but we both have our lives in very different parts of the country. I'd never ask you to up and move to North Carolina. You'd be leaving all your rental homes and your family. You love Buttercup Lake."

Cash nodded slowly, but he wouldn't take his eyes off

mine. "I've seen the highs of love and the lows, Maya. I know what it's like to lose someone you think is going to be your forever."

My throat tightened from his words. Was he falling as hard for me as I was for him?

"But I would never give up the highs I have to avoid the low."

A tear ran down my cheek, and I wiped it away. "You're a freaking poet, Cash Knox."

He shrugged. "Just the way I see it. So, am I willing to lose you in order to try to have you?"

He didn't answer his question, but I knew.

"You get me, Maya. You've seen my scars. You hear me when I don't even speak. You understand parts of me I try to forget." He rubbed his palms down his face. "That's not easy to find."

Another tear ran down my cheek, and I sniffled.

"I didn't mean to make you cry," he said. Cash's voice was tender, but his gaze could melt a wall of bricks.

"They're part happy tears." I sniffled again.

He pulled me into him and hugged me as Chewie jumped off the couch.

"How about we try to stay focused on the here and now?" He straightened and smiled at me, holding his giant pinkie finger up. "We vow to enjoy what we have for the next three weeks and not worry about what happens after."

I let out a deep sigh and nodded, hoping I could stick to that. I wrapped my finger around his and smiled.

"What did my grandma want you to do about your brother and Daisy?" I asked, snuggling into him.

"They want me to wrangle my brother up here at the end of the month for a party."

I laughed. "Which Daisy will undoubtedly show up for."

Cash chuckled. "I wouldn't be surprised if she were the guest of honor."

"Poor thing."

He smiled at me. "Feel free to warn her."

"No way, no how. I'm not getting in the middle of Grandma Millie's matchmaking deals."

Cash kissed my cheek. "You're as bad as she is."

"Not even."

"Not gonna lie," he said softly. "I'm going to miss this."

I smiled and nodded, feeling his hand in mine. "The nights with you have been the best."

His brows shot up. "Oh, yeah?"

"Not just *that*." I chuckled. "I mean this . . . hanging

out with you on the couch, watching television, staring at the lake, eating popcorn."

Cash's smile fell slightly, and he nodded. "The nights have been unforgettable."

I stretched my legs and wiggled my toes in my socks. "Look at that. No hideous boot holding me back. How about we take a dip in the lake?"

"Right now?"

I nodded. "Even though it's October, it was like eighty today."

"Just wait." He smiled. "The night temps are cold and have already lowered the lake temps. Guaranteed."

"Are you a pansy?" I teased, standing up.

"Never," Cash growled.

I shook my hips a little and let out a little moan before saying anything else. Heat roared through his gaze as he stood up.

Taking a couple of steps back, I pulled off my sweatshirt and kicked off my shorts.

"What are you doing?" he asked, coming closer.

I tugged on my pink camisole so it went over my hips and covered my cotton underwear.

I smiled at him and winked. "I'm too lazy to get my swimsuit. Think this will work?'

Cash brought me into his arms and kissed the crook of my neck softly. "It will work if I don't pull it off you first."

"I dare you." I narrowed my eyes to his and escaped his clutches, starting toward the door.

"Ope. The doctor's orders are to keep it slow," Cash called after me.

"Doctor, Schmoctor," I yelled as Chewie jumped up and down.

I'd made it outside and left Cash in the dust to shoo Chewie from the door and close it. I had a huge head start, but within seconds, he was next to me.

Cash picked me up and threw me over his shoulder as I swatted his rear. He was still fully clothed and ran into the frigid lake with me.

I shrieked as the cold spiked into my bones, but I couldn't help laughing.

I couldn't help but love Cash Knox a little more.

He dropped me into the water and pulled me into him.

Cash swept his mouth over mine, and I laughed into his lips, feeling like I could take on whatever the world had to throw my way.

He pressed his mouth against mine and parted his lips as I let out a happy moan. His tongue fearlessly swept through my lips, tasting me as he gripped my hips with his hands. I felt his erection grow hard as our frenzied kisses created a heat that made me forget we were in the lake.

Cash parted his lips from mine, and he held me close.

"You're shaking," he said. "It's time to get inside."

I looked into his eyes, begging for more.

He obliged and picked me up, carrying me out of the lake as my arms stayed looped around his neck.

"You're my perfect Thor," I whispered as he let out a soft growl of approval, and I think . . .

a quiet *I love you*.

Chapter Thirty

Cash

I promised Maya that I wouldn't lie to her again, and I technically hadn't. I needed to pick up some items at a big box store for my new rental, and it was cheaper and easier to just go down and haul everything up than to try to get them to deliver.

Letting out a sigh, I climbed out of the truck to see the gently rolling hills of Sunset Perch. I'd always hated the name, but the place had the best views. I swallowed the familiar tightness that threatened to suffocate me, but this time, it was different. This time, I felt like I needed something more than to kneel and pray.

Large oak trees clung to the last of summer, sprinkling a colorful quilt on the thick grass. It was quiet here.

Always was.

I clutched the pink daisies as I wandered through the

park-like setting, and I pretended I was anywhere but here.

Freya.

Today was our anniversary.

The monuments dotted the landscape in various shades of stone—white marble, black granite, grey limestone.

But it wasn't the cemetery I needed. It was the beautiful public park that was connected to it from behind. Freya's favorite lake. After her passing, I donated to the park, and they made a monument in her honor set in the middle of flowers with a nice park bench. It had taken me days to come up with the inscription that spoke to who she was.

I wound down the path to where an angel draped over a granite bench beckoned me as I wiped away the tears threatening my resolve to stay strong.

I knelt in front of the bench and touched the cold stone as the angel smiled at me. I'd found an odd comfort in that angel's smile up until today. Today, I wanted the warmth of the woman I had loved. Her wisdom.

Just her.

Because I needed to know that it was okay.

Okay to love again.

I let out a slow breath, feeling the rough letters of Freya's name carved onto the plague, and shook my head.

"I miss you, love. I miss you as much today as I did

the night you never came home." I wiped my nose and looked at the horizon before turning back. "And I am so sorry that I was such a fool. Such a forgetful, self-absorbed fool. All I had to do was remember to pick up one thing. And I failed you. I failed us."

I fell from my kneeling position and sat in silence.

"Rusty passed four months ago. It was like he was my last connection to you. He was the one thing I could hold onto, knowing you held him too. But I now have Chewie. She's not quite as regal as an Irish setter. Actually, she's a teacup Pom. Long story, but I saved her life. She certainly wouldn't impress your dad when it came to a hunting trip, but she's done the job. She brings lots of laughs."

I cleared my throat and wiped my eyes again. "But I have to tell you that after six years of going in circles, I still suck at life without you. I think I'm known as the town hermit or the town crank." I laughed.

"Shit. Maybe both, but I've been so heavy without you, Freya. You were my light. But about a month ago, I started to see a little spark flicker again. And I'm scared shitless that I'll do wrong again. And her life is already complicated. Remember Millie? It's her granddaughter. And she called her 'the hot-mess express'. And that's being generous. The woman got herself stuck in a wall. Kind of like you got yourself trapped in the outhouse."

Only the birds chirped. I didn't know what I expected coming here, but I knew I had to do it.

I shook my head and continued. "I see similarities. I see her openness to the world. I see the possibility of light again. But I don't want to disappoint you. I want to honor you and make things right." I laid the pink daisies down and hung my head in my hands. "I want to make you proud."

When I looked at my watch, I was shocked to see that hours had gone by. It had felt like minutes. There was no way I'd make it to the store tonight.

I stared at the angel cradling the bench and read the words. The words I had memorized haunted my life and everyone who knew her, who loved her.

Gone too soon . . .

But . . .

God needed her light to keep the moon aglow,
to keep the world spinning,
to keep the angels singing.

I touched the monument, expecting the chill of the stone, but felt warmth instead. I closed my eyes and brought in a deep breath, vowing to make the right decisions and to be open again.

Open again.

And it started today.

I would drive back home and tell Maya how I got my scar.

How I knew what I wanted for the future.

Where I was today.

I would be open.

I stood and nodded, witnessing the beautiful sunset over the lake. This was where I'd proposed, but it was totally Freya. Not many women would be thrilled about their big moment being attached to the back of a cemetery, but she chose to see the beauty.

I started up the gentle hill toward the sea of monuments with legacies shortened, souls drifting away too soon, and stories never heard.

But I wanted to do better by Freya.

I could embrace my past while still maintaining a future. Ghosts didn't have to haunt me. They could uplift me. They could be my angels.

Walking over to my truck, I climbed in and turned on the radio. It was time to start from scratch with Maya. If this was going to work, we both needed to be honest. Were we going too fast? Too slow? Who knew?

But what I felt deep inside was that Maya came into my life for a reason.

And whatever the outcome, we had to vow to make one another's lives better by the end of it or the start of it.

As I pulled onto the county road heading back to Buttercup Lake, I let the eighties rock drift through the cab. I'd tell Maya the truth, and maybe she'd want to hitch a ride with me to get the supplies tomorrow.

Maybe it was okay to think of tomorrow with Maya.

By the time I pulled down the road to Maya's rental, the sun had set, and sprinkles of moonlight flickered through the pines.

And then I saw it.

Police cars.

Red and blue lights flashing.

An ambulance.

My heart pounded in my chest as I veered off the road onto the gravel, barely avoiding a group of lanky pines. I turned off the truck and jumped out, tumbling in between fallen pine tree limbs and river birch branches. Scrambling to my feet, I ran through the front yard to the front door, where a county deputy stepped in front of me.

"You can't go in there."

My hands flew to my head. "What? It's my house! What's going on in there?"

"It's an active investigation, sir."

"Is she okay?"

"I'm not at liberty to say. It's an active—"

"I don't give a shit." I always had the utmost respect for law enforcement.

I shoved my way through right when the officer shouted for me to stop.

Nate appeared down the hall. "It's okay. Let him go. He's fine."

I shrugged the county officer off me and apologized as I charged down the hallway.

"Outside," he started.

"Is she alive?"

"Yes, but—"

"No but." I shook my head and moved forward when I saw him.

Rob sat in handcuffs in the corner of the family room.

My family room.

His head had a laceration and swelling.

"What the hell is he doing here?" My pulse didn't soar. It attacked my body—hearing loss, dizziness, crazed.

I shot toward Rob as Nate lunged for me.

"What did you do to her?" I yelled, swinging at him.

Rob sat smugly with raging eyes.

Dark pupils in the center with even darker rings.

He licked his lips. "She tastes just as sweet as I remember."

Blind fury shot through me as Nate tackled me.

"Don't do this, Cash. He's not worth it. He's already going away," he whispered.

Nate grabbed my arms and helped me up.

Rob flicked his chin at me with a smirk, and I swore to God that my fists tingled.

This wasn't the sign I was looking for, but it would feel so good to make things right like this.

"Don't do it," Nate snapped under his breath. "Go outside to Maya."

I turned slowly and nodded.

Nate leaned into me. "And since when don't you answer your Goddamn phone?"

I closed my eyes and shook my head. "Shit. I'm sorry. I just . . . I was at Freya's. It was our anniversary."

"And the plot thickens," Rob said, overhearing.

My fists clenched as Nate pushed me toward the doors leading to Maya.

"I'm so sorry," he said softly. "I should have

remembered. I was a damn groomsman, for Christ's sake."

I shook my head and looked straight ahead of me as I got to the door.

Maya had a blanket draped over her shoulders, but she was facing the lake. A female officer was kneeling in front of her, speaking quietly.

"I called for county backup. This property is right on the edge, and they have more resources."

"Resources?" My voice cracked.

Maya turned around slowly to see me, and my world spun out of control.

Chapter Thirty-One

Maya

Cash!

He was here.

I turned slowly to see him, but it was as if I were looking at a shadow of a human, his eyes fiery with something I didn't recognize.

Nate whispered something to him, and he took a step toward me.

And another.

With each step, the fire turned to something else until I was in his arms. His hands slid up my back to my head, his fingers tangling in my hair.

"My, God, Maya. What happened? What happened?" he muttered with his mouth pressed against my forehead.

I tried to speak, but I couldn't. The words stayed in my throat, tucked deep in my mind.

I'd been so wrong about Rob. My job was to read people. To help people.

I didn't even recognize the signs right in front of me.

Seeing the terror and anger running through Cash's gaze made me feel even worse. He could have lost me tonight.

Something could have happened to another woman he loved because of stupidity.

My stupidity.

I should have told him about the letters.

About Rob making a move again, intimidating me.

I drew a deep breath, but tears fell quickly down my face as Cash knelt down to wipe them away.

"Let it out, my love. Let it out." He held my head to his chest, but his heartbeat was quick and powerful—not the gentle rhythm that I'd always found comforting.

Because of me.

It was so absolutely ridiculous to believe that with an upbringing like mine, I could find and maintain a *normal*.

The chaos of Rob stuck to me like glue. It didn't matter that a nice guy with a heart of gold could promise me safety.

No, I'd somehow ensured that I'd screw it up.

By hiding the truth.

By hiding my reality.

The dirty, messy world that came riding on my back when I rolled into Buttercup Lake.

Cash deserved better.

"Hey, we're taking him in now," Nate told us. "If you want to go around the corner so you don't have to see him, Maya . . . totally fine."

I straightened and shook my head, turning to face Nate. "I want to see him in handcuffs."

Cash rubbed my back as we waited for a glimpse of the man who'd spent years making my life hell.

But I'd let him on some level, right?

No. It wasn't true.

I held a Ph.D. in psychology and had practiced for over a decade.

I knew better.

I knew better.

Yet, he sank his infected claws into me.

I swallowed down my fury and pride and waited for Rob to come into view. As the officers walked him out of the family room, I saw him. He limped with each step.

His head hung down until he saw me.

Rob stopped and turned, much to the surprise of the officers, and spat at me.

"Whore."

Cash's entire body turned rigid before he shot away from me and through the door.

His entire body became Hulk-like as he torpedoed into Rob, barreling him to the ground. Both officers looked at Nate, who shook his head while Cash sank his fist into Rob's chin, followed by another punch to the cheek.

Nate leaned over Cash with the help of the other two officers and picked him up. His eyes clouded with fury. He looked like a wild animal, glancing at Nate and the other officers.

"Do we?" one of the officers started to ask.

"Nah." Nate shook his head. "I didn't see anything. Did you see anything?"

One of the officers stared at Rob quivering on the floor. "Well, I did see him trip. Maybe? I don't know. I wasn't really paying attention."

Cash's gaze lightened as he came to and caught my gaze. He mouthed a simple *sorry*, but all I could say back was *thank you*.

Nate let out a nervous chuckle. "Okay, so I think we should try this again." He pointed at the officers and Rob, who they picked up quickly and escorted all the way out of the house without incident this time.

And for the first time, it was as if Cash was getting a

view of what had transpired within his house. The kitchen cabinet doors had been opened in my search to find something to stop Rob. The drawers were opened, and contents littered the floor in my attempts to stop him. Lamps were tipped over in the family room, cushions no longer on the couch.

But I did it. I managed to beat the bastard off with the 911 operator recording everything.

All the would-be threats and taunts were finally captured.

"Chewie," I screamed from nowhere. "Where's Chewie?"

Panic drilled through Cash's expression. "Oh, no."

He darted into the dining room, calling for her as I hollered for him.

"Cash, she tried to attack him. She barked at him and bit his ankles."

"Shit," Cash muttered, calling for her with every loud step upstairs.

I started shaking as I lifted the cushions and checked under the table and chairs. The loud stomping upstairs made my stomach clench with dread.

And his dog too?

He didn't deserve this.

Oh, God.

No.

Cash's footsteps stopped.

Silence.

Oh, no. He'd found her.

Tears welled in my eyes. My knees felt like rubber.

Not our Chewie.

Footsteps trotted down the steps, but I was afraid to see.

I was a coward even though I'd caused this.

Keeping my gaze to the floor, I wept. "Cash, I want you to know she was a fighter. She made him bleed. She slowed him down. She bought me time."

Cash chuckled, and the sound felt like a gift from heaven. "That's because she's a goddamn hero. This one? That's right. Who's my ferocious teacup?"

I lifted my chin and swallowed down the tears to see the orange pom-pom staring at me with her pink tongue hanging from her mouth.

"Is that blood on her chin?" I asked.

Cash lifted her wiggling body up to check. "Would you look at that? This girl takes after her mama. She takes no shit from anyone."

I chuckled at the thought, wishing it were true. I'd taken a lot of shit and kept on asking for more.

Until now.

I was done with it.

Cash brought over Chewie, and all I could do was take her little fluffy self and nuzzle her softness while Cash hugged me.

"What in the H-E-double hockey sticks happened in here?" Grandma Millie shouted. "And how can I kick his ass to the moon and back? Oh, let me get my hands on him."

Nate laughed and shook his head. "I think Cash already took care of that for you, Millie. He's in the cop car headed up to county."

My grandmother eyed Nate and leaned in. "Does he really have to make it to county, Nate?"

"I'm afraid, ma'am, that he does."

"Cryin' shame." She shook her head, making her way over to me and pulling me into her arms.

Chewie squealed, and Millie hopped back.

"She already went through a few of her nine lives," I told my grandma. "We don't need to squish her to death."

My grandma furrowed her white brows and chuckled. "She's not a cat, Maya. That's a cat thing to say."

I shrugged, slowly starting to feel like myself. "Says who?"

Grandma Millie gave me a funny look. "The world,

Maya. The world."

Chapter Thirty-Two

Cash

"How are you holding up?" I asked, holding Maya's hands in mine.

"Oddly well." She looked across the lake where a father and son were fishing before the inland trout season ended in a few days. "But I don't think I'm ready for dinner with your parents."

I nodded.

"I think I'm still freaking out about Chewie. I thought something happened to her." She shook her head. "I'm still scattered."

I shook my head, feeling the knot in my stomach. "Nate said you really sank a good one onto Rob. He has an enormous lump on his head."

"Good." She smiled wickedly. "I knocked him out."

I nodded. "That's what Nate said. He'd arrived, and

372

the dude was out cold."

"I owe you a lamp." She grinned. "You can take it out of the deposit."

Laughing, I let out a sigh.

Maya had been through so much throughout her life, and then last night . . .

It just blew my mind how resilient she was.

Here we were the next morning, sitting out by the lake, almost as if nothing had happened.

Until I looked into her eyes.

Then I could see the emotions swirling around, and that was what concerned me. She wasn't letting me in.

Shouts of glee echoed through the air from the father-son duo as the son brought a small fish into the boat.

Maya stood up and clapped, and I chuckled.

After a few minutes of silence, I turned to look at her.

"I feel like there's something you're not telling me."

She nodded slowly. "That's true."

"You've been through a lot."

"I have." She pressed her lips into a fine line.

The morning sunlight soaked into her soft brown eyes, highlighting golden flecks and the kindness I'd fallen in love with.

"But the thing that kept me from going back home to

North Carolina was Rob. The thing that drove me from my home was Rob."

Her words dug deep. I didn't like where this was going.

"Now that he's in jail . . ." Maya didn't finish her sentence. She just stared at the fishermen.

"You want to go back?"

She turned to look at me and nodded. "I should. It's where my business is headquartered. I have a home there. I have a life in North Carolina."

My throat tightened.

This was bad.

Way worse than I expected. I knew this scenario was a real possibility, but I thought I at least had until October.

I'd started drinking the Kool-Aid of the book club. I thought I had a shot of convincing her to stay.

I cleared my throat, and she reached for my hand. "Okay. Are you planning on heading out earlier than your original date?"

She drew a breath and nodded slowly. "I am. I just want to get back to my normal life."

I debated what to say. I didn't want to sound desperate or unsympathetic.

Or like a jerk.

Like, *What about me?*

"You know what's waiting for you back there." I rubbed my hands through my hair. "You've been through a ton of trauma, and I get it."

Her expression almost fell. "You do?"

I cupped my hands together and pretended to blow in them when all I wanted to do was hide the sniffle that was trying to betray me. "I don't want to force you to stay somewhere you don't love, with people you don't know, or with the uncertainty that can't be predicted."

"But . . ." She stopped herself and nodded. "No, you're right."

I laughed and shook my head. "Well, it wasn't my idea. I'd have you stay for the rest of fall if I could."

"Really?" Her eyes stayed on mine.

"Yeah, but I get it. We both knew this could happen. It's why staying a distraction would have been a better idea." I pushed my legs out and put my hands behind the back of my head, feeling my arms stretch. "And once again, Rob is effing up our time together."

"I hadn't really thought of it that way," she said softly.

"It is what is." I cleared my throat and stood.

Never in a million years did I think I'd wake up this morning and be rejected by the one woman I'd fallen in love with.

Just looking at her made me want to stomp and shout that she needed to stay and that I was falling in love. That I needed her. That I saw a future.

Our future.

But it wasn't just about me.

If she wasn't seeing it, feeling it, what could I do?

I moved my hand to my temple and pressed it hard while I stared at the lawn.

This seriously couldn't be happening, but it was.

"I mean it when I say to take everything out of the deposit," she told me, standing.

"Oh, is that it?" I smiled, scoffing. "We're back to business?"

"I don't know what else to say?"

I rocked back on my heels and dug both hands into my pockets. "Really? Nothing comes to mind?" I couldn't hide the gruffness from my voice.

But really?

Couldn't she come up with anything else?

"I've enjoyed my time here." She stood and put her hand on my chest for a brief second. "And most of that is because of you."

"But I'm not enough."

She drew in a sharp breath. "It's not like that."

I nodded and looked over her shoulders toward the empty lake. The temperatures were dropping quickly.

"No, it actually is." I scratched my chin and brought my eyes back to hers.

I saw pain circling through her gaze, but I knew there wasn't anything I could do. She'd made up her mind, and she was a Bailey.

They were hell on wheels.

"Does your sister, niece, or Millie know?"

She shook her head. "No, not yet."

"Your niece loves having you here."

"I know." She let out a deep groan. "Look, Cash. It's not an easy decision to make, but I figured it was better now than later when our emotions are even more tangled up."

"Right."

Mine already had been.

"Last night, when you saw me back here with a blanket draped over my shoulders . . ." Her breath stuttered. "I was mortified. I'd brought this mess of a life, my mess of a life, into your world. The world where your parents are in love and your brother stops at their house to get their help with a cold bath. I'm the woman who wouldn't even know where to find my parents, what street corner to look for them on. I'm the woman who couldn't even cry about my mom passing away."

"That's not true. You cried."

"But not for the reasons you think." She hugged herself and shook her head. "I'm not the person you deserve. I've been giving it a lot of thought, and you've already been through so much loss."

"So have you," I said quietly.

"It's not the same."

"Who's to judge?" I eyed her cautiously.

It looked like she was ready to flee. In fact, I wouldn't be surprised if she didn't have her bags packed.

"Look, Cash. I'm probably making the worst decision of my life, but it's the best one for now." Maya's shoulders stiffened as the weight of the words hung in the air.

"Like you said. Better now than later."

"I've never felt so loved and protected." Her bottom lip trembled, but she continued. "Being with you made me think anything is possible. I'd never had that. I had to bury myself in psychology books and self-help books to pat myself on the back. But you just did it naturally."

I shook my head. "So, you just want to throw that away?"

"I want us to be friends."

"That's not going to work for me. I can't just be friends with you, Maya. Not after everything we've been through."

I knew the words that would save this, but that wasn't fair to her or to me.

Those words meant something. They were what started a forever, not ended one.

Devastation seeped through her expression, but her lips stopped trembling.

"Grace is picking me up for breakfast out with Izzy and Millie. I should go get ready." She started toward the house.

"Are you going to tell them?" I asked. "At breakfast?"

She stopped and looked behind her and nodded. "Yeah. I'll let them know."

But the moment she went inside, I felt it.

My heart fell and broke into a million pieces, but this time, I would piece it together again myself. I wouldn't do anything stupid.

Even though I knew that this had been our goodbye and that Maya wouldn't be here when I got back, I straightened my shoulders, called Chewie, and went to my Jeep for a drive.

Chapter Thirty-Three

Maya

I'd never seen Grandma Millie look so disappointed in me. Her expression clung to my soul as Grace and Izzy tried to persuade me to stay.

To give it time.

But they didn't understand that Rob's breaking into my rental and scaring me to death wasn't what made me want to go home.

It was that Cash had to be the one to pick up the pieces, *my* pieces.

Again.

It wasn't fair to him.

I almost got his dog killed, for crying out loud.

My life's problems weren't going to get easier, especially now that Rob was in jail.

Cash didn't need to be a part of that.

He might seem gruff and rough around the edges, but the guy had a spirit that reached deep.

I didn't want to be the one who broke it.

The only problem was that my sister had booked a flight out here at the end of the month. We'd planned it so I could see her before returning to North Carolina. So, that meant I'd have to come back to Buttercup Lake.

It was our one chance to be together as sisters, and it had been a long time. We needed to figure out what to do with Mom's ashes. I knew I'd be back.

But I'd definitely be staying at the lodge.

My rideshare finally pulled up in front of the house. I looked around the foyer, and all the emotions from the first time I walked inside came rushing back. The excitement, the grief, and the headaches from my ex, and the grumpy landlord.

My heart tugged as I thought about Cash.

His beautiful green eyes always felt like they were peeling back my layers and getting to the heart of my issue— no matter what it was. Which was exactly why I couldn't let him see my weakness when I told him I was leaving.

I knew he'd read between the lines, and he'd know I wasn't doing it for myself. I was doing it for him.

Then he'd convince me to stay, and he'd be fine.

But it was too big of a risk.

I opened the door as the woman walked up to the front of the house.

"Hey," she said, glancing at my bags. "Need any help?"

I nodded. "That would be great."

"So, you're a fan of Disneyland and Minnie? I love her too." She rolled my largest bag through the door, and I didn't bother to correct her.

Instead, I thought about Cash.

The way his lips tugged into an unrelenting smile when I teased him, or the way his eyes lit up when he'd talk about his projects.

I pulled my smaller bags out the door and closed it behind me.

"Going to Disneyland?" she asked as I put the last of the luggage into the trunk.

"Nope. Just home."

"Where's home?"

"North Carolina," I said softly.

"Never been, but I've heard it's beautiful."

I nodded my head. "It is, but it's different from here."

She climbed into the driver's seat as I climbed into the backseat. She looked at me in the rearview mirror.

"You don't seem too excited to leave."

"My family is here," I explained. "I'll miss them."

"Family is everything," she said, nodding.

She pulled out of the drive and onto the main road. I'd managed to book a ticket last-minute from one of the smaller regional airports with a connection in Chicago, but it was worth it. I just wanted to get on the plane and be on my way.

I had a lot waiting for me back home, and I had a lot of explaining I needed to do.

As we made our way down the road, I froze.

Cash's Jeep had pulled into a driveway, and Daisy came bounding out of the house.

My throat tightened and my chest clenched.

It was fine.

That made sense.

This didn't.

We kept driving by, and I slid down the seat, praying he didn't see me.

I'd left it exactly how it needed to be left. I couldn't bear to have him see my pain, and I knew the coldness that he directed at me was deserved.

And he didn't fight it.

Almost expected it.

There was a moment in the end when I wondered if

he was going to say something he'd regret.

To say the four-letter word that I'd wanted to say for days.

But he didn't.

I slid out my phone and answered some emails resting in my inbox and noticed there was a voicemail from my attorney.

I held it up to my ear and listened.

A prickle went over my skin as the good news soaked in.

I was no longer being sued by Rob. His attorneys dropped him as his latest shenanigans came to light, and Rob withdrew the petition through them before they parted ways.

I chuckled to myself, wondering if that was Rob's first phone call.

Rob.

The man who couldn't love ended up with a woman who needed love more than anything.

Maybe that was the problem.

I knew I wasn't easy to love, or maybe it was that I didn't believe I should be loved.

If my own parents couldn't find it in their hearts to love me, why would a total stranger fall for me?

I nodded to myself, realizing that was precisely it.

After all the schooling, all the therapy, all the helping others, I finally realized I didn't deserve to be loved.

Or at least that was what I had thought.

Until Cash.

And the thought downright scared me. I never had to give anything to Rob because he didn't want it. He didn't want to listen to my problems or hear about my feelings.

Cash did.

Whenever I opened my mouth, Cash dropped everything and acted like what I had to say was the most important thing in the world.

It wasn't.

But he believed it was.

My heart felt like it was going to burst.

How had I not seen this until now?

I looked for emotionally unavailable, bordering on sociopathic, men who wouldn't hear me, who wouldn't do anything but use me to make themselves feel better.

Was that what I did to Cash?

He'd been vulnerable with me, let me see the sad with the happy. And I'd walked away.

My shoulders deflated.

Who was I kidding?

Our relationship felt alarmingly close to something

that could last forever, and it had barely begun.

"And I threw it away."

"Pardon me?" the driver asked.

"Oh, sorry. Just talking to myself."

Our time together had been beautiful.

So why make it ugly?

"I hate to do this," I said to the driver, "but can we turn around?"

The woman winked at me in the rearview mirror and nodded. "Absolutely. Where are we headed?"

I glanced down at my phone and drew a deep breath in and gave her the address.

The one thing I hoped for more than anything was that I didn't screw it up forever.

But if I did, at least I knew why, and I was ready to make a change from within.

I deserved to be loved.

When we pulled up to the house after about thirty minutes, my heart clenched.

The one place I could always count on to make me feel better.

Millie's vegetable garden, surrounded by deer fencing, had been swapped for a sunflower patch. The bright green shutters on her home, the bright green porch swing and rockers, and bold orange mums sprang to life from the pots staking the door.

It was home.

Grandma Millie's smile widened when she saw the car pull in. She stood and walked slowly toward us with a purple shawl wrapped around her shoulders.

I hopped out of the car with tears in my eyes.

"I wondered when you'd come back. I thought it might take you landing in North Carolina before you realized you'd made a terrible mistake."

"When will life be easy, Grandma Millie?" I hugged her and slid a kiss across her cheek.

"When you stop fighting it and accept the obvious?"

I took a step back as the driver popped the trunk for my luggage.

"And what's the obvious?"

"That Cash Knox has fallen head over heels in love with you," she said, shaking her head. "And he'll do anything to get you back."

I let out a sigh and pulled out all of my luggage, setting it out of the way of the driver.

The woman waved and stuck her head out the driver's window as she smiled. "Looks like you've found a home in Wisconsin, after all."

I smiled and waved as she turned onto the country road.

"I didn't know you were a Minnie Mouse fan." My grandma looked surprised.

"I'm not. I just like the polka dots." For which I will be buying a new set.

She took a small bag, and I stacked the rest on the big one as I followed my grandma into her home.

The moment I stepped inside my grandma's house, I knew I'd come to the right place.

Grandma Millie would fix the mess I'd made, one way or another. She always did.

Chapter Thirty-Four

Cash

"What in the hell died in here?" Hunter asked.

The sound of my front door opening and slamming shut told me that Hunter had let himself in.

"What are you talking about?" I grunted from the couch. I'd propped up enough pillows to keep the light out from my eyes as I lay in silence.

Until I was so rudely interrupted.

"Sounds like you're doing about as well as expected from this breakup," Hunter mumbled. "Where are you?"

"Family room," I mumbled, refusing to remove the pillows.

"I brought a six-pack, but I'm guessing that wasn't a great idea." My brother smacked my two feet, which were the only things sticking out from my pillow fort.

"Don't sit on my dog."

"Where is it?" Hunter asked, glancing around. "Is that what smells? Did you forget to feed it?

"It doesn't stink in here," I grumbled.

"Well, you do."

"I showered this morning."

"In a bottle of whisky?"

I chuckled, tossing a pillow right at the sound of my brother.

"Ouch. Damn. What was that for?"

I sat up, glaring at my younger sibling.

Maybe he and my older brother had it all figured out.

Just keep it casual.

"Looks like things went as expected with Maya Bailey." My brother twisted his lips into frustration. "But at least you didn't let it get too far."

My brows rose, and I reached for the flat Dr. Pepper to sip. I'd left it overnight, but it would do the trick.

"Dude, how old is this pizza?" My brother held up a slice of pepperoni.

"Last night. Not so big of a deal that it didn't make it to the trash last night. I'm on vacation."

"This is your idea of a vacation?"

I stretched my arms toward the ceiling and looked around for Chewie. I knew what would get her going.

"Here, Chew-Chew." I opened a bag of almonds.

The sound made her come running down the stairs, nearly crashing into my ankles. As I fed Chewie half an almond, my stomach tightened.

This was Maya's trick to get Chewie to listen, and it was magical.

Everything about Maya was magical. I shook my head when her words rushed through me from that conversation. She thought I had the perfect family and was out of her league.

Which was absolutely crazy.

Asinine.

I froze and thought back to all the times she'd told me she was a mess and implied that she didn't deserve love. She didn't necessarily come right out and say it, but her eyes said it. Her actions said it. It was like she wore the shackles of her parents' choices as her own.

"I need to fly out to North Carolina," I told Hunter.

His eyes widened. "I don't think that's really the way to go at this point. We've headed down this path, and look where it's gotten you."

I scrubbed my face with my shirt. "I'm fine. I've been self-reflecting."

"You haven't answered any of our calls." My brother

shook his head. "You don't need to get into this any deeper. She's gone."

"I'm already deep, man. Maya deserves to be loved by someone who knows how amazing she is."

"I don't disagree." Hunter nodded. "But that doesn't have to be you."

I pressed my lips into a frown. "You wouldn't understand."

Something in me had been resurrected.

The fight. Why would I just let Maya walk away? It probably just made her feel even more certain that she didn't deserve to be loved and wasn't worth the fight.

I glanced at my brother. Of all the people assigned to give me a pep talk, it seemed odd that Hunter was chosen.

"Big brother," Evie's voice rang through the air.

"What's my younger sister doing here?"

Hunter chuckled right when Evie rounded the bend and scowled. "Why is Hunter here, and why does it reek?"

I shrugged. "My parents sent him in after me."

She put her hands on her hips. "No. They sent me in after you because I'm more sensitive. He just overheard."

"That makes more sense."

She waved a hand in front of her nose and walked toward the trash. "But seriously . . ."

"It's just Cash," Hunter quipped.

"You're just jealous because I haven't smelled a day in my life." I laughed. "But my trash had some chicken in it from two days ago, and I guess I just got used to it."

"Enough said. Hunter, take this out." Evie pointed at the trashcan, and my brother swiftly obliged.

"How do you do that?" I whispered. "He never listens to me."

"Female power of persuasion. He listens to his mom, me, and whoever he has under him."

I cringed at my little sister saying something like that.

She cocked her head and laughed. "Come on. It's Hunter. We know what our brother is like, but it's you I'm concerned about."

"Don't be."

She looked at my house and back at me. "Your place is a disaster."

"Doesn't matter. I'll clean when I get back."

"Back from where?"

"North Carolina," I explained. "I let Maya go, and I shouldn't have. I should have fought for her."

Evie nodded, lending the first sympathetic ear I'd had all day. "How so?"

"I think . . ." I bit my lip and shook my head. "I think

393

Maya, for some unfounded reason, feels unworthy, and I didn't help by letting her just declare that she's leaving, and I waved her out the door when we'd connected on such a deep level."

"But if you connected, why did she leave?"

"Because change is scary. Being loved means exposing a vulnerability."

Hunter walked in with the empty can. "Oh, God. Not this vulnerability crap again."

Evie scowled at our brother. "You could learn a thing or two from Cash."

"Anyway, she flew to North Carolina a few days ago, and I should have stopped her, but I didn't. I just hope it's not too late."

Evie smiled and clapped her hands. "Mom will be thrilled to hear this. She was worried you'd given up the fight."

"Not when you hear Hunter tell the story."

"That's because Hunter is afraid of his own shadow."

"Afraid?"

"Oh, yeah. You are one big scaredy cat," our sister teased.

"While you two figure this out, I'm gonna go pack." I darted up the stairs, and Chewie followed behind me.

The one thing I'd failed to mention was that I'd sent Maya texts.

She just never answered them.

Chapter Thirty-Five

Maya

"Here's the thing," I explained to Grace. "You are in a happily-ever-after relationship, and prior to Jackson Jr., you had Tim. You two had a wonderful marriage and brought an amazing little girl into the world. You've been the epitome of stability. And then there's Nina."

Grace studied me carefully as she drank the hot cider that Grandma Millie had prepared.

"Nina took all the wildness and uncertainty of growing up with our parents and became this cool Bohemian woman who never overthinks things and just lives. Lives with the plants and lets the world guide her. She's a free spirit. She's made her life work."

"I don't know where you're going with this or why you're hiding away at Grandma Millie's house while the man you love is texting you and wishing things had gone differently." Grace shook her head. "You have a Ph.D., Maya. It's not like you're exactly dropping the ball in your court."

I narrowed my eyes at my sister. "Do you know why I have that much schooling?"

"Because you wanted to help people?" She eyed me right back.

"Absolutely." I straightened in the chair. "And I wanted to figure out why I felt so . . . confused."

"Did the schooling help?" Grace teased.

"Obviously." I chuckled.

"Have you ever thought that maybe you overthink things too much?"

"The thought has occurred to me," I said wryly.

Grandma Millie wandered into the kitchen and traded a look with Grace.

"Listen, why don't I take you out for coffee? I need to pick up Izzy anyway when her shift ends. Speaking of perfect unions, Izzy and the half-brother she never knew she had are hanging out with Caleb tonight for movies at the house." My sister gave me an *I-told-you-so* look. "So, looks are deceiving."

The thought of wandering around town and bumping into Cash made me feel like I was going down on the Titanic. I couldn't breathe. My heart raced. My palms got sweaty.

There was absolutely no way I was ready to see Cash. No way. No how. I'd been taking the last several days to work on myself, to heal, to become whole again.

Running into him would absolutely blow all my work out the window. I'd even started doing yoga again.

Just the possibility of bumping into him made me feel like I was about to get a case of hives, and that hadn't happened to me since fifth grade when my teacher read a love note I'd written to a boy, egged on by Nina the night before.

I shivered at the thought. So, no . . . I didn't need to be pushed into doing something I wasn't ready for.

"You've been moping around the house long enough," Grandma Millie said. "You need some caffeine or anything that makes it look like you aren't part of the walking dead."

"Thanks a lot, Grandma." I pretended to scowl at her, and she chuckled.

"You're gorgeous even when you look like a zombie," she tried again.

"Let's just stop with the compliments."

"Well, I need some pumpkin in my veins, and Abby has the perfect combination of decaf coffee, pumpkin spice syrup, and organic whipped cream that makes my unborn child do flips."

I chuckled, realizing it was a losing battle. "Fine. I'll go. But don't expect me to change. I like my sweats and flip-flops."

"That's a shoe choice for North Carolina in mid-October, not Wisconsin. Where's your sense?"

I laughed and shook my head. "If you haven't noticed, all sense left me when I broke up with the one man who completely understood me and liked me for me."

Grace handed me a hair tie. "At least put your hair in a ponytail so people can't tell it's been days since it's seen a brush."

I stuck my tongue out at her. "It hasn't been that long. Well, maybe."

When we stepped outside, the crisp air swept over my skin, and I reveled in how quickly things changed in Wisconsin.

One minute, Cash and I were bouncing together in the frigid lake, and the next, it seemed like snow could fall.

"If I didn't know better, I'd say it felt like November," Grandma Millie said, shivering. She bundled her goose-down coat around her.

"It doesn't snow in October, right?" I asked.

"It can, but it just doesn't stick," my grandma explained.

I grinned. "Ah, I see."

As we piled into the car, I started to feel a little better, a little less guilty for leaving Cash in the dust.

I still didn't want to bump into him, but I felt like I could breathe again.

Grace started the car as I buckled into the backseat.

"Izzy and I are going to the pumpkin patch on Saturday. Wanna come with us?" Grace asked.

I drew in a breath and thought about my odds. Would I run into Cash? Could I hide from Cash if he happened to be around?

It wasn't that I didn't want to see him, but I didn't want to see him. I'd acted like an idiot, and even though it made sense to me at the time, it didn't soon after.

But the damage had been done.

And I needed to get brave enough to confront him and apologize.

It also didn't help that word got around about Rob, and I had to do lots of damage control. It wasn't that I was protecting Rob. I was protecting my brand, which in this case meant empowerment.

After several conference calls and Zoom meetings, I felt better in control, and I'd also made the final decision to close the office and let all employees work remotely. I'd also planned a getaway at Buttercup Lodge next summer for employees and their families. I'd wanted to put on a retreat for a very long time, but it was something Rob was opposed to, and that no longer mattered.

The thought made me nearly giddy as my sister pulled in front of the coffee shop. I poked my head around, looking for any sign of his white Jeep, and was relieved it didn't appear to be lurking. I did still wonder why he'd been parked at Daisy's house, but it wasn't my business. I'd broken up with him. We still weren't together, so he could be up to all kinds of shenanigans.

And I could fully pat myself on the back for that.

Grandma Millie got out of the car before Grace had even turned it off. She stretched before trundling into the coffee shop.

"Does she remember we're with her or . . ." I teased, and Grace chuckled.

"Are you okay going in for coffee?" she asked.

I laughed. "Oh, now you're concerned?"

"You know what I mean."

I smiled and nodded. "I do know, and yeah. As long as I can dive behind the counter if Cash shows up, I'm good."

Grace shook her head and climbed out of the car, followed by me.

The moment we walked in, Izzy lit up and waved. Abby spun around to greet us, but she was already talking to my grandma.

"Hey, Mom," Izzy said. "Craving the pumpkin one again?"

Grace laughed and put her hand on her barely-there belly and laughed. "I am, and I think I need a slice of pumpkin brownie."

I stared at her. "What the heck is a pumpkin brownie?"

Izzy groaned. "Oh, it's so good. It's like pumpkin bread with brownie batter swirled through the middle, sprinkled with nuts."

"I'll have that too, and I'll try your mom's drink."

"Coming up." Izzy wandered to make the drinks as Grandma Millie wandered over with a cup of tea.

"It's all set." My grandma sat down.

"What's all set?"

"The party on the thirtieth."

I stared at her blankly.

"You know, the one at the apple orchard? Cash's parents?" she prompted.

I'd been so wrapped up in my drama that I'd completely forgotten that there was a get-together at the end of the month.

"You're coming, right?" Grace smiled as her daughter brought over all of the food and drinks.

"We'll see. I don't want it to be weird. It's only a couple of weeks away."

"It will only be weird if you make it weird," Izzy told me with raised brows.

"I'll take that into consideration. Thanks."

She spun on her heels, and Grandma Millie grinned. "She's a smart one."

"Takes after her aunt," I said, sipping my drink.

It felt like someone had bottled up every amazing thing about fall and shoved it into this drink. I was addicted. Another reason to stay in Buttercup Lake.

I'd slowly started to come to the conclusion that even if Cash didn't want to accept my apology or try again, I still wanted to stay here. My family was here, and it was growing. I was excited to see Nina, and I was thrilled beyond words about a tiny new nephew or niece. I saw my future here.

And if it wasn't with Cash, I'd have to learn to deal with it. Granted, seeing him wander around town when he started to date again would be rough.

Maybe torturous, but I'd whip out my therapy skills and think about how lucky I was to have had him for as brief as it might have been.

Exactly.

I was a professional.

And on that note, I was tired of everything about me all day. "When's Jackson Jr. coming back from tour?"

Grace beamed at the mere mention of her fiancé. "Four days and six hours, not that I'm counting."

Grandma Millie chuckled. "Of course not."

"I'm so happy you reconnected with him, Grace. It's like the stars aligned."

Grace laughed. "With the help of the Sunshine Breakfast Club."

"Oh, brother," I groaned.

"It's true."

Grandma Millie looked at me and took a sip of her tea. "Which is another reason you and Cash need to sort this out. We have a nearly perfect record, and you two are wreaking havoc."

"What about Daisy and Cash? That didn't work out," I pointed out.

Or at least I hoped it hadn't worked out.

Grandma Millie shook her head. "Doesn't count. Once we get Daisy matched up again, we can keep our score intact."

My brows rose. "Your score? Wow. And that's where Hunter comes in?"

Grandma Millie drew in a sharp breath. "Cash told you."

I shrugged.

A text from Cash flashed on my phone, and my stomach flipped.

"What?" My sister looked at me funny. "Why do you look so startled?"

"Cash is headed to the airport. He's flying to North Carolina to see me." I scooted from the chair and stood. "Can I have your keys?"

"Absolutely." She handed me the huge set, and I didn't even want to know why she had like thirty keys attached to a golf ball for a key chain. "Don't mind stranding us here. We'll be fine."

I leaned in and gave her a hug before dashing out the door, but for some odd reason, I felt like I needed to make a stop first. I just hoped it wouldn't make me too late.

Chapter Thirty-Six

Cash

I didn't know why I bothered sending Maya the text that I was coming. She hadn't responded to any of them so far.

But I wasn't going to let that keep me down.

I shook my head and scooped Chewie into my arms. "Now, you be good for my sister. Evie has a good heart."

The moment I'd managed to book my flight, I'd stuffed everything into a duffle bag, and Evie volunteered to stay at my house and watch Chewie.

The flight had two layovers to get me to Charlotte, and I wouldn't technically be arriving until tomorrow afternoon, but at least I'd be there.

My sister came into the entryway to give me a hug and take Chewie from me.

"Just put the naysayers out of your head and go do what you've got to do." She smiled. "I'd be flattered if a guy jumped on a plane for me."

I laughed. "Thanks."

"But remember, play it cool. Make her the center of your conversation."

I nodded. "I got it, but thanks. I'm going to miss my flight if I don't leave now."

Evie nodded and let out a deep breath, glancing at her phone. "Oh, and if the timing works out right, maybe you can smuggle me back some North Carolina-style BBQ."

"Yeah. I don't think that's a good bet."

Evie shifted her weight. "Then at least a T-shirt from the airport."

I gave her another hug and started toward the door.

"Oh, and —"

Chuckling, I turned around to see Evie's wide eyes. "I really am going to miss the plane. Text me any more bright ideas."

She nodded just as the doorbell rang.

I pointed behind me. "Are you expecting someone?"

"I wouldn't invite someone to your house." She laughed. "At least not while you're still standing in the entryway."

I smiled and opened the door.

There, in front of me, stood the most beautiful woman

ever.

Her big brown eyes looked up into mine, but I couldn't say a word.

"Hey, stranger," she said, a faint blush creeping up her cheeks. "I got your texts, and I thought it might be a waste for you to fly out."

I didn't say anything. I couldn't.

Maya was beautiful with a heart of gold and more understanding than any human I'd ever met, and I'd let her go.

I just stared.

"I didn't mean to ghost you," she said, sucking on her bottom lip and drawing in a nervous breath. She had both hands behind her. "But I'm not easy. I'm a complicated mess who is working really hard to simplify herself."

"I like your complicated mess," I said, putting my duffle back down. "I like everything about you."

"Everything?" She leaned over and put something on my porch.

I nodded as she glanced at whatever she had left.

"I've been lying to myself about a lot of things. About missing my mom. About being scared shitless of Rob. About . . ." She swallowed and looked back up at me. "About you."

Maya's gaze flashed over my shoulder, and she froze.

All the color drained from her face, and she parted her lips to speak but snapped her mouth closed.

I turned around to see what Maya was looking at, and my heart stopped.

"I should probably go," she muttered. "I thought since you texted, you were into me and—" Maya nearly tumbled over her own two feet.

I grabbed her so she wouldn't fall, but I didn't let go.

"That's my sister." I smiled, liking that she had a reaction. It showed she did care. "Evie is my younger sister."

Maya let out a huge sigh and looked up at me sheepishly. "I mean, you're a grown man and can do whatever. It's not like I—"

"I should never have let you leave," I told her. "You looked like you had your mind made up, and I'd felt off and on that you didn't really want anything serious."

"I was a fool," she said softly.

Maya brought her gaze to mine, and my chest tightened. "We both were."

"Come on in," I said, pulling her hands with me.

She stepped into my house as Evie wandered toward me with Chewie.

"My job here is done," Evie said, chuckling. "You take the dog."

I held Chewie and watched Evie slide her shoes on and stand in front of Maya.

"You must be Maya," Evie said.

"That's me. Unwashed hair and everything." Maya grimaced, and I shook my head.

She was beautiful.

"It's wonderful to meet you. I've heard all about you nonstop from my parents."

I looked at my sister. "You have?"

"Yup, and I can see why. She's wonderfully normal."

"She's more than normal. She's extraordinary," I said, nearly barking my words.

Evie chuckled and nodded. "You're probably right."

My sister gave me a quick hug and smiled at Maya. "I know my brother tends to grunt his answers, but he means well."

Maya chuckled, and I soaked it in. I thought I might never hear it again.

Just having her standing in my house made me feel lighter.

It was as if everything I'd been searching for in life had all boiled down to one concept.

Love.

I'd had it taken away before, and maybe I held on to

my past too long, but it all brought me here.

Evie walked out of the house, and Maya's big, beautiful eyes stared at me. I set Chewie down, and she promptly ran off to the family room, probably hoping for some pizza crumbs.

"I've been thinking," she said softly.

"Oh, no."

She chuckled. "I am the first to admit that I might be an overthinker, but I'm working on it."

I smiled, brushing a loose lock of hair from her face. She'd pulled it all up into a messy ponytail and looked like my dream girl.

"I wanted to wait a few more days before talking to you, but when I saw your text about going to North Carolina, I knew I had to stop you."

"Why did you want to wait? To make me crazy?"

She shook her head. "I was trying to work on myself."

"And you thought it would only take a week or so?"

Maya snorted, and it was like my life was complete.

But I knew there was something I still needed to tell her.

"I was using North Carolina and my company as an excuse. The truth is that everything I care about is here at Buttercup Lake. There's Chewie, Grandma Millie, Grace, and

Izzy."

My brows arched.

"And some hot landlord who thinks he's God's gift to women."

I laughed and shook my head. "I do not."

"No, but you could. You are that sexy."

"You're making me blush," I teased.

Bringing Maya into my arms, I kissed the top of her head, taking in every incredible second of this moment. I honestly thought I might never see her again.

"I'm sorry for being stupid and not chasing after you." I kissed her again. "You deserve to be chased. I mean, not like Rob did, but you know, a normal, friendly pace."

Maya laughed and took a step back. "This last month has been wild."

"One way of putting it."

"And I wouldn't have it any other way," she said softly, resting her palms on my chest. "Did you ever make it down to that store to get what you needed for your new house?"

So much had gone on, I hadn't even told her what else I was doing that day.

"No. I still need to head that way. I haven't really been feeling myself lately."

She hopped on her toes. "Oh, I almost forgot. I'll be right back."

"Okay?" I watched her dart to the front door, fling it open, and bend down to get whatever she'd put outside. She kept her hands behind her and spun around.

"I didn't want to give these to you until I was certain this would be headed in the right direction."

"Or?" I prodded.

She laughed. "I would have just taken them back home with me. They're my favorite. Okay, so maybe they're more for me than you, but I thought it might soften you up a bit."

She closed the door behind her with her foot and made her way toward me.

"I know we have a lot to work on, but it will make it a lot easier with me in Buttercup Lake. But I wanted to start by saying that I'm truly sorry. I don't want to be the woman who breaks your heart." She whipped flowers out from behind her, and my world suddenly stopped.

Pink daisies.

Pink daisies wrapped in the same tissue and ribbon I'd taken to the bench.

Maya's expression froze. "What? Are you allergic?"

I shook my head, taking the pink daisies while I tried

to keep it together. Today was about Maya.

Maya and me.

"You couldn't have picked anything more perfect." I held them and smiled, pulling her into me with my free arm.

"Really? I was worried pink might freak you out, but . . ."

"You have no idea how much these mean to me." I drew a breath and closed my eyes, feeling the intensity of the moment. "No matter what we face in the future, we can't run away. We have to be open and honest."

She looked into my eyes and nodded slowly. "I know. I realized that on the way to the airport. I realized a lot of things."

"Like?" I asked as we slowly started toward the kitchen.

"All these years, I believed in my heart of hearts that I wasn't lovable." She let out a sigh. "That if my own parents couldn't love me, then why would a complete stranger?"

"So, you found Rob who fit that mold."

She nodded. "A self-fulfilling prophecy. But you started to show me that maybe I was likable. I think that was when the panic set in."

Maya stopped walking and looked around the kitchen and family room that looked like a frat party had been thriving the last week.

"I just need to tidy up a bit, take out the pizza box from yesterday and stuff." I shrugged, laughing.

She turned around and smiled. "Maybe you didn't do so hot without me?"

"Not at all."

"In the vein of being open and honest, I didn't just back away because of my insecurities. I was worried I'd hurt you, and you've already been through so much. I didn't want to be the one who put you there again."

I nodded and let out a deep breath. For the first time in days, it felt like I could finally exhale and not feel trapped.

"Since we're being open and honest . . ." I tugged on the bottom of my shirt and lifted it over my head.

My eyes connected with Maya's. "This scar right here, the one you asked about and I shut it down?"

She nodded, her eyes staying locked on mine.

"I did it to myself."

Maya flinched, but her eyes never left mine. "I was being reckless. It hadn't even been a month after Freya's passing. It was winter with minus twenty temps, and I took the snowmobile out at midnight with no gear on. I was wasted, but I didn't care." I shook my head. "Within minutes, I'd crashed into a tree."

Her hands slowly rose to her mouth. "Cash, I had no idea."

I nodded. "Even though I was out of my mind, I had enough sense to call my brother. He was with my dad, and they found me down the road from my house. I was lucky I didn't bleed out or freeze to death, but I think since it was so cold, it helped with blood loss. I don't really know."

Maya hugged me. "I'm so sorry."

"My dad and brother always thought I was trying to do myself in. Maybe on some level, I thought about it, but I wouldn't ever want to do that to my family. I think I was just being an idiot and my guardian angel said, *not today*."

Maya nodded, but she didn't say anything. Maybe this would scare her off. It was why I hadn't told her before.

"And that day I was going to pick up supplies for the new house, I had another place to go."

Maya swallowed. "Yeah?"

"It was my wedding anniversary."

"Oh, my gosh," she whispered.

"I went to where I felt closest to Freya, to a public park that has this gorgeous lake and beautiful gardens."

Maya just listened quietly.

"It was where I'd asked her to marry me."

"How beautiful."

I laughed and shook my head. "It's attached to a cemetery called Sunset Perch, so I'm not sure it would be that many females' romantic dreams, but it was Freya's."

Maya chuckled and nodded.

"Anyway, I told her about you and that I vowed to keep an open mind and heart. I think I was secretly searching for a sign. I left her favorite flowers on the bench I'd had made for her." I looked at the pink daisies. "And I walked away knowing that I could finally leave the ghosts of my past behind me."

"I'm so sorry, Cash." She looped her arms around my waist as I set the flowers down, and she looked into my eyes. "What were her favorite flowers? Freesia? Roses? Alstromeria?"

I let out a sigh and shook my head, bringing Maya in for a hug. "Pink daisies."

Maya clung to me. "Oh, Cash. Sometimes, the signs are so vivid and pointed that it makes it even harder to believe. I'm sorry I left. I finally understand that I am worthy, and I'm not going to be afraid any longer. If I hurt you, I'm sorry in advance, and if you hurt me, I'm coming for you."

I chuckled as she unhooked her arms from my waist.

"I almost said this last week," she explained softly, "but I want to say it now."

I held up my hand. "Don't."

"Don't what?"

I wanted to say it first. I swept her back into my arms and ran my mouth along her exposed neck. "Maya Bailey, from the moment I met you, my world was turned upside down. I love you more than you'll ever know."

She stomped her foot and giggled as my mouth found hers. Tasting her laughter was the best feeling in the world.

"I love you too, Cash Knox," she said in between our kisses, "but I can't handle this any longer."

Maya took a step back and twirled around to see the disaster of a house I'd been living in.

"I didn't expect you to come here. You've seen how amazingly clean my houses usually are."

She snickered, and a snort popped out. "Give me thirty minutes, and I'll have this place whipped into shape."

"I got it." I stopped her. "Seriously. I can think of other things we could spend our time doing."

But Maya didn't listen. She turned into a whirlwind of activity, picking up magazines to recycle and gathering cups and paper plates, while I grabbed a broom and started to sweep the kitchen floor.

When she'd finally slowed down enough, I reached out for her wrist and tugged her toward me.

"You remind me of a pixie on speed."

Her brows rose. "You've met a lot of pixies in your day?"

"We can do the rest tomorrow," I growled, moving my lips to hers.

"Fine," she muttered with her lips pressed to mine. "Then take me to bed, and don't expect me to rise early."

Chapter Thirty-Seven

Maya

Our kisses filled my soul and told me I'd finally been right about love. I was supposed to feel something, and whenever I looked at Cash, boy, did I feel something. We'd basically spent the last two weeks of October making out, making our way to bed, and making up excuses as to why we'd turned down every single invite around town.

But today's invitation couldn't be ignored. Cash's parents were having an autumn soiree—Cash's mom's wording, not mine—and for whatever reason, we were expected to be there.

I had a sneaking suspicion it had to do with Daisy and Hunter and the Sunshine Breakfast Club. Regardless, the setting was beautiful, and my sister Nina had arrived a few nights ago.

Rows of apple trees lined the property, and a beautiful

red barn perched over the rolling hills set the beauty in its place. Large boxes near the barn were filled with pumpkins that we could choose from tonight to take home.

Several picnic benches had been lined under an archway of apple trees where white lights and red globes dangled. Several heat lamps had been sprinkled in between the tables and chairs to keep us all warm. There wasn't a thing that Cash's mom hadn't thought of, and I was grateful I finally got to meet her a few mornings ago for coffee. It made tonight less strange.

"You want something to drink?" Cash asked.

I nodded. "Sure. I'll take a cider with some kick."

Cash winked at me as Nina wandered over. She wore a tan moleskin skirt and a beautiful, flowing orange top along with several dangly necklaces with all kinds of stones. Her dark hair's waves had been swept back into a long braid with a scarf tied around the base.

"How do you do it?" I asked Nina.

"Do what?" She took a sip of some kind of apple martini.

"Always look like you're ready to hop into a Volkswagen bus and tour the countryside with an easel and a paint palette in your leather pouch."

She leaned toward me and winked. "Because I am."

I chuckled. "And I believe it."

"Did Grandma Millie tell you the good news?" she asked. "I haven't told Grace yet."

"What is it?"

"I'm moving into Grandma's house until I get my bearings."

A mixture of surprise and worry darted through me. Nina was my older sister, and we'd always gotten along. Partially because we were all each other ever had growing up.

But a roommate?

I smiled and nodded. "Wow. That's awesome news."

"Grandma said you were never at the house even though you had a bedroom there."

"Did she say that?" I laughed as Cash brought over my drink.

"She did, indeed." Nina winked at me. "And I can see why you wouldn't bother."

I took a sip of the cider, and the fire of liquor ran down my throat. "*Whoo!*"

"It's some kind of cinnamon liquor."

Nina chuckled. "Goldschläger, I bet."

Cash nodded. "That was it."

"That's good stuff. Enjoy!" She lifted her glass and trundled to Grace.

"So, what did Nina have to say?" Cash asked. "You looked like you choked on a cayenne pepper."

I chuckled. "She said that she's staying in town and will be living at Grandma's house."

Cash smiled. "That could make it cozy."

I nodded. "Grandma is always at Jackson Sr.'s, but I haven't lived with my sister since I was a teenager."

Cash eyed me with a funny look. "You do realize you spend all of your time at my house, right?"

I grinned and took another sip of my drink. "Only because you told me all of your rentals were booked up and I can't figure out how to work Grandma's thermostat."

"Likely story," he hummed.

"Isn't it crazy that nearly from the moment we met, we've lived with one another?"

Cash nodded. "I was just thinking about that. Who knew that playing nurse would lead to such good things?"

"I could say the same about being a patient," I teased.

"Being with you has been so easy," he said, taking a sip of his drink.

"Minus the guy running after me in your home and trashing the place, a lawsuit, and criminal proceedings."

"Well, yeah. And you forgot your broken foot."

I let out a happy sigh as I watched so many people

wandering around with cinnamon-apple donuts and drinks, chatting with their neighbors, and enjoying the season without mosquitos.

"Do you think this thing between your brother and Daisy might work out?" I asked Cash, and then a thought popped into my head.

"It could. Even I must confess that the book club has a good track record." He wrapped his arms around my shoulders and pulled me in for a quick kiss.

"You're finally a convert."

He laughed and nodded. "I suppose I am."

"Remember how we promised we'd be open and honest with one another?" I asked, spinning around to look at Cash.

"Uh, yeah. Kind of hard to forget."

"Well, I have to confess that when my driver was taking me to the airport, I saw your Jeep in Daisy's driveway."

He smirked. "And?"

"And I was just curious what you were doing there."

His smile widened. "You wouldn't believe me."

I crossed my arms over my chest. "Try me."

"I went there to warn her about tonight."

I gasped as my hand flew to my chest. "You wouldn't."

He shook his head. "I couldn't. Once I got to her house and she started chatting away, I realized that she might actually be an amazing match for Hunter. There's something about the damn Sunshine Breakfast Club."

"If Hunter will take the hint." I glanced around the property, not seeing him. "Speaking of, where is he?"

Cash slid out his phone. "Good question. It was my job to get him here."

"Nice work, slick."

Cash laughed and dialed his brother's phone and looked at me. "Last I spoke with him, he was just grabbing a coffee at—"

The moment we both heard what he was saying, the color drained from our faces.

A coffee shop first thing?

It had to be Brielle.

"Oh, no," I muttered right when Hunter answered.

"Hey, Bro," Hunter said. "We're just pulling into the parking lot."

Cash stared at me while he spoke to his brother. "You're not alone?"

"Why would I ever go to a party stag unless it's a wedding?"

I rolled my eyes and tried to keep in a chuckle.

"Who's with you?" Cash asked.

"Brielle."

Cash bit his lip and didn't say anything other than 'bye before hanging up. The moment he did, his eyes widened.

"Mom is going to kill someone tonight. I don't know if it's going to be him or me."

"You couldn't have guessed this would have happened."

Cash shook his head. "I implied six ways from Sunday to come to this thing sans-date."

"It sounds like he listens as well as his brother," I teased.

I glanced up the hill to see Hunter and Brielle walking toward the gathering. Nina's laughter stopped, Grace froze, and Grandma Millie started hacking as Hunter's date tripped and tumbled down the hill with Hunter running behind her.

"Well, that's one way to make an entrance," I said, chuckling as the crowd rushed over.

"If Brielle didn't wear thigh-high black leather boots with six-inch heels to a farm, I think her luck would probably change pretty drastically," Cash whispered, and I nodded in agreement.

Hunter helped her up as she smoothed down her

cashmere dress that left nothing to the imagination. Although, it did remind me to ask her who her plastic surgeon was in case I want a little nip or tuck someday.

"Do you like butts like that?" I asked Cash, taking him by surprise.

"If that's how you were born, I'd love it."

"You don't think that's how she was born, do you?"

Cash laughed. "Not on her best day or her worst. I think whatever used to hang around her waist magically got stuffed into her rear, but I'm no doctor."

I squeezed his hand and rested my head on his shoulder. "This is what I love about you. We can talk about anything."

Cash kissed the top of my head as Brielle and Hunter made their way over.

Brielle still looked mortified, but not quite as much as I would have been.

"Nice to see you again," I said, smiling.

She cocked her head. "Have we met?"

My brows rose. "Uh, the camping trip?"

"Oh, right. Hell on wheels."

I shrugged. "I really enjoyed it."

She eyed me. "You would."

I scratched my head and took another sip of cider,

unsure of what that actually meant, as Hunter whispered a sorry to Cash.

Cash's mom, Nancy, trundled over with a puzzled look on her face. She eyed Cash and then Hunter before sticking her hand out to Brielle.

"Nice to see you again."

"You too, Mrs. Knox."

"Oh, you remember her?" I asked.

Cash chuckled as Hunter attempted to kick his brother.

Nancy glanced at me and smiled.

"Brielle didn't remember me."

"Didn't you two go on the camping trip together?" Cash's mom asked.

"We did." I smiled, and his mom gave me a knowing look.

"Well, Hunter, honey, I have someone I'd love for you to meet. She is sunshine on a platter." Nancy's grin couldn't get any wider.

Cash leaned down to my ear and whispered, "Get ready for a ride."

"I can't wait," I whispered back.

"Um, Mom," Hunter said flatly. "I don't think tonight is the night."

"Oh, don't be ridiculous, Hunter. Brielle, you're a confident girl, aren't you?"

Brielle looked at Hunter and cocked her head before answering. "Yeah, I think so. Am I, Hunter?"

"Mom, I'm serious," Hunter tried again.

"I think she'd be a perfect fit for your bar," Nancy continued. "She is the absolute best bartender in the Midwest, and you'd be missing out if you didn't hire her on the spot."

Relief spread through Hunter. "Wait, you're not trying to set me up?"

"Why on earth would I ever do that when you clearly have someone worth having on that very eligible arm of yours?" Nancy plastered a smile on her face. "This is purely business. In fact, she's up here in Buttercup Lake bartending at the lodge, but I think she'd like to spend the winter in Madison." Nancy clapped her hands and took a deep breath. "And I know you're always looking for help."

Hunter nodded happily. "Absolutely. I'd love to meet her."

I shifted my weight from one foot to the other and polished off my cider. This really was getting good. Nancy was a master. She reminded me of my grandma.

"Oh, Millie," Nancy called. "Would you mind finding Daisy and bringing her over to meet my son?"

My grandma gave her a thumbs-up and wandered away.

Cash turned to me. "Need another?"

I chuckled and nodded. "I think I might."

Nancy looked at Brielle as we waited.

"So, honey." Nancy smiled. "What is it you do for a career?"

"Oh, I don't work." She shook her head. "I don't need to."

Hunter's mom scowled and turned to him, worrying that he was taking care of her.

"What was it you told me, Brielle?" I asked. "You married well and divorced even better or something like that?"

Brielle laughed and looked at Nancy. "It's true. I have a knack."

Nancy smiled and eyed me. "Ah, what a skill to have."

"And it is a skill," Brielle added as I watched to see whether Hunter was registering any of this.

I had to admit I was completely confused. Hunter was a really attractive guy, probably about thirty. He owned a successful bar and could have any decent human out there. But he got Brielle?

Cash came over with a drink for each of us right when

my grandma came wandering over with Daisy behind her.

I'd just taken a drink when I saw Daisy. She was gorgeous. Her hair had been twisted into a French roll, and she wore a pair of jeans with a simple yellow jacket.

There was something about her that was just stunning tonight. I snuck a look in Hunter's direction, and it looked like all words had evaded him . . .

Forever.

So, the brothers suffer the same plight around women they like.

I hid a smile.

"Hunter, this is Daisy. She is the best bartender in the Midwest, possibly the country." Nancy grinned. "She makes the best Old-Fashioned in the word."

Hunter smiled and nodded. "It's nice to meet you, Daisy."

Daisy glanced at Brielle and then back at Hunter. "It's really nice to meet you too. Is this your wife?"

Hunter straightened. "This is Brielle."

Nancy leaned into Daisy. "His girlfriend."

Cash flinched, but he nodded. "My mom mentioned that you might like to work in Madison over the winter."

Daisy nodded. "I think it would be really fun." She turned to look at Brielle. "Are you okay? I saw you take that tumble. I have a First-Aid kit in the car."

I turned to Cash and grinned as he grimaced and looped his fingers over mine to tug me away from the table.

We slowly walked over to the grove of apple trees near the buffet, and he pulled me into his arms. We were tucked away just enough that we had a bit of privacy.

"Did I tell you how beautiful you are today?"

I smiled, looking into his gorgeous green eyes. "A few times, but it never gets old."

"Good." Cash's low, velvety growl tickled my insides as he brushed his lips against my neck.

"Oh, Cash," I whispered. "How can you even make an apple orchard sexy?"

He brought his gaze back to mine. "It's all you, babe."

I smiled and shook my head, looking into his eyes. "I don't know what I did to deserve you, but I'm forever grateful."

Cash smiled and took my drink from me and set it on a picking ladder next to us.

"I know this might seem crazy, but I can't wait for a second longer."

"What are you talking about?" I cocked my head.

"I know my mom will want to do a big blowout when she finds out, but I don't want that. I just want this," he continued.

"Want what?"

He kissed me, and the kiss was scorching. I parted my lips, and I tasted the sweetness from the apple drink on his tongue. I let out a little moan, and he moved his fingers through my hair.

"This is what I want," he said, breaking our kiss. "You. Right now."

I glanced around the trees and shook my head. "Cash, I really don't think this is a good idea. People would most definitely see. I know we've been pushing the limits the last few days, but . . ."

Cash laughed and brought his lips to mine with a brush of a kiss.

"I meant that I want to love you forever." He smiled and reached up high on the ladder and bent down on one knee, taking my hand in his with the stuffed chipmunk in the other. "I want us to take on great adventures, plot an amazing story, and live it together. But what I know is that I don't want to live another day without calling you mine. I want to be the one who pulls you out of the walls and picks up the luggage you trip over. Maya Bailey, will you make me the happiest man in the entire world? Will you let me be your Thor? Will you marry me?"

Never in a million years did I expect this, but it was what I wanted more than anything in the world.

My hands cupped his cheeks as I pulled him and the chipmunk up, and I kissed him all over as tears ran down my face.

Kiss after kiss.

I couldn't get enough.

Cash swept a tear from my cheek, still holding the chipmunk, when I heard a familiar voice behind me.

"Well, Maya?" Grandma Millie asked. "What's the answer?"

I snorted and nodded, kissing Cash again as he untied the ring from the stuffed animal and slipped the ring onto my finger.

"Yes, a million times over, Cash Knox."

He nuzzled my nose as I glanced at my ring.

"Cash," I said louder than I expected. "It's huge."

He chuckled. "I'm glad you like it."

"I like it, and I love you. You were never just my distraction. You were my forever," I told him softly. "Forever and always."

"Forever and always."

Grandma Millie stepped away, and hunger filled his eyes.

"Do you trust her to keep it a secret?" I asked.

"I give it ten minutes, tops." He grinned with a smoldering look resting behind his gaze.

And I knew what was in store for me tonight and any night for the rest of my life.

Cash set the chipmunk back on the ladder and looked at me.

Cash's gaze blazed through me, leaving a flutter in its wake, and I knew I was about to get the best kiss of my lifetime.

I closed my eyes and felt his mouth against mine, and I finally knew without a doubt that I was worthy of his love, and he'd always be worthy of mine.

Forever and Always.

Dear Reader,

Thank you so much for reading Pinch of Love! I mean it from the bottom of my heart! Cash and Maya's story stuck with me long after I wrote it, and I hope you loved reading about them as much I loved getting to write those two. Buttercup Lake and the Sunshine Breakfast Club continues to come alive and that's because of you. I can't thank you enough for embracing my latest series, and I hope you continue to enjoy stories from this little Wisconsin town. Starting a new series is always a leap of faith as an author, and I am so relieved and happy so many have come to welcome this meddling book club into their libraries. If you'd like to join my Facebook group, we'd love to have you! We chat about my books, recipes, everyday things… It's a great group of readers. Don't want to miss out on my new releases? Join my newsletter at KariceBolton.com

Also, Daisy and Nina's stories will be coming up next in the series. Sprinkle of Love (Sunshine Breakfast Club #3) and Christmas of Love (Sunshine Breakfast Club #4) are available for preorder. If you'd like to read more romances from me, try the Cloudberry Inn Series, Silver Ridge Series, or Island County Series! Keep reading for an excerpt from Imagining You (Cloudberry Inn #1). Enjoy!

Hugs and Happy Wishes,
Karice

BOOKS BY KARICE BOLTON

THE SUNSHINE BREAKFAST CLUB SERIES
DASH OF LOVE
PINCH OF LOVE
SPRINKLE OF LOVE
CHRISTMAS OF LOVE

CLOUDBERRY INN SERIES
IMAGINING YOU
REMEMBERING YOU
LEAVING YOU
LOVING YOU

ISLAND COUNTY SERIES
FINDING LOVE IN FORGOTTEN COVE
LOVE REDONE IN HIDDEN HARBOR
TANGLED LOVE ON PELICAN POINT
FOREVER LOVE ON FIREWEED ISLAND
TEMPTING LOVE ON HOLLY LANE
CHANCE AT LOVE ON MYSTIC BAY
IRRESISTIBLE LOVE AT SILVER FALLS
LUCKY IN LOVE ON HOUND ISLAND
MISTLETOE MISCHIEF
ACCIDENTAL LOVE ON MEADOW COVE LANE
DISCOVERING LOVE ON CRANBERRY LANE
CHRISTMAS ON FIREWEED
IMAGINING LOVE ON WILLOW ROAD
CHRISTMAS CRUSH ON FIREWEED ISLAND
WAITING LOVE AT HAWTHORNE AVENUE
FOREVER CHRISTMAS ON SUGARPLUM LANE

BEYOND LOVE SERIES
BEYOND CONTROL
BEYOND DOUBT
BEYOND REASON
BEYOND INTENT
BEYOND CHANCE
BEYOND PROMISE
BEYOND the MISTLETOE

SILVER RIDGE SERIES
A HAPPY TRUTH ABOUT LOVE
A LITTLE SECRET ABOUT LOVE
A FUNNY THING ABOUT LOVE
A SURPRISING FACT ABOUT LOVE
A SIMPLE WISH ABOUT LOVE
CHRISTMAS AT SILVER RIDGE

LUKE FLETCHER SERIES
HIDDEN SINS
BURIED SINS
REDEMPTION
MIA

V MAFIA SERIES
BLAKE
DEVIN
JAXSON

THE WITCH AVENUE SERIES
LONELY SOULS

ALTERED SOULS
RELEASED SOULS
SHATTERED SOULS

THE WATCHERS TRILOGY
AWAKENING
LEGIONS
CATACLYSM
TAKEN NOVELLA (A Watchers Prequel)

AFTERWORLD SERIES
RecruitZ
AlibiZ
UprisingZ

BLOOD TORN DUET
BLOOD TORN
BLOOD CURSED